LIZZY

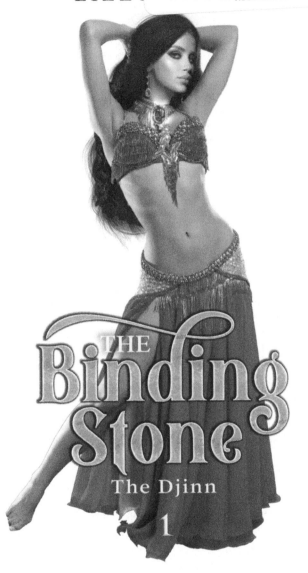

THE Binding Stone

The Djinn

1

CITY OWL
PRESS

This book is a work of fiction. Names, characters, places, and incidents either are products of the author's imagination or are used fictitiously. Any resemblance to actual events or locales or persons, living or dead, is entirely coincidental and not intended by the author.

THE BINDING STONE
The Djinn, Book 1

CITY OWL PRESS
www.cityowlpress.com

Cover Design by MiblArt. All stock photos licensed appropriately.

Edited by Tee Tate.

For information on subsidiary rights, please contact the publisher at info@cityowlpress.com.

Print Edition ISBN: 978-1-64898-048-0

Digital Edition ISBN: 978-1-64898-047-3

Printed in the United States of America

PRAISE FOR THE WORKS OF LIZZY GAYLE

"A promising paranormal romance debut with intricate backstory, a fun cast of characters, and a trio of Djinn who'll have you rooting for their freedom to pursue true happily ever afters. A magical gem that will have readers wishing for the next in the series." – *Luna Joya, Author of the Legacy series*

To my mother, Sharon.
Her "yes, you cans" makes all the "nos" in the world meaningless.

1

AWAKENING

THE MAGIC IS PALPABLE. IT TINGLES AS IT RADIATES UP AND DOWN MY arms. My eyes snap open the moment I feel it.

I let the power drift over and through me, soaking it up like a human does sunlight. My fingertips crackle with it. Voices become clear now, and sounds assault my ears like daggers after the blissful silence of nothingness. I prefer to sleep. When I do, there is no need to think. Or remember.

Whoever dares disturb my century-long slumber will suffer my wrath. That's a promise.

"Really? Only ten?" The voice of a young man attracts my attention.

He is close, but my senses remain dulled from my sleep inside the gemstone, so I choose to be cautious, staying invisible to human eyes. His voice, warm like honey, soothes the edges of my anger. But some qualities can be deceiving. I know from experience.

"Jer, remind me not to bring you along when I buy a used car," comes the voice of another young man. "Your haggling skills need some serious work."

I stand in the center of a modern marketplace. It is small but cluttered, centered in front of a brick house with several people milling about the lawn and walkways. Whatever time I'm in, the women wear far less clothing than I remember. Near the outskirts of the unkempt grass, I spy a girl who is closest in appearance to me. A small child tugs at her arm, but the woman is distracted. A smile pulls at the corners of my mouth, and I quickly change from the draped fabrics of my last master's time, mirroring her outfit. I nod in approval. I'm going to enjoy this century.

Now to locate and destroy the source of the threat. It is not difficult. I follow the same girl's blushing gaze toward the honeyed voice I'd heard before.

"I'll take it."

He stands a mere table's width from me, and it is clear he is indeed the One. His aura glows like none of the others. A rainbow of iridescent colors pulsates and bleeds around him like a force field. This is too easy.

A gasp draws my attention. It's the young mother, frozen in a state of horror. I've seen that look before, so I follow her stare to find the toddler examining a flower growing in a crack in the concrete. A machine of some sort zooms toward her, so big it will surely crush the child in seconds. Time slows as I raise my fingers and invisible hands lift the young one out of harm's way, setting her securely back near her mother. No one has seen, save the woman who will likely never again be so negligent.

Focusing on the rainbow aura, I raise my hands. All it will take is one blast, directed at the handsome man busy handing a piece of green paper to an elderly woman. He will cease to exist. But I feel it as I let go, and even before it bounces harmlessly off his aura, I know. So I scream. It is not as though anyone can hear it. Not yet.

"Never figured you'd go for the whole bling thing," says the one with glasses and a dull, human aura. "Try it on."

I watch helplessly as Jer slips the ring on his middle finger. The large opal in the center gleams a little too brightly, and I tug at the choker around my neck, running my thumb along the matching stone. I hope the ten-paper is worth more than it appears. Why must I care so much for the innocent after all these years? If I'd let that machine crush the child...

No. I am not, nor will I ever be, one of the human Magicians. It is what sets me apart, and the only thing that may make up for some of my past sins. The ones that were within my control.

"Great. Can we go now please?" It seems by his rush that the friend does not like it here. I cannot blame him. My nose wrinkles up as I scan the rest of the market—a few scattered tables covered in odd objects, dusty boxes stacked and interspersed between them. Most things I don't recognize, but it all looks like junk to me. So how did I end up here? Just one more indignity to add to the list.

I trail behind as the two boys move away and down the wide street. The homes surrounding the market are similar to each other, yet closer together than in my last master's time. It saddens me to find far fewer trees and greenery to balance all the brick and mortar surrounding us as we walk.

The chilled wind carries the ozone-tinted scent and humid feel of a body of water nearby, which pleases me. It is refreshing after my sleep. I let my bare arms stretch out behind me, allowing goose bumps to prickle along my skin. A few buildings away, the men amble up the uneven brick walk, scattering fall's last crisp leaves from the single maple tree in front, before bursting inside the four-story rectangle. I've seen worse. Although I'm certain this "Jer" will be upgrading soon. I continue following them up creaking metal steps and into a small room, containing a sagging, cushioned seat big enough for two, a square table and chairs, a well-worn bed, dresser, and a desk.

"Do you think it's real?" Jer's friend inspects the ring.

"I don't know, Gabe. There was something about it. Like I couldn't put it down."

Of course not. You sensed the power. My power.

I suppose I should reveal myself. If I do not, the stone will force me, and at least this way I can have a little fun with the friend.

I loosen the invisibility and freeze Jer's friend before he can touch the ring. I will teach him not to touch things that do not belong to him. I grin and let my eyes glow green with power so there can be no doubt as to my nature.

My new master's reaction is immensely satisfying. About to sit in the chair near the desk, he spies me and misses, falling to the floor with a *thud*. His face is pale, his eyes huge as his gaze darts between me and his friend. I would not be surprised if he fainted. Instead, he licks his lips and clears his throat.

"Hel...hello?"

Well, that's different.

2

RULES OF THE GAME

"Greetings, Master." The taste of the last word is bitter on my tongue, but I cannot avoid it.

"Master?" he repeats, his voice barely a whisper. I incline my head slightly. No doubt he will ask me to kneel soon enough. They all do.

"I'm sorry but, um, who the hell are you? And how did you get in my apartment?" he asks, finding his feet. He is tall compared with my petite frame, almost two meters tall.

"My name is Leela, and I am Djinn. It would appear you purchased more than a ring." I let my eyes relax and adjust my stance so that he gets a good glimpse of cleavage. I've had many masters and find the best way to gain some control is through flirtation. I do not mind, now that I have a better look at him. He is young, but well formed. His eyes remind me of Achan's. They are dark as oil. Enough years have passed, yet still my throat clenches at the thought.

His gaze darts downward and quickly back to my own. His Adam's apple wobbles. This may not be so bad after all.

"I'm Jered. Jered Archer. So you're saying you're, like, a genie?" he asks, falling back into his desk chair. He manages to hit his target this time.

"Is that still the term humans use? Yes, I suppose I am 'like a genie.'"

"Yeah. Right. And I'm LeBron James." His smile falters at my expression. "You aren't, like, an escaped mental patient or something, are you?" he asks.

"No."

"This is a trick, right? Gabe put you up to this." He looks over to his friend as though expecting him to burst out laughing. "Not bad, Gabe. I never knew you were such a good actor. Hidden talents." When Gabe still does not respond, Jered turns to me, swallowing audibly.

I finger the opal in the choker around my neck, and his eyes widen with understanding. He stretches out his fingers in front of him, staring at the ring like it's come to life.

"That's not possible. You're attached to the ring? How? How'd you end up in a yard sale?"

I focus on his question regarding the yard sale so I won't have to reveal my past. "I wish I knew. I've been asleep for quite some time."

"Unbefuckinglievable! So if this is real, how does it work? I get three wishes?"

"No. That is just a child's story." I incline my head toward his friend, whose glasses have slipped to the edge of his nose.

"Gabe! Oh my God." Jered jumps up from his seat, sending it wheeling into the desk with a *bang*. "Um, can you? I mean, is he..."

"He is fine. I thought it prudent to reveal myself in privacy. I have learned through experience that the fewer people who know, the better."

Jered passes a hand in front of Gabe's face, studying him for a reaction. When he gets none, he straightens to look at me. "He's cool. I mean, sure, he can be annoying sometimes, but he's still a good guy. You can let him go."

"You may command it, Master, but I warn you—others have been murdered by those they call 'friend' after taking possession of the stone." I lie on the bed now, propping my elbow on the soft mattress and resting my head in my hand. My black hair falls over the simple blue blanket, coiling like snakes. I pose for his benefit.

My last master would have beaten me for speaking out of turn. I sense this one may be a bit more pliable. Still, if a normal human murders him, thinking he will get the stone...as much fun as the boy is, freedom is far more appetizing. On the other hand, if too many people know, another Magician may find out, and that would not be good.

I study him while he debates the fate of his friend. His skin is fair next to mine, his hair the color of sand. His body is that of a man, with muscles lean and well-defined. His mind, well, I will reserve judgment until I know more. Time has taught me many lessons. Most important of all is caution.

"No. You have to let him go. That doesn't count as a wish, does it?" he asks, collapsing to sit on the opposite end of the bed.

"I told you, no finite wishes." I climb onto my knees and scoot behind him. "Think of me as yours. Yours to command. Yours to fulfill even the most impossible wish." I whisper the last in his ear, letting my breath send a shiver down his neck. He swallows again but remains still. I reach my hand out over his shoulder and snap my fingers—just for effect. Gabe comes back to life with a yelp.

"What the—? Who the—? How the—?"

"Intelligent, is he not?" I ask, letting my eyes glow green for him. *Yes, boy, I am dangerous.*

"Chill, Gabe. This is Leela. Leela, Gabe."

"Shit. Where'd she come from?" Gabe asks, voice shaking.

I smile and drape my arms around Jered's shoulders. I feel him tense, hear his heartbeat speed up. His aura shines red.

"The ring," my new master croaks.

I nod.

"She was in the ring?" Gabe drinks me in. "You mean trapped or something? Is she a zombie? Because suddenly, having my brains sucked out through my ears doesn't sound so bad."

"I know not of this zombie," I snap. Friend of my master or not, the power builds at my fingertips.

"Sorry," he says, and I relax a bit. At least he has some manners. "Is she a ghost?"

Do I look like a ghost? I'd love to question him out loud, but I mustn't be too harsh with my new master's friend. He won't survive long now that Jered has me, however. They never do.

"She's a genie," says Jered.

"Djinni," I correct.

I can see it dawn on Gabe, understanding gradually lighting up his eyes. "Hell yeah! We get three wishes each," he says, dancing around like he is in danger of soiling himself. "You'll give me a turn, right?"

I lean over my master's ear again, letting my hair shield us. "See?" I whisper.

"It doesn't work that way, Gabe. She explained while you were frozen." The way my master's voice cracks pleases me.

"I was frozen?"

"Sorry." I shrug. *I'll show you ghosts.*

"Explain it to him, please," Master says, slipping out from beneath my arms so he can see me. "I'm still not sure I get it." Damn. He gave me a direct order. Polite, but direct. Now I am compelled.

"Explain what?" I sit back on my heels. It all depends on how he words it.

"The rules. Tell us the rules of having a Djinni."

Double damn.

"First, only the one with magic can control the Djinni." I may as well get it out of the way. "Second, I am tied to the stone in the ring. If you own it, you own me and all my power. Of course, even my power has limits. Third, I go free only if you command it or you are murdered without a new master taking possession of me." I collapse back on the bed and stretch like a cat. I do enjoy the sensations of the corporeal body. I always have.

"I think she's got you confused with someone else." Gabe laughs, and Jered's face turns a deeper and deeper pink. I raise my eyebrows in question.

"He means I don't have magic. Well, unless you count that disappearing coin trick from fifth grade." Master blinks his big eyes at me. Those eyes, Achan's eyes, were once my greatest weakness.

I rise and saunter toward him. "You do. It is not much compared to mine. If humans had that kind of power, no one would have bothered enslaving Djinn. But it is there. I can see it as plainly as the dimple in your cheek." I run one finger along the side of his face, enjoying the shiver it elicits.

"I really don't," he says, his tone breathy.

"Let us do an experiment," I say. "I am going try to kill Gabe, and you will stop me." A dagger materializes in my hand, and before he can say a word, for surely he would command I stop, I throw it.

I know that to him it is merely a second. But for me, time slows. The aura around him spikes and throws itself outward. I help guide it, to illustrate my point, and it flies between the tip of the blade and Gabe's head.

Time resumes, and the dagger hits an invisible shield, clattering to the ground. Both boys stare unblinkingly at me, Master's hand outstretched toward Gabe. I smile and bat my eyelashes.

"You tried to kill me!" Gabe says, face burning like embers.

"It was perfectly safe. I told you Master would stop it." I shrug and conjure a fistful of grapes, which I start popping in my mouth one by one. The sweet and sour taste explodes across my tongue, a pleasure I have not experienced in quite some time.

"You shouldn't have done that," Master says, and I cringe.

"I have upset you, Master. Forgive me. I merely wished to demonstrate your own power."

"Don't do it again."

I answer his glare with my own. He has given me a direct order. He is learning his place a bit too quickly. I quell the look as soon as I catch it, but he has already seen. I brace for punishment, but none comes.

"How do I know it was me that did that and not you?" he asks instead, running a hand through his hair. "I mean, this could be some kind of trick. I've never used magic in my life, and poof, here you are, and suddenly I can?"

"You are very clever, Master. No. I do not deceive you." *At least when you ask me directly.* "You asked me the rules, and I answered."

"Jer, you know what this means?" Gabe paces before the dresser. I feed a grape to my new master. He spits it out because I have taken him by surprise. I smile and offer another.

"This means," Gabe continues, "that we can have anything we want. Anything."

"My master can have anything," I correct him, hoping I will not be forced to obey this mindless human as well. I am used to humiliations, but that is too much.

"Call me Jered. Or Jer. Please, Leela."

I nod, trying not to let my shock show. This must be some trick designed to lull me into complacency. Well, I will not let it. I am a thousand years older than him. He will not best me.

"One thing's for sure," Gabe says, sitting on the edge of the bed. "We are going to be famous."

3

THE BEGINNING

I HAVE WATCHED HIM FOR MANY MOONS AND STILL DO NOT TIRE OF HIS beauty. He is a shepherd who loves a girl. A foolish girl who does not return his love because he is a shepherd. Humans are odd. We Djinn have monitored their progress for millennia, and humans are far more entertaining than the Neanderthals that preceded them. I know I am not the only one who has taken to watching more carefully...to imitating.

In fact, I followed Taj through the veil the first time, mimicking his behavior. I was unprepared for the reality, despite his stories. I find myself overwhelmed by the stimulation this world provides. Such decadence. Such intensity compared to the world from which I come, where most human senses do not exist.

On the other side, we do not have a physical form. Our essence exists in the nothing of space, intermingling with each other, communicating through thought alone. It surprises me that here, where everything is so vivid, so vibrant, we are unable to share our thoughts in the same way. Instead, Taj tells us, physical contact elicits other reactions, ones "surprising but undeniably pleasant." Ones I have been dying to try out on my shepherd boy, Achan.

It did not take me long to find Achan once I made the transition. The moment I saw him, all interest in Taj's pursuits ceased. Something about this boy—the way his body moved beneath his robes, the way he stood so straight and sure, the way his hair as dark as human night fell around his face—stole the breath from my chest. Truly, I could observe him until the end of time.

Since that moment, I've taken the form of a human girl. Much like the girl who captured and then destroyed his heart. Only better.

The way he speaks to his sheep is fascinating. He thinks they do not listen. Do not hear. But I do. I know him. And if I were human, I would love him.

Today is the day. I could wait forever, hidden. But I have seen the way the others watch him near the well. The way the girls' breaths speed up, their eyes drink him in. He is bound to notice these others eventually. Bound to seek the many pleasures available to him.

I feel no guilt as I step out from behind the rock. Others have masqueraded in human form; Taj and Rhada do it all the time. These humans cannot tell. Cannot truly see. And I understand the draw. The impossible pleasure this new body is capable of experiencing. The colors, the feel of the soft silk against my skin, the sound of the sheep or the birds in the sky, the taste of the desert sand. Most of all, Achan's scent on the breeze.

"Welcome." He addresses me with ease, though I know he cannot understand from where I come.

"Greetings," I say, enjoying the timber of my own voice. I want nothing more than to touch him, but I have watched long enough to know that is not how they behave.

"Are you lost?"

"In a manner of speaking. I am a traveler. My name is Leela." I heard the name in one of Taj's tales. I liked it. It felt right.

"I am Achan, and I am at your service."

And it is at this moment that I vow he will be mine.

4

TEST FLIGHT

"No one else need ever know of my existence," I say, wrapping my arms around Jered from behind. Again, he stiffens beneath my touch. Interesting. Perhaps he would prefer Gabe...

"We are not shouting this from the rooftops," he says to Gabe, and then turns to face me. "But certain people I'm going to have to tell." I resist the urge to choke him. I would only end up hurting myself if I tried.

"Jered," I say, moving around to look him in the eye. I am taking a chance by stepping out of line. But if he is as naïve as I suspect, it is a chance worth taking. "I am sure you are wise beyond your years, but I have centuries of experience with humans. You have already put yourself at risk with the boy—"

"I have a name, you know," Gabe says.

"Your name is of no consequence." I focus on my new master. "Power is a temptation stronger than you can imagine." I do not add what I am afraid of. I will not say any more unless I am asked. But if Jered has magic, he inherited it from another Magician.

Jered lifts his hand as though he wishes to take my own, but hesitates with it hanging in the air. His hands are large and lithe, and I wish he would not have stopped. I would enjoy seeing what they feel like.

"I understand your concern, Leela. I'm sure you know a lot more than me, but you don't know my mom or my friends."

I bite down on my lip to prevent going too far. Memories of my last master are still fresh in my mind.

"Jered, you have a GENIE. Stop talking about your mother, and do something cool."

We both look at Gabe. The glint in his eye is hard to miss. I would recognize that anywhere.

"What are you thinking?" Jered asks, suspicion clouding his words.

"Let's take her for a test flight." Gabe rubs his palms together so vigorously I fear they will start a fire.

"What is your desire, Jered?" The feeling of his name on my tongue is foreign. It tastes like freedom, and I do not want it to. That is an illusion, which cuts too deep.

"Well...um..."

"Wish for a car. A Maserati," Gabe interjects.

"My mom—"

Gabe grabs Jered by the shoulders and shakes him. I do not hesitate. I flick a finger forward, and Gabe is thrown across the room. He hits the wall and sinks to the floor in a heap.

"Gabe!" Jered runs to offer Gabe a hand up, and I cannot hold back the laugh I feel when I see the smoke curling in wisps from his shaggy dark hair.

"Leela, do not hurt Gabe! Don't hurt anyone. Ever. Okay?"

Uh-oh. "Jered, you may want to rescind that last command," I say, panic lacing my words.

"No. If you are going to be my Djinni, you need to follow my rules, right?"

"Very well," I say, prostrating myself on the floor so he cannot see my face. Anger pours through my body, and I fight the tears that have not threatened me for hundreds of years. He has no idea what he just did. One little mistake...

"Leela, don't bow, okay? It feels weird. I mean, I want you to be yourself around me. Gabe, are you okay?"

"That was fucking awesome! I'm with her. What if you need her to, I don't know, take out some carjacker or something some day?"

I do not know what a carjacker is, but for the first time, Gabe makes sense. I wait for Jered's response as I stand again, keeping my head lowered so that my hair shields my face.

"If that happens, I can still tell Leela to transport them to jail or something. Right, Leela?"

"Whatever you say."

"See? There's always another choice," he says with a smile that would bring the queen of Persia to her knees. He is so unaware of his own powers. Magic and otherwise. "Now, for that test flight."

"Now you're talkin'," Gabe says. He licks his lips.

"This is hard. I have to think it through. I mean this is real magic, and this whole planet needs a lot of work." Jered paces as he gestures wildly, his excitement clearly building.

Gabe's gaze slides from side to side as he watches.

"The problems in this country alone: kids going hungry, no health-care for people who need it, animals going extinct. And what about other countries like North Korea? And the whole Middle East situation?"

"Come on," Gabe says. His leg twitches like he wants to try choking Jered again. I narrow my eyes.

"Okay, here goes," Jered says, clearing his throat in preparation. "World peace?"

"Jered, I did mention that there are limitations to my power, did I not?" I ask.

"Oh." He sits on the bed, and his face falls. I am impressed though. His first wish, and it was for everyone else. Usually they start out meaning to get there, but the more they wish for themselves, the more self-centered they become. I've ruined many souls. They deserve no less for enslaving me. "What do you suggest, Leela?"

"Surely you have a whole list of things you want," I say, not trying to hide my disbelief. I tick them off on my fingers. "Usually they start with money, clothes, home, pleasures of the body..."

"Oh yeah, that's what I'm talkin' about," Gabe says, rising and moving toward me. The boy practically drools. I curl my lip in distaste. Jered throws out a hand to stop him and stares him down. It is impressive, and I feel a strange flutter in my stomach.

"Your friend seems to wish to fly. Perhaps that would suit you?" I ask, attempting to focus.

"Fly?" they both ask in unison.

"If you desire it, Jered," I say, stepping close enough to let my body brush his.

"Won't people kind of notice that? You said I should keep a low profile." His voice lowers, and the sound reverberates through my body.

"Not if we are invisible." I wait for the command, and he nods. I flip my palms upward, and we rise toward the ceiling, slowly at first and then faster. I smile at the sound of Gabe's scream as we pass through the roof and into the sky.

5

NEW SKIN

BOTH BOYS WHOOP AND HOLLER AS WE TUMBLE THROUGH THE AIR. I SPIN into the wind, relishing the tingling sensation as it washes over me. When I open my eyes, Jered is watching me. His stare is so intense, I almost believe he has forgotten where we are. I reach for his hand and pull him toward the nearest gabled rooftop, where we land with a gentle thump. Above us, Gabe chases birds.

"He'll be busy for a while," Jered says.

"No doubt." I wrap my arms around myself, throw my head back, and inhale deeply.

"You must be cold," he says, glancing at my outfit.

"Actually, I'm never cold. But if you like, I can change. I picked this because I hoped to please you." And myself.

"What? No! I mean, yes, you look amazing, but please don't dress for anyone but yourself." He stops and clears his throat. He's wavered so many times between mature and naïve, this man confuses me.

"How old are you?" Normally, I would fear asking anything of my master. But somehow, with Jered, it feels different. Perhaps it is the way he examines his hands before glancing up at me as though hoping I'll say something else.

"I just turned twenty." I hear the undercurrent in his voice. The uncertainty.

"The first human I ever met was eighteen—younger than you are now. He was perhaps one of the most powerful Magicians I have ever encountered and no less of a man because he was young." I do not elaborate.

"Thank you." His shoulders relax, and I am rewarded with a second heart-stopping smile. "It's hard to believe you aren't my age either. I mean, no offense, but you barely look twenty, let alone a thousand."

"I'll take that as a compliment." The truth is that, because of the stone, I am not only unable to alter my appearance without a direct command, I have also never been given a chance to grow up. But how would I begin to explain that?

"Guys, what is wrong with you? This is amazing! Come on!" Gabe shouts.

Jered turns his head toward his friend and laughs. I look and see that the boy is upside down, flapping his arms like wings.

"You go ahead, we'll be up in a minute," Jered calls.

"You surprise me," I say.

"I surprise you?"

"Yes." I watch a cloud drift lazily through the sky. "You are not acting like the typical master."

"Well, maybe I'm not typical. Seriously. Times have changed. When was your last, um, you know?"

"Master? She died in the year 1895 without passing on the stone. I have been asleep since then. What year is it now?" I ask.

"It's 2021." He waits for my reaction. I show him none. This is not the first long nap I've taken. He shivers.

"Are you cold?" I ask. Before waiting for a reply, I concentrate, and he wears a jacket lined with fur.

"Um, you really need to learn a few things about clothing," Jered says with a grin. "In fact, you should probably get caught up on current events...if you're going to be hanging around."

"I can take care of that, if you command it."

"I guess I do," he says.

I raise my eyebrows.

"I do, but Leela, there's something I want you to know first."

"Yes?"

"I didn't forget what you said about being free. And I don't want you to have to wait too long, but I'm not stupid, and I need to know that's a safe thing to do. To the world. I get the feeling you'd be a force to be reckoned with."

I have no words. So I choose to fulfill his command. I stand and fling myself into the air, straight toward Gabe.

"What the—" His muscles tense with shock in anticipation of my assault.

I collide with his body and squeeze inside. He would not be my first choice, but he is convenient enough, and I would not dare invade my master's privacy. I open myself to Gabe's mind and let his experience flood through me. At the same time, I am aware of his body, lanky and awkward. His memories fly past as I probe his mind, searching for information about this modern world I find myself in. I deftly avoid all irrelevant thoughts until one moment catches my eye. I cannot help but sneak a look when I realize the significance.

I—that is, an eight-year-old Gabe rides his bike harder and faster than he should, loving the feeling, like he is so close to flying. He closes his eyes for a moment, pretending that he is a superhero. It is then that the other boy crosses his path on his Razor scooter.

Jered is so recognizable, even ten years younger, with his dark eyes and sandy-blond waves. Both boys lie in a tangle of arms, legs, and metal before struggling to their feet. Gabe is frightened. He is afraid this other boy will be angry. Will find out he was playing a game of pretend.

"Are you okay?" Jered asks, picking up Gabe's bike and trying to straighten out the handlebars.

"Yeah. Um, are you?"

"Yeah." Jered shoots him a nervous smile that has that same heart-stopping quality he has as a man. "I'm sorry. I guess I wasn't paying attention. My mom's going to kill me. I'm not supposed to be out without her, but sometimes I—" He looks like he wants to say more but clamps his mouth shut.

"I'm Gabe. You can come over to my place if you want. My mom makes

some awesome chocolate chip cookies. But I have to warn you, my baby sister is annoying."

"Leela!" Jered calls me, and I am pulled back toward him like a magnet. I land far more gracefully than Gabe could ever manage on his own and grin. "Are you? Did you? Oh my God."

I force Gabe's body away from me and step into the sun. He stumbles around a bit, and Jered lays a supportive hand on his arm. I wonder if he feels it now. The way his own magic bends to his will. Right now, it is feeding Gabe strength and support.

"I told you to leave him alone!" Jered shouts, and I flinch.

"You commanded me not to hurt him. I did not. You commanded me to learn about your time. I did. I now know everything Gabe knows." *Which isn't much.*

"You stole my thoughts?" Gabe sounds like a wounded child.

"Don't be ridiculous. You still have your thoughts, or you would be a vegetable. I merely listened in on your experiences, so that I could better understand your world. Don't worry, I only saw the parts that were relevant." I snap my fingers, and they are both covered in leather jackets. The type I now know Gabe hopes for. This does seem to appease him, as I knew it would. Jered, on the other hand, not so much.

"I hope now you know doing something like that is wrong," my new master says. "And you won't do it again. Or any other crazy, amoral thing."

I incline my head, letting my hair swing in front of my face. Inside I leap for joy. He did not make it a command. He simply hopes. That is good. That is what Gabe would call "catching a break."

6

THE BEGINNING

ACHAN'S LAUGH WARMS ME LIKE THE SUN. IT IS DEEP AND RICH AND MY favorite sound by far. He still watches her—the one named Kitra. It frustrates me because I do not understand. My hair is softer, shinier. My skin is smoother. My eyes are as two emeralds shining in the sun. Others have commented over and over about their color, staring into them in disbelief. She is nothing compared to me. Yet he still fancies her.

Perhaps he will not like her when I turn her into a viper. It isn't necessary though. She is far from interested in Achan. Rather, she enjoys crushing him. She insults him in public, laughing with her friends. I see the hardness in his eyes when she shows her cruelty. The way he clenches his fist when she ignores his advances. But his smile remains secure.

I coax, and I cajole, until finally one night Kitra goes too far, and he is mine.

"You want me, don't you?" she asks, her face in his. I watch from the corner of the marketplace, hidden behind a wooden cart covered with scarves and other wares.

"Yes, if you will give me the chance."

"You will never have me. I have no use for a shepherd boy." She spits in his face. He bows low and sweeps off, hurrying from the town and back toward his sheep.

I follow. Bring him wine. I know he's tempted to dismiss me by the way he tenses his body, but I kneel and feed him cheese and wine. Listen as he talks. Hold him as he cries. Kiss away his tears. They taste of him. Salty and sweet. His lips find mine, and he presses forward with all the frustration of passion withheld. And my human body experiences pleasures I never could have imagined.

His hands are calloused and warm. They send tremors through every inch of skin that they touch. I pull him to me, urge him on, and he is as lost as I am. We roll in the sand, our bodies melding into one. I relish every moment. Even the pain. And I am rewarded with sensations beyond my wildest expectations.

At the moment fire explodes within me, I lose control of my powers, and fire also explodes without.

Achan screams in fear as his tent bursts into flames.

7

MEETING MOM

EIGHT DAYS HAVE PASSED SINCE JERED PURCHASED MY STONE, AND FOR once, I have him to myself without Gabe. I watch him from the bed, where I sit cross-legged, a pillow in my lap. Jered insists that I appear like a "normal woman." This is fine with me, considering I enjoy the freedom the clothes of this century allow. I quickly found my favorite combination of jeans and low-cut shirt, which I now wear.

Jered leans over his textbook, attempting to complete work assigned at his college. I enjoy the idea of my master being a scholar, but I am frustrated that he won't allow me to grant him an instant degree of his choosing. Today, he studies for a calculus exam. I don't believe he's completed one problem since starting. For one thing, he hasn't flipped the page in the last half hour. For another, I've seen how his eyes continue to slip toward me, how he chews his lip and taps his foot each time.

He's so intense with everything he does that I'm surprised his book doesn't melt beneath his gaze. I have certainly come close when I am the object of his attention. Achan was intense as well, but somehow, Jered's focus always has to do with bringing out the best in everyone around him. I admit it's taking longer than I thought it would for the stone to corrupt him. Perhaps I can corrupt him instead.

"Something I can do to help you relax, Jered?" I ask in my most innocent voice. If I can't grant him a diploma, at least I may be able to distract him with more enjoyable activities. After being inside Gabe, I know that he's confessed some experience with women, so there's little doubt of his attraction to my human form.

"Leela, I've been thinking," he says, spinning toward me in his seat, and resting his book on his lap. He stretches out his long legs before him and sinks down in the chair. "I'd like you to go to campus with me. So...so I can keep an eye on you." Clearly, he doesn't realize that I am always tied to him, nearby, watching, even when I'm not visible.

Tears well in my eyes as I was not expecting this. I struggle to keep them from falling, but he sees and drops his book to the ground, rushing to kneel by my side.

"Leela, what is it? Tell me what's wrong." He voices it as a command, so I am compelled to share more dangerous information with this master.

"It's just that I am afraid," I say, fighting the tears, hoping he will not press.

"What could you possibly be afraid of?" He asks.

"Buildings." I avert my eyes.

"Buildings?"

"The lead. Inside the paint. Lead is dangerous," I whisper, climbing off the bed and hugging myself.

"Only if you ingest it," he says, standing and placing his hand on my arm.

"For Djinn, it is poison. In great quantities, its presence weakens me, and touching any of it is pure pain. In fact, the more I am exposed, the worse I feel. I know it sounds silly, and I find it a miracle there isn't any in your apartment. But I still do not wish to be exposed to other sources." I hesitate and then add, "As punishment, my last master would force me to stay inside a house covered in paint with lead in it. It was quite painful." I don't know why I reveal this to him. He did not ask.

"I'm sorry," he says, and when I look, I grimace at the gentleness in his eyes. "You should know that we now understand lead-based paint is dangerous for everyone. It isn't really used anymore. I'm sure your last master didn't know how it affected you."

A bitter laugh escapes my lips. "She knew all too well, Jered. The paint peeled from the walls, and she'd make me press my palm to it. It was like a hundred knives imbedded in my skin."

I examine my hands, unable to stand the pain I see mirrored in his eyes.

He tilts my chin up to face him. "I promise to keep all lead far away from you." I find his smile painfully pleasant and don't want to pull away when he folds me into his arms. I feel...safe.

He decides to tell others that I am a student as well, but does not press me to attend classes. That's fine with me. At least this way, I don't have to pretend to pay attention to the instructors.

The first person he tests this new identity on is his mother, who lives within walking distance. Gabe often teases him about the amount of time he spends "checking in" with her. Thus far he has avoided telling her about me, and although no sign of magic presents in her aura, I am pleased he has chosen to heed my advice. Now it is time to compromise. Or so he explains. This way she can meet me without knowing what I am. I find this acceptable and am the picture of manners when we are officially introduced the following Saturday afternoon.

What jumps out at me the moment she answers the door is that she's gone to the trouble of putting on some makeup and fixing her hair. Normally her sandy waves are twisted up in a clip, her face drawn. The resemblance to Jered is remarkable, everything except for her star-tling gray eyes, so different from the deep, dark pools that seem to bind me whenever I look at her son. I immediately feel a rush of affection for this woman who cares enough to change her appearance just for me. I chastise myself for such a ridiculous reaction.

"Hello, Mrs. Archer," I say with my best smile attached. "Thank you for letting me come over."

"Nice to meet you, Leela. Please call me Corrie." She rakes me over from head to toe, searching for clues to my real identity. I can almost see the checklist in her head: drug addict, sex maniac, psychotic stalker.

Since none of those comes close to the truth, she moves aside to let me by.

Jered steps into view, and I smile. I see Corrie reacts much the same way. In fact, I've noticed how she rarely takes her gaze off her son. It's as though she's afraid he might disappear.

"So your major is history?" Corrie asks while I help her chop vegetables in the kitchen. It's a small room with chipped wood cabinets and a linoleum floor peeling up in the corners. But it is warm and comfortable, filled with the afternoon sunlight spilling in the sliding glass door. Family photos are spread across the refrigerator.

The photos are solely of Jered growing up. His father is missing from every one. This does not surprise me. Jered has already told me how his father ran off with another woman when he was young. That he rarely sees him despite the fact that he lives somewhere nearby. Although Jered has never met them, his father has another family now. I saw the obvious yearning in his eyes when he spoke of how he would love to know the siblings he has always wished for.

"That's right," I say, stealing a glance at Jered, who comes up behind me to snatch a piece of carrot from my cutting board. The warmth of his body so close to mine makes it hard to focus on what his mother is saying.

"Well, I'm glad you decided to come over for dinner. It's sweet of you to help, but it isn't necessary. If you two want to go watch TV or something..."

"That's okay, Mom. Leela loves to help out. Don't you, Leela?" Jered rests his hands on my shoulders.

"It's what I live for," I say, setting down my knife and wiping my hands. "I'm just happy that you've invited me, Corrie."

When I turn to speak to her, I find myself standing a hairbreadth away from Jered. I freeze, watching as he swallows and leans in toward me, drawn like a compass to true north. Corrie clears her throat.

"Jered, would you mind getting down the good dishes?" she asks, redirecting him to the farthest side of the room. I smile, but her eyes are sharp as daggers.

"So you're a social worker?" I ask, trying to change the subject back to her.

"That's right. I work with at-risk youth. It isn't a pretty job, but it's gratifying. You don't want to hear about me, though. Tell me something about yourself, Leela." She sets down the bowl of filling she's been mixing and crosses her arms.

I shift a little, uncomfortable.

"Not much to tell." I avert my gaze. We'd come up with a fake life story, involving me being a history major since I'd be able to answer so many questions with accuracy. But I don't like the lie, and I am far less comfortable with the truth.

"That's a pretty necklace," she says.

I cup my opal protectively. I feel exposed. "Thank you." My voice is a whisper.

"Is it an heirloom?" She reaches for my hand, and I take a step back with an audible gasp, hitting the counter, and knocking the knife to the floor so that it stabs the square of linoleum between our feet. She stops and retracts her hand, mouth slightly ajar.

"It's from her mother," Jered says, stepping in between us and retrieving the knife. "She died when Leela was young."

"Oh. I'm so sorry," Corrie says, and a shadow passes over her face. I believe she is. But that doesn't mean she isn't also wary.

When dinner comes, the room is filled with the clanking of forks on plates. Corrie sits between us at the table, and I have trouble looking at Jered. I'm afraid I've ruined everything. Afraid he'll be ashamed of me now because of my behavior.

"Pass the parmesan, Leela," Jered says.

I reach for the container at the same time as Corrie. My heart pounds, but I cannot stop it. I've been given a command. I must deliver Jered the stupid green can filled with powdered cheese.

Tears well in my eyes as I wrench the thing from Corrie's outstretched hand and hand it to Jered. His face is all it takes to push me over the edge. I watch as shock is replaced by outrage, which is replaced with dawning recognition.

After a hasty apology and exit, I reappear invisible in the kitchen.

Plates clatter with such vehemence, I'm sure Corrie is going to break something.

"Give her a chance, Mom. She didn't mean anything." Jered places a hand on Corrie's shoulder as she scrubs plates with such tense hands, I fear they will shatter.

"I don't think it's a good idea for you to see her anymore. I'm sorry, but something isn't right. Do you even know anything about her? Have you met her family?"

Jered sucks in his lip, and Corrie takes his hesitation as an answer. She stops what she's doing and turns to face him, hands pressed against the countertop, dripping water on the linoleum.

"I can't know for sure, but I think she might have been abused, Jered."

"And you want me to avoid her because of that?" Jered's face flushes; his eyes flash.

Corrie drops some silverware in the dishwasher and flips a towel over her shoulder, pausing to consider her son. She finally releases her breath and says, "I don't know what it is, Jered. But I know you. You're a good person, and the last thing you need is to get sucked into someone else's drama. She'll use you. I've seen this pattern before, over and over with the kids at work."

"Yeah, kids. We're adults in case you haven't noticed. You sure have it all figured out, though. Is this how you size up your patients? Say hello and decide what's best for them? Leela's a good person. I'm not going to stop seeing her."

"You're twenty, but that hardly qualifies as adult, I'm sorry to say. I don't want to see you get hurt."

Jered stares hard at Corrie, and Corrie stares right back. Finally, he storms out the front door and back to his studio apartment, where I appear before him, head down, hair falling in my face.

Will this be the point where he starts punishing me? I think of things I might say to stop it from happening. Offering to change his mother's memories perhaps. But the words catch in my throat.

"Leela," he says, and his voice is painfully soft. "Are you okay?"

I lift my chin. "I couldn't help it." Never once has an attempt to defend myself worked with a master. For some reason, I am still compelled to try.

"It was my fault. Not yours. I'm sorry, Leela."

Jered continues talking, telling me that I should stay hidden from now on around his mother. That he'll pretend he broke up with me so she doesn't ask too many questions. But my heart is caught on those first words, and I almost allow myself to hope that everything might be okay this time around.

8

DJINN TRACKER

I APPEAR IN THE PASSENGER SEAT OF JERED'S OLD COMPACT AFTER CLASS. I've taken the liberty of moving Gabe to the back seat. I ignore his protests and note the twinkle in my master's eye in response to my sudden arrival. I push aside the squeezing in my chest. What is wrong with me?

"Where are we going today?" I ask.

"Downtown Chicago."

I like that response. Finally, somewhere interesting. Thus far, he's dragged me through his sleepy suburb, asking me to fix people in the hospital, rescue cats from trees, and other humdrum tasks. He explains that every small act of kindness can change the world. I do not argue, just revel in his excitement and innocence.

I slide next to him and rest my head on his shoulder. I feel him tense, but I also hear his pulse speed up. I smile.

"You should put on your seat belt," he says.

"I will not be hurt," I say, playing with the corner of his jacket.

"I could get a ticket."

"I won't let the police pull you over." He frowns at me but doesn't argue anymore. I enjoy the feel of him, the musky scent that lingers in the air around him. I sit quietly the rest of the way downtown, silently moving traffic aside without his knowledge. At least, if he does know, he doesn't comment.

"The lake is beautiful," I say, watching it whiz by. "I've never lived near water."

"You like water?" he asks.

"Yes. It soothes me." I watch the line of deep blue sail by, finding the rhythm of the car's vibrations combined with the cadence of Jered's heartbeat lull me into a trancelike state. It is possibly the most peaceful I've felt since putting on the cursed necklace.

"Here we are," he says far too soon, pulling up to a rundown building. Shingles on the roof are missing, and graffiti decorates the moss-covered bricks. The entire neighborhood reeks of neglect, with brown, patched lawns and cracked sidewalks. My body vibrates with the thrum of the bass from some distant car's speakers.

I frown. "What is this place?"

"Good question," Gabe says, shutting the door behind him and shoving his hands in his pockets, protecting his wallet no doubt.

"Soup kitchen." Jered smiles up at the sad structure, positively ecstatic at the thought. "It's still a month or so until the holidays, and people don't usually notice that others are hungry until that time of year."

"You want me to feed them?" I ask, indicating two vagrants, now shuffling about outside the building, layered in tattered clothes and jackets.

"Put a fully cooked gourmet meal in the kitchen, enough for anyone who might stop by for the rest of the day. And leave some extra food in the cupboards." He smiles at me, eyes so full of hope and possibility. I bite back my own thoughts and fulfill his command.

"Anything else?" I ask.

"Leave clean clothes and blankets for all those staying at the shelter. And toiletries. And maybe some cash."

"They'll just use it to buy drugs and shit."

We both glare at Gabe, and he clamps his mouth shut.

"Just enough to buy them a hot meal somewhere else too. They can make their own decision what to do with it," Jered says. "Or can you make it so it disappears if they try to buy something harmful with it like booze or drugs? You know, just in case."

I wonder why he hasn't asked me for enough money so that his mother would no longer have to work. I don't want to ask it in front of Gabe though, so I nod and do as he commands.

"Can we go now?" Gabe asks.

"Yes. Let's go home," Jered says.

I wave an arm, and we are in his room.

"My car—" he starts, whipping around.

"Is in the garage. I don't know why you won't let me give you something better." I can at least say this.

"I didn't mean for you to bring us here. I meant I'd drive us back," Jered says.

"Jer, you gave her a command. You said 'let's go home,' and she brought us back. Don't say it if you don't mean it."

I nod at Gabe in approval for once.

He grins.

"You two are ganging up on me. Well, it isn't going to work." Jered takes out his homework and settles in at his desk.

Gabe shakes his shaggy head and folds his long legs beneath him and onto the floor while pulling out his phone.

"Jered, why do you never use my magic for yourself?" I ask, unable to hold it in any longer.

He stops his work and raises his eyebrows, jaw dropping open as though I've surprised him.

Gabe pauses the game he has started in order to look up. "Good question."

Jered shoots him an angry glance before swiveling back toward me. Those eyes make my stomach squirm. They do not belong on his face. They do not belong in my life. I focus on his hands instead.

"I'm afraid," he says simply and drops his pen on his open notebook.

"Afraid?" I take a step back. I feel as though I've woken in an alternate reality. One in which humans no longer follow a logical path.

"I've seen movies, read books where stuff like this happens, and it never turns out the way you expect," Jered says.

"I don't understand." I shake my head, confused.

"I think he means he's afraid you'll twist his wishes so that the exact opposite will happen," Gabe says.

"Oh. I must follow your command exactly. Have I done something that displeases you when you've expected something else?" I kneel beside him.

"No. Well, yes, but it isn't that. I don't think you mean to hurt me or anything." He is so young. So trusting.

"But you don't think like we do."

I cock my head to the side and consider him. One moment he says something so naïve. The next he notices something no one has bothered to notice in a millennium. He is a conundrum.

"I have never had a master like you," I say.

"I suppose most of them become blinded by power?" I nod, eyes wide as he smiles. "That's what's wrong with this world, Leela. Too many people think only about themselves, and how they can get more. Never mind who they have to use to do it."

"I have a question," says Gabe. "If you can step down off your soapbox for a minute, Mr. World Peace."

The light behind Jered's eyes fades. "What?"

"Does this mean you aren't going to wish for anything else?"

Jered rolls his eyes at Gabe as doubt creeps back to squeeze my heart. Jered may mean well, but he's still human.

"Can I borrow her?" Gabe asks. "You know, if you're not actually going to use her?"

"Gabe, she isn't a thing. She's a person."

"No. I'm not. I am not a person," I say, standing. "I look like a person. But I am Djinn. You would do better to remember that. I will wait for your command." I disappear in a puff of smoke. I wish I could be alone. But I must remain always near him. I know he does not understand this. That when I disappear from view, he thinks I go somewhere on my own. There is nowhere of my own though. Not as long as I wear the choker. And since I am bound to it for eternity, that is going to be a very long time.

"You really should lighten up, Jer," Gabe says. "She's obviously dying to show you those tits." Obviously, *he* doesn't think I am listening.

"I need to finish this homework, Gabe. Go play Zombie Squasher 4000 or something." Jered swivels again to face his desk.

"Naw, I think I'm gonna do a little research instead."

"Research?" Jered asks.

"On Djinn."

"Whatever." Jered picks up his pencil and scribbles.

I move over behind Gabe's shoulder to watch on the tiny screen. Most of the information is flawed, but as with any myth, bits and pieces ring true. Then he searches for an app. *Good luck finding one on Djinn,* I think, but to my surprise something shows up. An app called Djinn Tracker is available for free. I am as curious as Gabe, who darts a look over at Jered before starting the download.

It takes only seconds for an icon to pop up. It is an image eerily familiar to me. An eye inside of a sun with a moon and star orbiting it. My heart drops into my stomach. That is their symbol. How can it still be around? Impossible. He clicks on it.

Fingers of light filter out of the screen and climb through the air, searching sightlessly. Instinctively, I back up, dodging the probing beams. But even as I turn toward Jered, I know something is not right. His aura flares, colors washing over him, reacting like a magnet to the intruder.

I reach out with a cry, and the phone shatters in Gabe's hand, but not before the light connects, for just a moment, with Jered.

"Idiot!" I scream, revealing myself.

"Leela!" Jered shouts in surprise.

"He's done something," I say, seething. "He has alerted someone to your whereabouts. Someone that means you harm."

"What are you talking about? What's she talking about, Gabe?"

"I don't know. She's a psycho Djinni. She crushed my phone. I want a new one."

"Your phone is insignificant compared to Jered's life."

"What happened?" Jered says, slamming his book closed.

"I downloaded an app," Gabe says, casting his eyes downward. I smile triumphantly. "Djinn Tracker. But it didn't work. All I got was this cheesy logo."

"Oh, it worked, all right," I say. "You couldn't see it with your feeble human eyesight. Whatever that thing was, it found Jered, and it knows he's a Magician."

"I still don't buy that whole Jered's a Magician thing," Gabe says, daring to look me in the face.

"What you buy and don't buy is irrelevant. Except for that app," I state, folding my arms in defiance.

"Look, what's done is done, Leela," Jered says in a far too reasonable tone. "I'm sure it's no big deal. Even if there was something there, it's a Djinn Tracker, not a Magician Tracker, right?"

"But—" I protest.

"Fix Gabe's phone, please, Leela. And Gabe, don't be such an asshole."

"You didn't say please to me," Gabe says.

"Asshole."

It's hard not to smile despite the trepidation inside. That was strong magic. The kind that even a human knowing what he was doing would be hard pressed to design. And there was the matter of the symbol. The Magicians' symbol. Something is coming. I know it.

And I know it isn't good.

9

OLD FRIEND

"So you really think I have magic?"

Jered lies in his bed, covers up to his chin, lights out. The moonlight spills through the window and reflects off the black of his eyes, dancing like blue fire. I lie next to him, on top of the covers, close but not touching.

"I know you do."

"Can you teach me to use it?" he asks. His smile is contagious. It stretches to his eyes, and they sparkle even more.

I have to look away, so I trace my finger back and forth over the edges of the blanket, never quite coming to rest on his skin. I glance up enough to watch him swallow. I feel powerful.

"If that is your desire. I can teach you many things."

"Teach me, Leela."

"Close your eyes. Breathe deep." I enjoy watching him without him seeing me. "Now think about the energy around you. Can you feel it?"

"I think so."

"Call it to you. Focus on it. Pull it tight into a ball. Don't be afraid to use your hands." I wait as he strains. He reaches forward, gathering the air around him, causing his blanket to fall and reveal his bare chest.

His aura glows, and golden light streams through it, between his fingers. The entire vision is breathtaking.

"Good," I whisper. "Now hold it there and see."

His eyes flutter open, and he gasps at the sight of the miniature sun, glowing between his own hands.

"What do I do with it?" he asks, voice cracking.

"Whatever you want."

"Can I make it into a milkshake?"

I laugh. "Yes."

He concentrates, and the ball of light melts into a large cup filled with thick vanilla cream and two straws. I look at him quizzically.

"To share," he says, holding it out.

Not quite what I was going for, but sweet. And I must admit, it tastes divine.

After a minute, I extract the cup from his hands and lean over him, setting it on the nightstand. His breath is warm in my ear, and a shiver runs through my body, landing somewhere below my navel. I tilt my head toward his and smile. His gaze follows mine downward, and he turns such a deep red that I wonder if he can breathe.

"It's okay, Jered," I say, trying to keep the humor from my voice. "I don't mind, you know. You've been most patient and kind." I throw my leg over his lap and press against him, tossing my hair over my shoulder.

"Leela," he croaks, pushing me off and scooting as far to the side as possible without falling off the bed. "What do you mean I've been 'patient and kind'?"

"You've shown great restraint," I say, unable to hide my surprise. "Clearly you're interested. Besides, worse things have happened." I cannot stop a devilish grin from claiming my face.

"You're doing this because you think you have to, aren't you?" he asks, and he looks a little afraid.

Silence. I do want to be with him, but there's no denying I would not be here if it weren't for the stone.

"Oh, God. Leela, no!" He scoots toward me, tentatively taking my hands in his. They are still cold from the milkshake. "You mean someone's made you...but I thought it was just the magic. The wishing thing."

This conversation is not going the way I wanted it to. Which is to say, I did not want a conversation at all. "Wish fulfillment. Yes, Jered. That is my purpose. You are the first to have so much trouble with the concept." I tug at the choker again. Why has it been bothering me so much lately?

"You're telling me all of those who've owned this"—he holds up his hand with the ring—"have been *that* horrible? You mean they've used not just your magic, but...but *you*?" He looks disgusted, like he wants to rip it off his finger. He doesn't.

"You are the one who is different, Jered. You are the only one who sees me as anything other than an object."

"How can anyone think of you as an object?" he asks, his eyes flashing.

I cringe, remembering, and he reaches for me. I climb into his lap and lay my head against his chest. His strong arms wrap around me, and I close my eyes with a sigh.

I am wondering what Jered would do if I reached up and kissed him when I hear a voice from behind.

"Oh, it's you."

I leap off the bed at the sound, foreign yet familiar. Jered sits bolt upright and reaches for his lamp, knocking the milkshake off the nightstand.

The newcomer sits casually on the windowsill, one leg dangling loose. He's as tall and well-built as Jered, but his skin is dark and smooth beneath his open shirt, and his eyes are two sparkling emeralds, just like mine. I would recognize that impish grin anywhere.

"Taj," I say.

Part of me wants to throw my arms around him and dance. The other part wants to toss him out the window. One thing's for certain, he's trouble.

"Leela, it's been a long time. Who's the human?" His eyes flash appreciatively over Jered. Well, this is awkward.

"Who are you?" Jered asks. I can see he's nervous and rightly so. Taj is Djinn but not under his control. The question really is, why is he here? *How* is he here?

"Taj is an old friend," I say. "Taj, this is Jered. Jered, Taj."

"Friend?" Jered asks.

"Djinni," I confirm. "Djinni I haven't seen in a thousand years."

"Well, it isn't like they'd let us go to parties together," Taj says, sliding off the sill. He saunters over to the desk and examines the contents. Jered moves to speak, and I throw out a hand in caution. He quiets immediately.

"Are you," I begin. "Do you?"

"Have a master? Oh yes. A delightful woman bent on world domination. You'd love her, Lee. How about you, Jered? Any evil plots hatching? Armies? Fire ninjas? Flying monkeys?"

"Flying monkeys?" Jered asks.

"Oh, you wouldn't believe some of the ones I've seen. I'm sure Lee's had a few doozies in her day as well." His gaze connects with mine, and a million memories flash through my mind.

"Taj, how did you find me?" I ask.

"Lee, you're smarter than that. How do you think I found you?" he asks, taking my hands in his own.

"The app." I could strangle Gabe.

"See? I knew you caught on fast." He lets go with a blinding smile and continues perusing Jered's room. His eyebrows lift at the sight of the nearest poster of a car schematic, and he *tsks* softly and snaps his fingers, changing the image to one of himself bare-chested on a beach.

"Why are you here?" Jered asks. He is either very brave or very stupid. Perhaps a little of both.

"Now that's a much better question. And I think you deserve an answer." Taj strides over to the bed and sits, placing a hand on Jered's leg.

Jered is up and out so fast, I am sure he used magic.

"Nice pajamas," Taj says, drinking him in. "I hate to be the bearer of bad news, especially for someone as delicious as you. But..."

Taj's playfulness melts and is replaced by an expression of stone.

"I'm here to kill you."

10

THE BEGINNING

*Achan fills my life with a joy I never could have imagined in the
other realm. When the fire happened, I quelled the flames quickly, preventing
any serious damage. Though I believe he remains in the dark as to my true
nature, I must be careful. Stories have surfaced in towns and villages of
beings who are not of this earth. I imagine others have had mishaps similar to
my own while learning to control their new human bodies.*

*Kitra is all but forgotten. And why not? I give him everything he could
ever desire. Even those things he must never know I have provided. He is the
best-fed shepherd in the East. This I am sure of. He is also becoming the most
practiced in the physical arts.*

*The only adjustment I've had to make is ridding his belongings of lead. I
found I was terribly allergic to the thick gray cooking pots he had. I am sure,
since I am the one using them now, he does not notice the new ones made of
iron.*

*We travel together, through the desert, circulating from village to village,
town to town, in a rotation that Achan says takes three moons, at which point
we will be back at the beginning.*

*"I wish I had a sheep fat enough to make a trade for that blanket," he tells
me as we browse the market in the nearest town. One look into his eyes, and
my knees grow weak.*

"Why not check again, Achan?" I ask. "You may have missed one, the way they all move about."

He quakes with that deep, musical laugh that warms me from the inside and shakes his head. "You think I would miss that? Am I that bad at my job, Little One?"

"Check again, Achan. For me." I love the name he's given me. Little One. He is but eighteen, and I am infinite. Yet near him I feel young and new.

Later, when he finds the sheep I have hidden among the flock, he is delighted. "You are my lucky charm, Little One," he says, and he rewards me with a kiss.

These days are the happiest of my life. Wandering the world with Achan and his sheep. It is not the same for him, however. I tell him I am content with only him and the moon and the sun, but something dark and restless lurks behind his eyes, and I worry that I will lose him.

"You are the best of all of them, Achan," I say. "You are more man than the leaders of their villages. You could be king if you desired it. To me, you are king. King of the Desert."

"They treat me like a shepherd boy," he says.

"You are a shepherd boy to them. To me, you are king."

"What if I wanted to be more, Little One?"

"You can be whatever you decide."

"Perhaps with you, I can."

11

TAJ'S TASK

"Kill me?" Jered's voice cracks. He collapses back onto the bed, causing the blankets to fall in a heap on the floor and making Taj grin.

"Why?" I ask, edging forward so that I will be between Jer and Taj. I must find out what I can before I act.

"What makes you think I'm going to tell you anything?" Taj asks, moving so close, we are nearly nose to nose. Or more accurately, my nose to his chest.

"Because you want to," I say. "If you only wished to kill him, he'd be dead, and you wouldn't be here."

"True enough!" Taj smiles and puts a hand on each of my shoulders. "I've missed you, Lee."

"So you don't want to kill me?" Jered asks.

"Want to? Well, now, that is an interesting question. No. I don't particularly desire to kill you, especially now that I've seen you. There are so many other things I'd much rather do to you."

Jered's face drains of color, and I clear my throat to recapture Taj's attention. It isn't easy. He appears rather taken with my master, which I find annoying.

"Oh. Yes. Why? Well, I think you probably already know the answer to that one too. She commanded it," Taj says, moving over to trace the curve along the top of the footboard.

"For what purpose?" I press.

He turns to face me. "She wants you."

"She must not know, then." I wring my hands together as I attempt to reason this through.

"Know what?" Jered asks. He's found his feet now and is standing behind me.

"I told you before. If you are murdered and no one else claims me, I go free."

"You told him that?" Taj's gaze rakes Jered up and down. "He must be more than a nice body."

"Focus, Taj." I cross my arms and set my chin.

"Right. My mistress commanded me to torture the boy to find out if he has a Djinni, and if he does, force him to give you over and then kill him. I might have left that first part out though. I hate discussing such tedious tasks." He flips his wrist in an offhand way and disappears, only to reappear near Jered's dresser, which he opens and riffles through.

"So she doesn't know for certain that I'm here?" I ask, relief washing over me.

"Not yet. I'm supposed to bring you back though, so I don't see what difference it makes."

"What were her exact words, Taj?" I ask, removing a pair of boxers from his grasp and replacing them in the top drawer.

"Hmm. Why am I telling you all of this again?"

"Because you're a kind and generous Djinni who doesn't really want to hurt me?" Jered asks.

"Oh, I do like you. I wish you weren't so much...fun. I'm going to dislike this task."

"Taj!" I yell to get his attention.

"She said, and I quote, 'Find this Magician in Chicago; find out if he or she owns a Djinni; and if so, persuade him or her by any means necessary to gift me that Djinni. When the Magician does this, you may dispose of him or her as you see fit.' Oh! I've been a slave for so long I forget to pay attention to the exact wording of the command. Maybe I don't have to torture and kill at all. Perhaps I can persuade you in a more pleasant way?" He moves deliberately toward Jered, his emerald eyes gleaming, and runs a finger down the poor man's arm.

"Leela, help," Jered squeaks.

"Taj, he isn't interested."

"Is that true?" he asks, pouting close to Jered's face. My master looks about ready to pass out, and I can't blame him.

"Taj." I call his attention back to me.

"Yes, Lee?" Taj straightens and turns to face me.

"You will not harm him," I say. "I will not go to this woman. You know why I cannot."

"Of course I don't want you to. That would be catastrophic. But I'm not seeing a way out of this, Lee."

"Let us think," I say, placing a hand on his arm.

"If I'm not back by tomorrow, she will call me and re-command it. I really don't feel like being punished again, either."

"Punished?" Jered asks, his eyes growing darker, like small shadows on his face.

Taj looks at me in question, and I sigh.

"Most masters punish their Djinn when we don't do as they intend," I explain.

"Or step out of line," Taj adds, conjuring an apple and taking a bite.

"In what way?" Jered asks.

"In any way, kid. Lee's yours. You can do whatever you want to her. Sky's the limit, and she can't do a damn thing about it."

I am reminded of our earlier conversation and find it difficult to look in Jered's eyes.

"We have until morning. We will come up with a suitable solution," I say. "We must concentrate on the task at hand. I will not become this woman's Djinni."

Jered sits heavily on the bed and shrugs away from my hand when I reach for him.

"What is it?" I ask.

"It's what you said. Or didn't say. The way you put it. You can't be given to her, not 'oh no, I can't let Jered die.'"

"Don't take it too hard, kid." Taj sits so close, their thighs touch, but Jered continues to sulk as though nothing's happened. "She doesn't care. That's our nature. We don't want to be slaves. You wouldn't either. So as cute as you are, I'm sure Lee would be thrilled if you were killed and she were freed."

"Taj," I say in warning.

"I never looked at it like that," Jered says. "I didn't fully realize until tonight, but you're right. I never meant to make anyone a slave. I would never—"

"Jered, listen to me. You will be fine. We will find a way to fix this." I kneel on his other side, catching his eye.

"I think the way to fix this is obvious," Jered says, straightening his back.

"How?" I ask.

"I need to free you."

12

EXPONENTIAL

FREE ME. I AM SPEECHLESS.

"No can do," Taj says, and my hopes shatter. He claps once, and Jered winces. "Now that you said that out loud, Einstein, I took away those words. I have to persuade you otherwise. Get it?"

"What do you mean you took away 'those words'?" Jered asks.

"I put a spell on you. You won't be able to free Leela. Not for the next couple of days anyhow. We should have this all straightened out by then." Taj's grin is as wicked and wonderful as I remember.

"You're fr-fr..." Jered stammers, face burning red with the effort. "I really can't say it? I should have just done it."

I do believe I see tears behind his eyes. Fascinating. I've only ever seen eyes like those cry once before. But the situation was so different. The sudden realization hits me head on, and I drop to the floor at his feet.

"I'm so sorry, Leela."

"Sorry?" I whisper. "For me?"

"You know," Taj says, "if I want to see all this melodrama, I can turn on my Mexican soap operas. Don't look so glum, kid. You're seriously making me dislike this job. I should've just done it. Only after I saw you, Lee, I had to talk to you first."

"How did this happen?" I ask. "Who is this woman?"

"She's no innocent like Jerry here; I'll tell you that much."

"But how does she know?" I ask, digging my nails into the carpet.

"The knowledge was passed down to her along with her Djinni," Taj says, his green eyes boring through me. It's like he's trying to tell me something.

"You mean you?" Jered asks, trying to keep up.

"No. I don't usually talk about myself in third person, kid. I was a recent addition."

"What?" I stand now, power crackling at my fingertips. "Then she already has—"

"She's looking for lucky number three. That would be you, Lee."

"You mean she's collecting Djinn?" Jered asks, looking between the two of us. "What for? Any normal person would be more than happy with one."

"She's not normal. Haven't you been listening? Good thing you're good-looking." Taj shakes his head and tosses his apple core into the air, where it vanishes.

"Djinn powers are exponential," I say, standing to pace. "A human Magician's power is limited. Mine is far stronger, but still restricted. I cannot reverse time, for example. Slow it down if I know what's coming, yes, but what's done is done."

"Put two of us together, and you have some serious energy," Taj says, waggling his eyebrows.

"Three with no one standing in the way, and we could control the natural order of the world," I say, coming to a stop in front of Jered.

"We're talking natural disasters of Biblical proportions. Enslavement of millions. Et cetera, et cetera." Taj puts an arm around Jered's shoulder.

"And no one's ever done this before?" Jered stands.

"No." I sigh and lean against the edge of the desk. "There are very few of us, spread all over the world. Humans were not supposed to even know of the possibility." I meet Taj's eyes and know we are both remembering the moment it was decided.

"It's an epic story, kid," Taj says. "Someday maybe I'll tell you, but for now, we need to put our heads together and come up with a way around the command. I'm notoriously slippery, but I can only hold her off for so long before she adjusts her command."

"But if you really don't want to follow a command—I mean, even slaves can rebel, right?" Jered asks, sitting back down like he doesn't know what to do with himself.

"It's magic. We have no choice. Remember the parmesan?" I ask, stroking his arm as I sit beside him.

"Show him," Taj says.

I grimace but understand the importance of Jered's clarity on the subject and nod.

"Tell her to hurt herself."

"No. I couldn't. I—"

"Give her a command you know she would never follow of her own volition," Taj says.

"I won't make her hurt herself!" Jered leaps to his feet. Taj's eyes flash in response to his sudden temper, and I know my master is treading a very fine line.

I snap my fingers so that Gabe appears in the room, wearing striped pajamas. "Tell me to do something nice to Gabe, then."

Jered swallows, taking in his best friend's confused expression.

"What the...where the...how the...?"

"Fine. Leela, kiss Gabe." Before Gabe can register his words, I press my mouth to his. He tastes like toothpaste. I nearly gag. Gabe, on the other hand, responds with enthusiasm, pressing his lips against mine and reaching around me with his arms. I feel his tongue worm inside my mouth.

"Enough!" Jered shouts.

I push Gabe away and wipe my mouth on my arm.

"Whoa," says Gabe, stumbling back. When he realizes he has an audience, he fumbles for Jered's desk chair, arranging it in front of him, a deep shade of garnet coloring his face and neck. "What the fuck? Don't tease me like that. And who's the Antonio Banderas wannabe?"

"Is that your boyfriend?" Taj asks Jered. "Because if he is, I am so disappointed." He is back to his calm demeanor, but I know how tenuous this situation is.

"I think I've been humiliated enough for one night," Gabe says.

"The point is that I cannot disobey a command," Taj says. "So unless you want to die, I suggest you help us figure this out."

13

THE BEGINNING

"Achan, where have you been?" I ask. I have given him his privacy today because he has asked for it. I have spent my time preparing a meal I know he will enjoy, forgoing my magic and using my human hands instead. I worry it will be difficult for him, coming back full circle to the town we started from.

When I see his handsome face, I find something new there. Or perhaps it is the way he walks, with more confidence.

"The people in this village have made a very important discovery, and I have convinced them to make me a part of their Council."

I nearly drop the basket of dates I am holding. "Achan! That is wonderful." Perhaps now he will be at peace, and we can live happy and free.

"What was their discovery?" I ask.

"They've found a way to make mud into gold. A way to never go hungry. They've found a way to use real magic."

"Magic?" I repeat.

"Indeed."

"What a lucky discovery that is." My stomach clenches at the thought. I could have done that for them. But I am not interested in solving all the world's problems. Just Achan's.

"You are my lucky charm," he says, with a blinding smile.

"I was not even near you today," I say, feeding him a date.

"You didn't have to be with me. You've changed me just by being near. Others see the change too."

"Like the Council?"

"Yes. They believe I am one destined to wield the new power. But I will need your help, Leela."

"Me?"

"Without you, I am nothing."

"You could never be nothing," I say, delighted.

He scoops me into his arms and covers my face and neck in kisses.

"Achan, the food!"

"Let it burn," he says, laying me down on the ground and running his hands over my body. I could not agree more, and I tell him so with my own caress. Yes. I believe this change is good.

Now he will be content.

14

SMALL WORLD

I CANNOT BELIEVE THEY THINK GABE'S CRAZY PLAN WILL WORK. WHY DID I have to bring him into this anyway? I should have let Jered tell me to cut off my arm or something. It would have been less destructive.

"You loved it," Gabe says, sidling up next to me. I wish I'd never heard that *don't hurt anyone* command.

"Let's get on with this," I say. Ignoring him is the best I can do. For now.

Jered gives a solemn nod, ready to issue the command and set the plan in motion. "Leela, go find another Magician nearby and bring that person here."

Permission to leave his side. Normally, I would be ecstatic, but now, I can't help worrying about Jered alone with Taj and Gabe. Jered's stubbornness nearly killed him once tonight; I can only imagine what clumsiness Gabe might unleash. Taj is a land mine waiting to go off.

I pick up the pace. The cold air stings my face as I soar through the city, invisible, phasing in and out of homes so I can observe the auras within. I allow myself an indulgent smile, reveling in the feel of the wind, the blackness of the night.

It doesn't take me long to find what I seek. And given the choice presented in this one suburban house, it is easy to pick. I settle down beside the small bed with its white lace canopy and pastel quilt, leaning forward, ready to transport us both back. Yet at the last moment, I hesitate.

The sleeping child is beautiful, with hair woven of sand and gold, and skin the color of cream. I study her form. So peaceful. So small. The rhythmic pulse of her life's breath rises and falls beneath the blanket that she clutches in her tiny hand. Innocent. For now.

I shake myself. What is wrong with me? I have a command. I have to get back. I saw the strong aura shining through the covers in the master bedroom. Perhaps I ought to take the parent...no. This child is the safer choice. A full-grown Magician—who knows what problems he might create? I inhale sharply and will myself to be seen.

"Hello," I say, placing a hand on her forehead. Her eyes flutter open, and in them I see waves of confusion and then fear, followed, most curiously, by recognition.

"You're real," she whispers back.

"Yes, child."

"I dreamed about you."

I smile and find that I am gently stroking her hair, which is as soft as the finest silk. "What is your name?"

"I'm Sophie."

"Sophie, I'm going to take you for a ride, okay?"

"Can I tell my mom?"

"No. We will be back before she even knows you are gone. I promise."

"All right."

Well, that was easy. I scoop her into my arms, letting the blankets slip back onto the bed. She clings to my neck and buries her head against my chest. She is warm from sleep and smells pleasant, like strawberries.

I fly out the window and through the night, back to Jered at lightning speed, setting Sophie down gently on the floor before the others. Even Taj raises his eyebrows at my cargo.

The child takes us all in without alarm. Mild curiosity would be a better description. And even with her pink pajamas, tangled hair, and sleep-laden eyes, she seems at ease. It is hard to believe she is not intimidated by four strangers twice her height.

"You brought back a child?" Gabe's voice is so high, I'm surprised the glass in the window doesn't shatter. "That's kidnapping. We'll go to jail."

"I kidnapped no one," I say, staring him down. "She came willingly. Not that it matters. What needs to be done, needs to be done."

"I don't know about this..." Jered says, stepping forward.

"It is perfectly safe. There will be no need to harm it," Taj says.

"It's so comforting, how you call her an *it*," says Gabe, and I see that I was right to be concerned about the volatility of the situation. Before Taj can strike, the child's voice rings across the room, and four sets of eyes focus on her.

"Hi, Jered."

"You know her?" I ask.

"There's something familiar about her," he says, stepping forward and kneeling before her. "Hello."

I wish I'd brought the adult instead. Or that one of the other two children in the house displayed the glistening aura of a Magician.

"Daddy misses you," she says. She reaches out a small hand to poke him on the nose.

"Oh my God," Jered breathes, but I remain as confused as ever. "Is it possible? Where did you get her?"

"At a house not too far from here," I say, not happy with the way the others are looking at me. "It was she or the adult. I didn't want to risk using a full Magician who may be aware of his powers."

Sophie beams up at Jered. "You know who I am, right? Isn't that why you sent Leela to me? She's yours, isn't she?"

"How does she know this?" I ask. I hear my voice rise in volume, feel my pulse speed up. This child is dangerous. I should know better than to trust appearances. I—

"Jered is my brother."

15

COMPLICATIONS

JERED DROPS TO HIS KNEES IN FRONT OF SOPHIE. "YOU'RE MY HALF sister?" A grin slowly spreads across his face. "But I still don't know how you know me. We've never met." He holds out a hand, and she shakes it, giggling.

I recall the longing in Jered's eyes when he spoke to me of his father and siblings. How he wished for a relationship with them.

"There's a bond between family members; still, its powers must be very strong." Taj bends to examine her. "I take back what I said before. We may have to destroy it."

Jered pulls Sophie behind his back and stands to face Taj, anger burning behind his dark eyes. It is hard for me to bear. To see those eyes burn like that again.

"You'll stay away from her!" It is the first time I've heard him sound this fierce. I almost believe he could handle Taj. But no human's that strong.

"Whoa," I say, stepping in between. "There will be no need to harm the child." Taj sees the real message in my eyes. *We will deal with this threat later.* After all, the grown Magician with two Djinn and the danger to my master's life must take precedence.

"I will trust your judgment, Lee. But do not push me," Taj snarls at

Jered as he backs up toward the bed. I step behind my master's shoulder so I can keep Taj in my sights.

"You said Dad misses me," Jered is saying. "How do you know that? Does he talk about me?"

"He thinks about you. A lot. He doesn't know I'm listening. I don't want to tell him because he'll make it so I can't hear. You won't tell, will you?"

"No," Jered says, glancing toward me and then Gabe.

"Can you hear everyone's thoughts?" I ask.

"I hear Daddy. And Jered now that I'm here. But that's it."

"But you dreamed about me?" I ask.

"Yes. You were hugging me and protecting me from the bad person." She giggles again, startling me after her pronouncement.

"What is funny?" I ask, looking around.

"Jered likes you."

"Of course I do, Sophie. Leela is my friend."

I feel his focus on me and fight the warmth creeping up my neck. I don't care how much time has passed, I will not make the same mistake twice. *I will not.*

"How cute," Taj says. "It does tricks."

"Stop calling her an 'it,'" Jered snaps, straightening to his full height, shoulders back and at attention. His aura swells and flows around him, scarlet and sparking.

The hairs on my arms stand up from the power sizzling in the room. I fear I won't be able to distract Taj this time.

"Jered, why am I here?" Sophie asks, tugging on his fingers in an attempt to get his attention back. She feels it too, then. *Good girl.*

"We have a gift for you," I say. I hold out my hand, and a doll appears. It is a good likeness, I think. With raven hair and almond skin in a traditional harem outfit. Me if I were an eleven-inch doll. Sophie's crystalline blue eyes shine with recognition, and she reaches for it, hugging it to her chest.

"My very own Djinni!" she exclaims. "I'm going to call her Little Leela."

"But I'm afraid I'm going to have to ask you to give it to Taj." I nod toward the other Djinni.

"Then it isn't much of a gift," Sophie says, still clutching it to her.

"No, I guess not," I agree. "But if you do give it to him when he asks, Jered will let me give you another doll, if that is what you want."

"Ohhh-kay," she says. I smile encouragingly. Whether more for her or Taj, I cannot say.

"Give me the doll for my master's keep," Taj says, flinging out an open hand.

"You didn't say please." Sophie pulls the doll behind her back.

Taj's muscles tense to the point I'm afraid they will explode. I tilt my head in a nod, and he takes a long, slow breath. "Please."

Sophie kisses her Djinni doll tenderly on the head and hands it to him. "Take good care of her." He rolls his eyes, and the doll disappears from view.

"Okay," Jered breathes. "Problem solved. A Magician in Chicago with a Djinni who's been persuaded to give it over to you."

"Wonderful. Now we have until I give it to my master tomorrow and she explodes in anger, punishes me, then questions me, and reorders your specific destruction in every gory detail." Taj sits on the bed and pulls a jeweled goblet from thin air, wine sloshing up and over the edges as he raises it above his head. "How about a toast?" he asks, and we each have a matching glass.

"To the worst plan ever!"

16

THE BEGINNING

"HUMANS HAVE FOUND A WAY TO USE MAGIC," I SAY.

Taj's boisterous laugh stops cold at the pronouncement. We meet in the treetops of the oasis, balancing like birds on the thin olive branches in the sky. We are invisible to humans, so we can truly be ourselves.

"Is it not wonderful?" I ask, continuing to dance around, leaping from limb to limb and spinning in the air.

"How have they managed it?" Taj asks, straddling one of the thicker branches and pushing aside the leaves.

"I do not know," I say, shrugging. "What difference does it make? Now they will be more like us. We will not have to hide much longer."

"Does Rhada know? She spends so much time with that woman."

"I do not speak with Rhada. She and Mira have little time for me since they have become involved."

"Mira tends to become obsessive on occasion," Taj says, laying a hand on my arm.

"I care not what choices she makes." I do not know why my chest squeezes when I say this. I remain perplexed by human behavior, including my own.

Taj looks as though he wishes to say more, but Mira herself materializes inches from me. Her beautiful face is creased with worry.

"I have not seen Rhada in a fortnight."

"Why should that concern me?" I ask with another shrug.

"She is probably playing with that human," Taj says.

"That woman is merely a distraction," Mira says. "She cares for me. She would not leave me for this long."

"She is obviously tired of you." I flick a hand in dismissal. "The humans are new and fresh. The physical form is so...delicious."

Mira disappears in a flash of green light.

"You should not be so cruel to her," Taj says.

"Why? She is not one of them. She is one of us. I am sure Rhada is simply enjoying the earthly delights she has discovered. Mira should not be so...what did you say? Obsessed. They have eternity to be together."

"Perhaps. But have you considered the possibility that not all humans are as divine as yours?"

"Do not be absurd. What are you even suggesting?" I pull an iris from the air and arrange it in my hair.

"I do not know. But I can tell you that I have already met a few that are now enjoying a life as rodents. Assuming, of course, they have not been swallowed by a snake."

"Taj! You should not interfere like that. And for what? Not appreciating your human form, no doubt."

"Perhaps they appreciated it too much and did not want to let it go."

"Scoundrel."

"Thank you, darling." Taj sweeps me into his arms and dances us higher, through the sky. We are both laughing and reveling in the warmth of the human sun....

Both Mira and Rhada are pushed aside like the clouds that swirl into nothingness as we spin through them.

Forgotten.

17

TAKING COMMAND

"WE MUST GO FAR AWAY." I PEER THROUGH THE WINDOW, HALF EXPECTING to find it's already too late and Taj has returned. "You should have me take Sophie home now so we can leave. It might be a good idea to ask me to erase her memory of this night as well."

I pace back and forth between the bed and the window while Gabe lies on the floor playing tic-tac-toe with Sophie and her replacement doll. Jered watches me with his relentless eyes.

"Slow down, Leela. It's going to be all right. There's no reason for this woman to suspect Sophie wasn't the same Magician from the app. Taj won't tell her if he doesn't have to, right?"

"No. Even he wouldn't be that impulsive."

"And I think I'd like to spend some time with Sophie, get to know her." He smiles toward his sister, now tackling Gabe in a fit of tickles. Jered's aura glows gold, and something within me leaps in spite of myself.

"She should be in bed," I say. "If your father finds out about me—"

"He isn't a bad man," Jered says.

"He left you." I regret the words the moment they leave my lips. His face hardens as he turns away. But there is risk in this, and he must see it.

"People make mistakes. He has another family now. Just look at Sophie, and you can see he can't be that bad." He wants me to agree, but I cannot. I know what other Magicians are capable of.

"Please," I whisper. "Please listen to me on this. I can take you far away from here. Somewhere they'll never find us."

"I won't leave, Leela. What about my friends and family? I'm not giving up my life because of some boogeyman."

"You can bring Gabe, then! I don't care." I grab his hand in desperation.

"Leela, stop. Just stop talking about it. I won't go. I can't leave my mom or Sophie or my dad, even if he never speaks to me again."

"So you have commanded," I say, pulling my hand away. I am unable to keep the bitterness from my voice. How can it be so much harder to take a command from him than from any of my other masters? At least since the first. Perhaps it is the level of freedom he's already given me. A taste is worse than none at all. Or maybe it's the eyes...

"Leela, I didn't...I mean...shit." He lowers his head, rubbing the back of his neck.

I disappear from view. The sting of tears is like pins pushing on the backs of my eyes. I don't understand where it comes from, but if I must bear this, at least I can bear it in private.

"You hurt her feelings," Sophie says, standing and approaching Jered.

"I thought you couldn't read her mind," he says.

"I don't have to. It's her face." She nods toward the place where I stand invisible, and my mouth drops open.

"You can see her? Is she there now?" he asks.

I shake my head at her. *No.*

"You want to come live with us?" she asks him instead. Her smile breaks free, and I wonder at the transparency of the young.

"I wish I could be with you more. I like having a little sister," Jered says.

"I like you too. We'll be together soon though. Daddy says you'll be ready this summer."

"Ready?" Jered asks. I dry my eyes with the backs of my hands.

"He thinks about it a lot," Sophie says.

"What does he think about?" I ask, reappearing.

"About being with Jered forever. Can I have something to eat?"

Jered focuses his energy between his palms and hands her a milkshake. It is impossible not to smile at the way her face lights up at the sight of it. I notice, as she takes it, the color of the ice cream changes to pink.

"Strawberry." She grins and takes a sip.

"When you're done, Leela will take you home. You do need to get some sleep." Jered leans down and rubs the side of her arm as she sips her shake, eyelids drooping.

"Seriously," Gabe says with a yawn. "My work is done here, so could you, uh?" I snap my fingers, and he disappears.

Sophie tries to stifle her own yawn, and I dispose of the milkshake before it hits the ground.

"Yep," Jered says. "Time for bed. Leela, take her home but don't touch her memories."

"Yes, Jered," I say, wishing I could use the word master to vex him. He said to "take her home," so I scoop the child into my arms and fly toward her house. She is already half asleep, clutching her doll and leaning into my chest. The warmth of her body against mine is pleasant and stands out in the chill air like a star in the night.

"Do not say anything to your father about tonight." I lay her tenderly in the bed.

"Okay," she says, tucking her doll in beside her. "Thanks, Leela, for taking me to my brother."

"You are welcome." I move to stand, and she stops me with her small hand. She smiles up at me and throws her arms around my neck. I wait patiently for her to lie back down.

"I love you, Leela." Before I can respond, she is claimed by sleep. I stay still for a minute, watching the delicate rise and fall of her chest, the way her small pink mouth sucks softly on nothing.

"Sweet dreams, Little One."

18

A BLAST FROM MY PAST

I watch Jered sleep. It is preferable to pacing the apartment halls alone. I sit perched on the windowsill observing, wondering what it is he sees in his dreams. If only I had the kind of power the child possesses. How's that for irony?

We argued when I got back. If I tried to bring up leaving again, my throat would swallow my voice, and nothing would come out. I tried to explain that Taj's master would be thorough. That she already understood things she should not. That she would surely be suspicious enough to wring every ounce of knowledge from Taj's mind. Jered would have none of it.

"We'll run the second he shows up," he said.

Assuming Taj will be able to show himself first. I was about to argue further, when he said the thing I haven't been able to put out of my mind for the past four hours. "Leela, I know you're looking out for me. I get it, and I want you to know I appreciate it. If I could, I would fr-fr..." He stops and takes a deep, shuddering breath, clearly frustrated at being unable to say the words.

"I'm so sorry," he continues. "But please trust me. I'll never treat you like a slave. I wouldn't hurt you on purpose."

A gust of wind breaks me out of my reverie.

"It *is* you."

I press my eyes closed for a moment at the sound of the familiar voice. I didn't want to believe the third Djinni was her. But here she is.

"Hello, Mira." I drink in face still fresh in my memory, the full, red lips, and the deep-set eyes.

"I'm surprised you're still here," she says.

"He wouldn't go."

"Not very smart. You should have persuaded him."

"He isn't easily persuaded," I say.

"Since when does that stop you from getting what you want?"

I flinch at her words like they are a whip. "What is your command?" I ask. She may hate me, but I have to believe she wants to prevent the worst.

"I have none. Yet. Though I can promise you my master will send me to clean up the mess when she figures it out, and she will."

"Then why are you here?" I ask, slipping off the sill to face her. "Just to torture me?"

"If only I could. No. Taj told me it was you, and I had to see for myself."

I nod, taking in this information. "How did you get away?"

"It is my night to patrol. So I'm patrolling here." She shrugs, swiping a finger over a line of dust along the back of the desk. "She sends us out on rotation to search for signs of magic. I won't have to tell her I found anything. I didn't find you. Taj did."

I force myself to look her in the eyes as she stops inches from me, swiping the thick layer of dirt from her hand. "You are still angry, but I couldn't have known."

"Then you were pathetic and blind. It doesn't surprise me." She sneers, and I wince in response.

"You're right. I was. But I'm not anymore."

"Bravo. Our race is enslaved for over a millennium, but you know better now." She claps her hands slowly in my face and then turns toward Jered's bed.

"Where are you going?" I ask, popping in front of her.

"To kill the Magician, of course. Then you can return the favor."

"No!" I should not have shouted because I see the understanding light behind her eyes.

"Methinks the lady doth protest too much."

"There is no need to kill him," I say.

"I think I'll take my time." She moves to push past me.

I throw out a hand to stop her, gripping her arm. "You're not listening, Mira. He's practically a boy. I can go, kill this master of yours, and Taj can retract his spell and—"

"Why risk it? Don't tell me you actually believe he's going to free you after this is over?" Her bitter laugh pierces the air.

"I will," Jered says from behind me, his aura wrapping around me protectively, like a hug.

I quiet the smile threatening to break through. I will not lose focus. I will not let her kill him. It isn't necessary.

"Leela, you are stupid," Mira says, narrowing her eyes. "A thousand years, and you still haven't figured it out? Humans suck. They're power-hungry, greed mongers with no souls. He will betray you."

"So let me make that mistake. It's only myself at risk. I thought you wanted me to suffer, Mir." I step toward her, pleading.

"Oh, I do. And it is only you at risk. This time." She looks past me, drinking in Jered's appearance. I feel his body close the space behind me. The warmth of his breath raises goose bumps on my arms. "Fine then. As long as I see him give the command for you to kill her and release us."

Jered rests his hands on my shoulders and spins me to face him. Turns me away from the threat.

"I can't tell you to kill someone," he says. He speaks softly, only to me. My heart sinks into my stomach.

"You must," I beg. I want to shake him, to force him to listen to me. "If you don't, you will die."

"I can't be responsible for something like that." His voice is stern, but his hands are comforting on my shoulders.

"I'll be responsible. Let me do this." I sound hysterical as I grasp his arms as well. "I want to do this. Simply say, 'Leela, you may do what you want to Mira's master.'"

"It's dangerous for you, isn't it?" he asks, changing tactics. He remains focused on me, despite my desperation to turn around and keep an eye on Mira. "She has two Djinn to protect her, this woman. She could order them to do something terrible, couldn't she? Leela, can they kill you?"

"It is irrelevant," says Mira, stepping into my line of sight. It doesn't help ease my nerves. She's now far too close to Jered. "If she doesn't know she's coming, she won't have a chance. I guarantee you that neither Taj nor myself will jump to protect her like Leela did for you."

"You're talking about cold-blooded murder," Jered shoots back. "There has to be another way." I am terribly aware of his hands still resting on my shoulders.

"Either you give the order, or you remain an obstacle I must remove." Mira takes one more menacing step forward.

"Jered, think carefully on what you say." It is the best I can do.

"One more question," he says, squeezing my shoulder.

"I tire of this." Mira throws her hands up in frustration.

"Think of the suffering I will endure if you are right and he betrays me." I try to quell the building inferno inside her. I used to be able to reason with Mira. She'd always been hotheaded but still logical. Has that changed after a thousand years of servitude? Does she want revenge on me badly enough to listen?

"I'm beginning to think you'd suffer worse if I freed you." She turns toward me, crossing her arms and narrowing her eyes.

"Mira, is there a way to free you and Taj without killing your master?" Jered asks.

"Only if she frees us. And that will never happen."

"What if we trick her?" He steps between us. "Make her free you by accident?"

"Bzzz. Sorry, your time is up."

The room around us rumbles as white flames shoot out of the walls. I feel the heat of the explosion through the protective bubble I throw around us. Time slows, and debris sprays through the air, pieces of

Jered's furniture and belongings reduced to shards. Fragments of Jered's life obscure our view as the inferno engulfs my shield. I have mere seconds to get us out before she sees.

On the ground outside, I turn to ask him to remove his restrictive commands, only to find him lying immobile on the grass.

19

WAKE-UP CALL

"JERED!" I SCREAM AND FALL TO MY KNEES BESIDE HIM. HIS SKIN IS PALE blue in the light of the moon. Dark splotches of soot pepper his face and chest. "Breathe," I say. And until I see him draw a breath, I realize I've been holding my own.

I heal him quickly, knowing Mira will be thorough with her search when she doesn't find me freed and waiting. He coughs, clearing his lungs, and I push away the smoke billowing out from the side of the building so it will not choke him.

"You have to tell me to help you. Be specific," I explain as he takes in our surroundings, wide-eyed. I've been commanded not to talk of leaving.

"Save the others." He coughs. "People live here besides me. Go, now!"

I vanish and reappear within the smoldering building. Damn him and his obsession with others. He could be dead by the time I'm done here. I search through the heavy smoke for any other signs of life. Thankfully, most are unharmed, yet dazed. I send them all away across the street to safety and am about to pop back to Jered when I spot her. Sandy-colored hair spreads across the lobby floor from beneath a beam fallen from the ceiling. Her eyes are closed, her face covered in grime. I don't know if she's alive, but I do know her face.

Jered's mother.

Exasperated, I throw the beam from her with the wave of a hand. I lift her in my arms and reappear before Jered. I am relieved to find him alone and unharmed below the crater that used to be his second-story apartment. Without a word, I lay his mother at his feet, and he gasps before throwing himself on her, crying and shaking her shoulders.

"Jered, move. I must save her." My body jerks toward them, desperate to fulfill my master's wishes. Jered nods and allows me access.

I examine the woman on the ground. I place my hands on her chest and focus my energy on her aura. *Breathe*, I will. She draws deep on the night air, and I feel Jered's hands on my back. I shiver despite the heat pulsing from the fire.

"You did it!"

"She needs a doctor, Jered. I can't reach her." I stand, searching his face. I watch the glow of the rapidly expanding flames reflect off the surface of his eyes.

"What do you mean you can't reach her?" He grasps my arms, jostling me like a flashlight he can make work.

"I tried. Truly. And she's in there, but...but I can't get her to wake up."

I would do anything to take away the pain I see through the flickering shadows on his skin. But I cannot. I feel helpless.

"Mira will find us any minute," I say. I must make him see the danger he is in.

"Take us all to the hospital."

I nod, and we are in the emergency room where, after a moment of chaos and confusion, doctors rush out with a stretcher for Jered's mother. We follow in their wake, two people who've escaped a horrible accident.

I hurry things along without a word. Once she is set up in a room and a nurse in light-blue scrubs has taken Jered's information, I squeeze his arm. He remains limp.

The nurse shuffles from the room with a smile that does not reach her eyes, and silence falls over the tiny space, punctuated by the mechanical beeps and whirs of modern medical equipment. The smell of rubbing alcohol burns my nose. I reach up, and the curtain that separates Jered's mother from the other bed snaps closed.

"We should—" I begin.

"I won't leave her." He says this without taking his eyes from her pale face.

"She won't know whether you're here or not," I say, cupping his face in my hands. "And if we stay, Mira will find us. She could kill every human in this hospital." I say this hoping his need to protect others may outweigh his need to be with his mother.

"I wish I'd never bought that ring," he says, and I believe he means it as a command.

"I can't rewind time," I say, dropping my hands and pushing back the lump climbing up my throat.

He nods. Swallows. As he turns to face me, a fierce new determination fills his eyes. "Take me to my father's house."

"Jered—"

"Leela, I've heard it said that you can't control the hand you're dealt. But I can stop avoiding it." He pulls a hand through his hair, and I watch the cloud of debris spread out from his fingers. "I guess I've always known I was different. I talked myself into believing that was how everyone felt. Well, I think it's pretty obvious now. So it's time I took control of the situation. I need to confront him. He's got to know about it. You said yourself he's a Magician. He can help me."

"Jered, you are hurt. You are in shock."

"Now! I gave you a command." I flinch at his words, but do as I'm told. I don't have a choice.

We materialize on the manicured lawn as dawn breaks over the horizon, bathing the large Tudor-style house in its own golden aura. The sky behind it is pink and raw, like the skin beneath a scab. Crickets still sing in the quiet of the early morning hour.

I reach for Jered's arm, but he shifts away from me, and my hand falls on empty air.

"I have to talk to him alone. Can you give us privacy?"

I disappear, grateful that he phrased it as a question and not an order. I don't want to leave him when he isn't thinking straight. What if Mira finds us? What if his father is as dangerous as I fear?

I watch as Jered rolls his shoulders and draws a deep breath in preparation.

"Good luck," I whisper, though I know he cannot hear.

20

THE BEGINNING

ONE MOMENT I AM KEEPING COMPANY WITH THE HERD, ENJOYING THE CLEAR *night sky, glittering with countless stars, the next I am falling to the earth, unable to control my own body.*

All I know is pain. Blinding. Incomprehensible. I have never experienced its like. It rips the breath from my body, tears my chest apart from the inside. I claw the ground, reaching for Achan, who I know isn't there. He is at a Council meeting.

I do not know how long I lie there, alone in the dirt, struggling for air, but when the hurt finally bleeds from my body, it takes with it a piece of my soul. I can feel it there, an empty hole in my heart, and I cry as though I have lost someone I love.

The sheep ignore me. I imagine if it were Achan convulsing on the ground, they might have at least bleated for help. But to them, I am merely a distraction. One that has taken their beloved Achan away.

"It is the Council that is doing it," I tell them, when I find my voice. "I am content to stay here, among you. It is their own hunger for power that steals his time. But if he is happier when he is with us, is it not for the best?"

I did not really expect an answer.

"See if I stop another beast from taking one of you."

I am desperate for Achan to come back. Certain that in his strong arms I will feel whole again. More than that, though, I worry that the pain I have just been through has something to do with his safety. Perhaps I ought to go find him. I know he has asked me to stay away from the village, but he does not need to know.

I am about to disappear when I see him running toward me, over the hill. I relax all over at the sight of his smiling face. He is not himself: he is more. I know he has not been hurt. On the contrary, he is dazzling. I have never seen anything like it. Colors surround him like pieces of light carved from the stars themselves, shifting, shining, and pulsing. It is almost too much to look at against the black backdrop of the sky.

"Achan," I whisper. "What has happened?"

He runs the last few feet, folding me into his embrace and cutting off my confusion with kisses. I respond, giddy with his happiness. And we make love like we did that first night, beneath the stars.

"You can see it, can't you, Little One?"

"Yes. It is beautiful. What is it?" I ask, tracing the muscles in his chest and arms. The scarlet light swirls where I pull my finger through.

"Magic, of course. I have it now. We all do. The three on the Council."

"There are only three of you?"

"The source is limited. We would have risked diminishing the power if we'd shared it. Besides, we will make the decisions for the others. We will lead them."

"Lead?"

"You said yourself, I will make a great king." He turns so that he is above me, his eyes sparkling brighter than the tiny diamonds in the sky beyond. His beauty takes my breath away.

"Show me your magic," I say.

To my astonishment, because I admit I did not completely believe it possible of a human, he pulls an iris from the air and lays it on my chest.

"It is beautiful." I smile, impressed. But I can't shake the twinge of apprehension that whispers through me. "What else can you do?"

"Not enough. Not yet. But soon. Soon, I'll be able to do so much more."

Any more questions I have are buried beneath the urgency of his kiss.

21

FAMILY TIES

"Jered!" Sophie throws open the heavy oak door and leaps into his arms.

"How did you know I was here?" he asks.

"I heard you. You shouldn't be mad at Leela. She wouldn't hurt anyone on purpose." She bobs her head, and her two neat pigtails swing back and forth like springs.

"You don't know that, Soph," he says quietly.

She looks at me. I shake my head, begging her not to reveal my presence. "Hmph," is her response.

The truth stings, and I wonder if I should have let Mira fulfill her purpose. I would be free. Free of masters who always manage to disappoint me.

"You're here to see Daddy," Sophie is saying.

"Yes." Jered sets her down on the gleaming hardwood floor of the entryway.

"He's sleeping. Come in and have breakfast, and when he gets up, he'll see you." She starts toward the kitchen, but Jered lays a hand on her shoulder.

"I'm thinking I should wake him, Soph."

"Oh no. Don't do that, please." She sounds frightened.

"Why not?" Jered squats to meet her eyes.

"If you wake him, he's mean. Like it isn't even him. If you let him get up on his own, he's much nicer."

"I'll take your advice then," Jered agrees with what I recognize as a forced smile. Apprehension creases his brow. Good. I want him to be careful.

We follow Sophie down the hall and past a sweeping staircase with a curved balustrade worthy of my last master's mansion. Sophie doesn't even bother with a glance. She simply continues skipping toward the enormous dining table to the left.

I take in the gourmet kitchen along with Jered. Marble counters, expensive appliances. Fine crystal and china in pristine lines behind the glass cabinet fronts.

Copper pots and pans hang from the ceiling in a pleasing aesthetic. I doubt they've ever been used.

Sophie doesn't notice Jered's expression of surprise. She bounds over to the cabinets and fridge to arrange two bowls of sugary cereal.

Jered ruffles her hair affectionately, and I see him focus on his magic until he appears clean and well-kept in nice khakis and a polo shirt. Impressing his father matters enough for him to resort to magic.

"Oh my God, there's a burglar! Call 911." A girl of about twelve is standing at the foot of the stairs, golden hair sticking up in all directions, fuzzy purple slippers on her feet.

"Relax, Mandy. It's just Jered," Sophie says.

"Just 'cause he told you his name doesn't mean he isn't some kind of perv or something."

"Wait, did you say 'Jered'?" A boy of about fifteen has joined the girl. "He's our brother, Mand. Right, Sophie?"

Jered approaches the two siblings and holds out his hand in greeting. The boy takes it gingerly and becomes more enthusiastic with each shake, a grin breaking over his face.

"I'm Chris. This is Amanda, and you've already met Sophie."

"What's going on down here?"

It appears the mother has joined the party. I see now where the golden hair and ice-blue eyes have come from. She's a petite woman, but judging by the expression on her face, I doubt she lets anyone intimidate her.

"Jered?" Her mouth drops open.

"You know me?"

"What are you...does your mother know you're here?"

"She's in the hospital," Jered says, turning away to collect himself. "I had to come. I have to talk to my dad."

"Well, you can't. You can't just come waltzing in to my house, unannounced at all hours of the morning demanding to see people."

"It's all right, darling."

I follow Jered's gaze to the man on the stairs above, and I gasp. How could I have missed it last night? Because his eyes were closed, I realize. And because he was only an aura surrounded by a blanket in the dark.

Achan.

But how? How is this possible? I am so stunned by his appearance, I hardly notice his hand glow on his wife's shoulder. The glassy look in her eye.

"Yes, of course it is. I don't know what's wrong with me. Kids! Time to get ready for school. Come on, now. Your father and Jered have to talk."

Sophie throws herself into Jered's arms for one last hug before bounding off after her siblings. But his eyes are only for his father. The man who betrayed me over a thousand years ago. It has to be a coincidence. It couldn't possibly be him. A descendant, perhaps?

"It's good to see you, son. But why are you here? And why so early in the morning?"

I want to shout at Jered not to fall for the deep and genial lull of his voice. But I keep silent. He has never taken my advice over his desire for family. Why would he start now?

"Mom...she's in the hospital. I thought you ought to know."

"What happened?"

"A fire. At my apartment building. She picked a bad time for a surprise visit. Somehow I got her to the doctor, but she...she may not wake up."

"I'm sorry." Jered's father places a hand on his son's shoulder, and I twitch, wanting to remove it. *Don't believe him.* "You will come stay with us. Until it's safe to move back in, of course," he says.

"Dad, I...really?"

"Of course. I planned on approaching you after college. I didn't want to add any stress to your plate. I've been wanting to be closer to you, but your mother refused custody and convinced me to stay away while you were working on your degree."

"Wait. *Mom* didn't want shared custody?" Jered takes a step back.

"Didn't she tell you? The court battle was ugly, but so long ago. Still, she keeps in touch enough to threaten me with restraining orders. I don't want to upset anyone, so I've let it go. But you'll have to excuse Elle's reaction when she first saw you here, considering."

"That can't be right. I always thought—"

"Son, I would never leave you on purpose. You're my flesh and blood. I need you in my life more than you could ever know."

I believed that line once as well, but I will not let anything happen to Jered. I can't. And I refuse to listen to the part of me that says I may not be able to stop it.

22

MISTAKES

JERED MUST SENSE SOMETHING TOO. I CAN SEE IT IN HIS FACE. SO THERE IS hope.

"I'm taking the kids to school now, Pete," his wife calls from the doorway.

"Bye, Daddy!" Sophie runs in to hug her father good-bye. "Kiss Little Leela good-bye too!" She giggles, holding up the doll.

I want to stop it, but it is too late. The recognition in his eyes is too much. I fight the tears that well up in my own eyes. This cannot be happening. Even Jered's face turns white when his father holds up the doll to examine.

"Well, well, well. Where'd you get this fine lady?" he asks.

Sophie looks at me, biting her lip. I try to smile. To let her know it is okay. But I'm finding it hard just to keep my feet firmly beneath me.

"It was a present," she says.

"I gave it to her," Jered says, taking the thing and holding it out to Sophie to kiss. "Have a great day at school, sis." He pats her head again, and I see his father's eyes fall on the ring. He clenches his fist at his side, an all too familiar gesture. By the time Jered looks over, he's recovered and grants his son a winning smile.

"Where were we?" asks Achan.

"You were saying you want me to move in with you while my apartment is being repaired."

"I wouldn't have it any other way, son."

Jered swallows as his eyes fill with unmistakable longing. He clutches Sophie's doll so tightly that I fear he may snap off its head. I want to go to him. To tell him not to believe it. That something here is not what it seems. But I cannot risk appearing in front of his father. There would be no time for explanations, and he would never let me do what I might have to in order to protect him. For the moment, I ignore the part of me that whispers, *He may not let you even after all is explained.*

"I'll be fine at Mom's house on my own," Jered says.

A muscle twitches in his father's jaw. "I believe in fate, Jered. This has to be fate's way of letting us know it's time to get to know each other."

I tense, ready for something, but Jered relaxes all over, flashing his own million-dollar grin back at his father. He sets the doll down on the table and laughs. "That's one way to look at it."

Achan chuckles as well, but his eyes appear sharp. "It's amazing how your mother barely survived, and you seem like you've just stepped out of the shower."

"I...I don't remember. It all happened so fast." Jered's gaze darts to the side.

"You're in shock. It's understandable. I'll tell you what, I'll make a few phone calls, find out what's going on at the apartment. I'll check on your mother's status too. You go upstairs, get settled in the guest room —it's the farthest door to your right—and then we'll talk."

"Okay." Jered nods, looking very tired, and turns toward the steps.

"Oh, and Jered. Don't worry about a thing. We're family. Family takes care of each other."

"Yeah." Jered forces a smile and, shoulders hunched, heads up the stairs.

23

THE BEGINNING

IT APPEARS WE ALL FELT THE DISTURBANCE THE NIGHT BEFORE. THE OTHERS are quiet. Hollow, like I have never seen them. Their legs dangle over the olive tree branches like willows in the breeze. I suppose I look the same. Never before have any of us felt pain like that.

"Perhaps this existence is not for our kind after all," says Taj. He will not meet our eyes. Mira wears her silence like a mask.

"You must stop being so negative," I say, pulling at his hands until he stands. "It is most unbecoming."

"I think perhaps I'm done with the pleasures of the flesh," Taj says, stroking my cheek.

"No!" Mira shouts, eyes wild.

"Mira?" I ask.

"We cannot go back until we find her. I won't leave Rhada."

Taj and I exchange glances, his bushy eyebrows furrowed low.

"Taj isn't serious, Mir. He could never give up on so much fun. Besides, I will not leave Achan. Not even if you cross back over without me." I pick through the leaves until I spot an olive that seems just right and pluck it.

"Don't say that, Lee." Taj's gaze is intense. "We're all connected. Leaving someone behind would be like cutting off an arm." He looks at Mira. "So no. We won't go without Rhada. I just don't like this pain thing."

I nibble at the olive. I do not say what I think. That Rhada should have come back like the rest of us after the pain. "Perhaps if we figured out what happened?" I suggest instead. "Then we may avoid it in the future."

"How?" Mira asks.

"I don't know. Achan is smart. I should ask him."

"You cannot!" Mira takes me by the shoulders, shaking me. She is clearly fragile today. "You must not tell anyone about us, Lee. I mean it."

"Fine, then," I say, discarding the olive. "Have it your way. I hope for your sake we can figure it out on our own."

24

SECRETS AND LIES

JERED CRIES INTO HIS PILLOW WITH DEEP, SORROWFUL WAILS THAT COME out slightly muffled. It is all I can do to stop from laying a hand on him. But if I do, he'll know I'm here, watching, and I don't want him to order me away. Not when he needs me near. I don't know which is the more pressing danger: Mira, Taj, and their master, or his own father. I'm beginning to wish Gabe were here. At least I now know he isn't a threat.

The guest room is easily twice the size of Jered's place, with plush white carpet and a queen-size bed, neatly made, in the center. There's a matching bureau, a nightstand, and an armchair tucked in the corner. Otherwise, the large room is conspicuously sparse. Jered spent quite some time wearing a path through the open space between the door and the long, tall window across the way.

Jered's father returned an hour or so after we'd come up. He said he'd called the hospital, that Jered's mother is still unconscious, and the doctors don't know how long it will be. He couldn't keep those eyes off the stone on Jered's middle finger the entire fifteen minutes he was up here.

After he left, Jered stared at the back of the door, unmoving for a full twenty minutes more, and then burst into hysterics. He is still crying. I wonder if I should reveal my presence but choose to wait until he calls, afraid he might order me away.

Finally, his quaking shoulders slow, and the sounds quiet to small gasps. He sits slowly up in the bed, taking a long shuddering gulp of air. His dark eyes are surrounded by bright red where the whites should be. He looks terrible.

"Leela," he says and clears his throat to repeat himself.

"Here, Jered," I say, appearing in front of him. I bite the inside of my cheek to prevent myself from launching into an attack on his father. *I'm smarter than this*, I think. What is wrong with me? I have to get control if I am to handle what is sure to come.

"Is he telling the truth?" he asks.

I swallow, trying to sort through the emotions I've experienced since seeing him on the steps. It seems my master is quite astute.

"I believe he is hiding something," I say, cautious of saying too much but eager to make Jered see the truth.

Jered looks away, blowing air out through clenched teeth.

"He used magic on his wife," I add.

"I was afraid of that," says Jered. "He might have just wanted to help calm her down though, right?"

This time I really do put a hand on his shoulder. He leans against it with his cheek, and a shiver runs up my arm. *Get control*. I realize that the anger and hurt inside me has dissipated. That Jered was just frightened and grieving.

"You need some sleep." I keep my voice soft, softer than it's been in quite some time.

"I don't think I can." He looks up into my face, so much pain written on his. He is very close, my hand still on his shoulder. His scent is familiar now. Comforting and exciting at the same time.

Gently, I turn his head away from me and grasp his other shoulder as well. I work out the tension in his back. I can't bear to see his eyes anyway. Not right now.

His head slumps forward after a few minutes, and I help ease him down onto the bed. I concentrate, and he is beneath the covers, clothes draped over the armchair in the corner.

"Be safe," I whisper, turning invisible and passing through the closed bedroom door. I put an alarm spell on the room, so that if anyone were to enter, I would be alerted immediately.

I find Achan downstairs in the step-down family room. I take in the sprawling Persian rug laid out beneath the glass coffee table, the large white sectional on which he sits, and the giant flat-screen television. The latter is off, but he stares so intently at the screen that I'm sure he sees something.

It's more what I don't see that bothers me. No signs of children in this pristine mansion. Nothing that tells of the family living here. Just expensive items on display.

I move around to face him, kneeling down on one knee to study his face up close. Echoes of emotion and snatches of memory filter through my head. I wince at the intensity of it. He is older, his face more lined and confident than I remember. But it is him, of this I am sure.

"I feel your presence," he says, and I jerk back my hand that was inches from his skin. "I know it's you, Leela." Any doubt about his meaning evaporates with the mention of my name.

Pulling in a deep breath, I materialize before him, posed confidently on top of the glass coffee table. His eyebrows raise a fraction of an inch. Otherwise, he betrays no reaction.

"How can you be here?" I ask with more venom in my voice than I'd intended. I don't like appearing emotional in front of humans. I have worked hard and long to prevent this. And now I have yet another reason I would like to kill him.

"I was going to ask you a similar question. How is it you are with my son, when you belong to me?"

"I will never belong to you again." He squirms slightly in his seat, and I smile, satisfied.

"You will. You must."

"Oh?" I ask, standing and striding as close as I dare. "And why is that?"

"Because we are meant to be together, Leela. Because our love is what has kept me alive, kept me searching all these centuries."

I freeze, feeling trapped. "You lie! How dare you try to use such obvious untruths? Do you think I am still a fool? After all these years?" I scream at him now, right in his face, shaking with fury. And before I realize what's happened, he pulls me down on top of him and kisses me.

My first response is to struggle, to try to pull away like a helpless human girl. But Achan has always been strong. He holds me tighter, fingers digging into my arms. And just as it occurs to me to use magic to repel him, I am overwhelmed by feelings I've fought to bury for a thousand years.

His earthen scent envelopes me. The touch of his lips, hungry and firm, moving against my own. His body, solid and warm. I part my lips to draw in air like a drowning person, and he slides his tongue inside.

And I kiss him back.

My body relaxes, and so do his hands, which he slips over and down, lingering at the small of my back. It is not until they travel up toward my chest that I pull away, backing into the table and gasping for air.

He smiles triumphantly, and I want to strike him. I realize as I try to raise my hand that I cannot. I cannot hurt anyone. Even him. I bite back the scream that rises in my throat and return his smile.

"Not that you weren't any good in bed," I say. "But now doesn't seem the right time for a romp. And your wife might not be too happy about it. I suppose you can always put another spell on her though. Is it damaging to her memory, Achan? To continually control her like that?"

"Don't act like you care about a simple human, Little One."

It is harder to keep control when I hear the nickname. I cannot retaliate anyway. "Back to my question, Achan." I enjoy saying his name, not calling him Master. "How is it possible you sit here before me? Tell me, or I will make you tell me." I pause and then shake my head, a grin spreading across my face. "On second thought, I might prefer that. Don't give in yet." He doesn't know about the command. He does know about my power.

He considers. "Left without a Djinni, I was forced to find a way to persist. To continue my fragile human life beyond that of mortal men. I found a way."

"That much is obvious," I snap.

He sits back down on the sofa, casually crossing his legs and slinging an arm over the back. "I use the limited powers I have to pass my soul into another body. It simply has to be a Magician. I prefer children of my own stock. Because of similar DNA, they cannot fight as proficiently as another full-grown Magician. And of course, I prefer male children."

Jered.

I cannot let my reaction show. I must keep it to myself. Keep it quiet.

"Of course," I say. "So what happens to the child?" I conjure a handful of grapes and offer him some.

"They struggle for a bit, but more often than not, their soul is released within the hour, and the body is mine."

"Your own children? How very coldhearted of you. Then again, it's hardly a surprise. I know firsthand how coldhearted you can be."

His laugh is the same deep, beautiful sound I remember. "I have many descendants who have remained unharmed, Little One. There is no shortage of mes running around this world, I assure you."

"Good thing you are still young enough to have more. Since Jered has me now, you won't be able to touch him." I search for his reaction, but all I get is another smile.

"Oh, I don't think that will be a problem," he says. "In fact, I look at it as fortune and fate smiling on me at last. Because once I take possession of his body, I will also have possession of you."

25

MEN TROUBLE

"And you think I'm just going to let you take possession of me again?" I laugh as though it's the funniest joke I've ever heard. Achan sets his grapes to the side and waves a hand, making them disappear.

"I've changed, Leela. I'm not the same man I was. And I doubt you are the same woman. We can be partners this time, you and me. It's what you always wanted, isn't it?"

It was. But I'd be a fool to take him at his word.

"What guarantee can you possibly give me? You have five seconds before I kill you." I watch as he considers me and am gratified to see the sweat bead on his brow.

"What is it you want?" he asks.

I borrow Mira's phrase. "Bzzz, wrong answer."

"Fine! I'll do whatever you want."

"That's better. But the truth is, there's nothing you can offer me short of freedom, and even that I'm not fool enough to wait for until you own me."

"What if I make Jered free you?" he asks.

I cannot help my eyes getting big. This is the last thing I expect him to offer. "Make Jered free me?" I repeat.

"Just before I take him over. Then you will be free, and we can work as equals—how it should have been in the beginning."

I cross my arms and sit back on the table to prevent from shaking. This has to be a trick.

"What makes you think I won't kill you then?" I ask.

"You love me. I love you. In all the centuries you've been around, have you ever once felt like you did when we were together?" He rises and leans down over me, those eyes penetrating my soul.

"No," I whisper. "No. But it is difficult to fall in love when you are a slave to the greedy whims of man. Not that I'd expect you to know that."

"I would say I'm sorry, but that will never make up for what I did. Actions are the only thing I have powerful enough to show you. Let me show you, Little One."

"Don't call me that!" I yell, standing. I let my eyes glow, but Achan does not notice.

"I know you still love me."

"Cocky son of a—"

He cuts me off with another kiss. I stiffen, but allow it. I want to see if what he says is true. If I could possibly still have feelings for him. He pulls me in, mashing against me with his body, which is at once familiar and strange. Sensations pour through me, thrilling and frightening.

I push him back onto the sofa and straddle him, placing a hand on his chest. He watches my face as I run my hand down his stomach. He lets out a deep sigh, as though he's been holding his breath, unsure what I would do.

"I know it's going to take time to make it up to you, but you forgave me once before for the unthinkable. And we will have eternity now, Leela. The two of us, forever. Isn't that what you always wanted?"

I did. Once upon a time. Do I still?

Not at Jered's expense.

I lean over him, kiss him again, just to shut him up. I don't want to hear anymore. I only want to feel. At least I can use him for this. Take this one thing. The sound of the key in the lock stops us. I take in his frightened features and disappear. Achan sits up and is still straightening himself out when his wife and youngest daughter burst through the door.

Of course! Sophie. Why hadn't I thought of it before? She can read his thoughts. She can see if he tells the truth. Before I can act, Jered calls me back, and I appear at his side, still flushed and confused.

"I didn't know where you were. Don't leave me again!" he says. Another inadvertent command. Now how will I speak to Sophie? I take in his messy hair and wild eyes. He sounds like a frightened child.

"You were asleep. I didn't want to disturb you," I say.

"I'm sorry," he says, running both hands down his face and over the stubble growing on his chin. "I guess I'm still freaked out. About everything."

"I understand," I say. This time I am softer. I sit on the bed next to him and brush some of his hair down with my hand. He does not pull away, only gazes at me intently as if he's trying to make a decision.

"I don't know what to do," he says.

"I will be here, whatever you decide." It is as true a statement as there is.

"I know that, Leela. And...and I want you to know that I trust you."

"You do?"

"Yes. I wasn't sure at first. I mean, I wanted to. But I was worried that you would try to manipulate me or, worse yet, kill me so you could be fr-fr...so you could be without a master." He watches me for a minute, but I only wait for him to continue. He was right to feel that way, after all. "I know now that you do care about me. Or you wouldn't have saved me from that explosion. I'm sorry I doubted you. Can you ever forgive me?"

Forgive him. I remember Achan's words. *I would say I'm sorry, but that will never make up for what I did.* I would have liked him to say it anyway.

"Of course," I say.

He takes my hand in his, which is still hot from sleep. The blankets fall to his waist, and I remember he is naked beneath the sheets. I blush as my whole arm tingles. He is very close.

How can I be feeling this way when moments ago I betrayed him?

"Thank you," he says, cupping my cheek in his other hand. I am aware of my chest rising and falling near his arm, his scent, different from Achan's but just as intoxicating. "And I should probably be honest and tell you..." His voice trails off.

"What is it, Jered?"

"I care about you too." He waits for my reaction, searching my face, and when I give none, he leans forward, lips falling on my own. So light and sweet, it feels as though a phantom is kissing me.

I close my eyes, enjoying the sensations that flow through my body, pressing forward with my mouth, enough to let him know it is all right. I lose myself in his kiss, the sensation of him. This is so gentle, so different from the passion I felt with Achan, but just as exciting. No. It is more. My entire being is lit with yearning. And although Achan's body was familiar, Jered's sets my soul aflame. The realization at once shocks and overwhelms me. The answer to my own question seems obvious. How can I be feeling this way? Physical need is one thing. Perhaps the only thing I've ever been able to control. But this, right here, is something more.

My heart isn't bursting from his touch alone. It is bursting because of him. Because of the man he is. So much more than Achan ever was. Because Jered could never have done what Achan did to me. And what I did downstairs makes my stomach turn, so I push forward, trying to wipe it away with this moment.

Not wanting him to stop, I guide his hand to my waist, wrap my own arms around his neck, tangle my fingers in his messy hair. He tastes like nectar, feels like heaven. He trails his hands up my sides, and I draw in a sharp breath as his mouth works its way down my jawline. My entire body is alive with anticipation. I climb over him, straddling him, pressing my body to his. Kiss him again with abandon. I run my hand down his arms. Tug the blankets out of the way.

I don't want this to end. But it does. Jered stops my hand with one of his own, gently reaching for my face with his other and wiping away some of the tears that have slipped unnoticed down my cheek.

He holds up his hand, showing me the glistening drops, question written all over his face, and I sob, crawling off him and onto the bed. He waits, far too patiently, until I contain myself. I don't deserve to have him look at me like that. Like he actually cares for me.

"Don't you know that I would never force you, Leela?"

"No!" I say. "That's not it, Jered. Please don't think that."

"Then why?"

"You are too kind. You should not be. You should be mean. You should force me to do that and many other things."

"Leela—"

"I'm not the person you think I am."

"And what person is that?" His tone is so full of gentleness and understanding that a fresh surge of pain overtakes me, and I cry again.

"Nice. Sweet. Innocent. I am none of those things. I'm not even a person at all. Not really."

"People have told you that so many times you believe it. But it isn't true, Leela. You are as much a person as I am, and you deserve to be treated like one." He reaches for my face, and I lean into his touch. "As soon as I can, I'll fr-fr..." He chokes on the words again, unable to say it, and beats a fist against the mattress.

I place a hand on his arm and smile through my tears.

"I believe you," I say. And I don't need Sophie to confirm it is true.

26

THE BENEFIT OF COMPANY

"I HAVE AN IDEA TO CHEER YOU UP," I say, FINGERING JERED'S CELL phone, which he's relegated to the nightstand. Each time it rings, he reaches for it eagerly. But when he finds it's Gabe and not the hospital, he abandons it again.

"What's that?" he asks. He is trying to be brave but looks so drawn and tense that I want to scream.

"Gabe," I say, and before he can protest, I wave a hand, and Gabe appears between us, wrapped in a towel. His wiry body is baby smooth and glistening with water.

"Hey!" he shouts, whipping around like a crazed animal. "My glasses—"

I snap, and they are on his face. He relaxes.

"Seriously, you need to stop doing that! It's very unnerving. What if I were still in the shower?"

"Then you'd be naked and covered in soap?" I ask, trying to hold back my laughter.

"I'm not here for your amusement," he says.

"No. You are here for Jered's amusement. Now, get to work and cheer him up." I clap my hands at him, and he flinches.

"I've been texting and calling you for hours, bro," he says, turning his attention to Jered. "What's going on? Where are we?" He looks around, adjusting his glasses with one hand while the other firmly grips the towel at his waist.

I suppress a smile while Jered explains the situation to his friend. I was right, of course. Having Gabe to confide in has brought back some of his spirit. I watch the colors in his aura spark and build.

"I'm so sorry about your mom."

"Thanks, man. I know. Now put some clothes on, okay?"

I snap, and Gabe is dressed in jeans and a black T-shirt. He frowns at me.

"These aren't the kind I usually wear," he says.

"Beggars can't be choosers. Besides, I hate those low-riders. I'm always afraid they'll fall, and I don't wish to be blinded by your scrawny ass." It feels good to be so brazen. Now that I am not so afraid of retribution by an angry master.

"So what do we do now?" Gabe asks, turning back to Jered with one final glare in my direction.

"*We* don't do anything," Jered says. "You need to go home and forget you even know me. At least until this all blows over."

Gabe and I exchange a look.

"No way. Nuh-uh. I'm in, and unless you plan on lifting the no-hurt ban on the Leester here, you're stuck with me," Gabe says.

"I can have her put you back," Jered says.

"I'll keep coming over." Gabe crosses his arms and plants his feet firmly on the ground. I have to admit, I'm proud of him.

"He does have a positive effect on you," I say.

"Wait a second, did you just say something nice about me?" Gabe asks. "Who are you, and what have you done with the real Leela?"

"Watch it, Gabe," Jered says, stepping up next to me. The air between us sizzles with energy. A genuine smile plays at the corners of my mouth.

Gabe's gaze darts between Jered and me as a huge grin breaks across his face. "You two did it, didn't you?"

I roll my eyes, and Jered turns as red as a beet.

"I knew it!"

"Actually, you know very little," I say. "I know firsthand. I've seen your brain."

A knock at the door stops me from saying more. Both men flinch.

"Jered?" Sophie's tiny voice calls from the hall. Jered relaxes and lets her in.

"You're home," he says as she bursts inside and flings her arms around his waist.

"Daddy says you're staying with us!"

"Only until my mother gets better," he says.

"Daddy doesn't think she will," Sophie says, playing with the bottom of one pigtail.

"He thinks if she could, you would have made Leela save her."

27

THE BEGINNING

"WHAT WOULD YOU DO FOR ME?" ACHAN ASKS, RUNNING A FINGER LIGHTLY *down my arm. I close my eyes, letting the shivering sensation pour through my body. Does he not already know the answer?*

"Anything," I say. "I would do anything for you, Achan." And to make certain he knows it, I thread my own fingers through his thick black hair and pull his face to my own.

He lets the kiss go on, caressing my body as I work against his mouth greedily. I tilt my head back with a moan of longing, and he laughs gently, his dark eyes twinkling in the starlight. He sits back on his heels, letting the strange colors that now surround him cover me like a blanket. It is like a million tendrils of pleasure careening over and through my body. I cry out in ecstasy.

"Pleasing you is easy, Little One."

"Only for you," I say. "Not everyone is so lucky."

"It is only the sheep and me whom you talk to, so yes, I hope so."

I hit his shoulder playfully and join in the laughter. It is hard to imagine anything more perfect than these nights with Achan in the desert.

"And have I not pleased you as well?" I ask, climbing to my knees to run a finger down his arm.

"Yes, you have," he says, and his dark eyes grow cold as he takes my

hands. "Yet I know so little of you. Where did you come from? It is none of the villages we visit on our route. So where, then? And why have you come? What bit of luck brought you into my life?"

"It was not luck, but fate," I say, studying the way the tent wall behind him billows against the wind. It will not break free; Achan has tied it down expertly.

"See? You haven't answered one of my questions about your past. Do not look so worried, Little One. I am content that you are here." He folds me into his arms, and I lay my head against his strong chest. Breathe in his scent. It is the scent of our desert. Of our love. "I do have a favor to ask," he says.

"Anything."

"Will you come with me to the Council?" he asks, tilting my chin up so that I look into his eyes. Their usual spark is back now.

"You want me to come to the Council?" I ask, unable to keep the surprise from my voice.

"Yes. I want to introduce you to the others. Show them my good luck charm."

"Of course I will come, Achan." A smile breaks across my face. He wants me to be a part of his life. A part beyond our nights together. He is proud of me.

The rest of my thoughts are drowned in the urgency of his kiss.

28

AN EXPERT AT CAUSING PAIN

"You heard about me in your father's thoughts?" I ask Sophie. How much does she know?

She nods, sucking in her bottom lip. Her blue eyes grow wide like she's afraid she's said something wrong. I put my hands on her shoulders and smile reassuringly.

"It is good that you tell us what he thinks, Sophie."

"But he's my daddy. I don't know—"

"He's my daddy too," Jered says, kneeling down until he's eye level with the child. "I want to be sure I understand how he feels."

Sophie cocks her head to the side and narrows her eyes at her brother, concentrating. It's no good pretending. She'll know what he's thinking.

"You're scared," she pronounces, moving her small hand to her hip.

"I am," Jered says.

"Sometimes he scares me too," she says, letting her gaze fall. Jered lifts her chin so she can see his face.

"Did you hear anything else about Leela?" Jered asks.

Sophie looks up at me, and my stomach twists into a knot. I hold my breath as she considers me with twinkling blue eyes. I cannot remember a time I've feared a six-year-old child.

"He's afraid of her," she says, finally. "He wants to go upstairs to the attic and get something he thinks will protect him."

Jered's snaps his head around, searching for me, eyes wild with fear. I focus on my face, being certain not to let my feelings show. Gabe backs up toward the bed and collapses onto the mattress.

"You should go to Gabe's house," I say.

"How does he even know?" Jered asks, a deep crimson boiling its way up his neck onto his face. Sophie flinches.

"It was my doll, wasn't it?" she asks quietly.

"It isn't your fault," I say, still watching Jered closely. "Your father knows me, Jered."

"How could he? You've been asleep for over a hundred years, Leela."

"He's...been passed the information from his father," I say. "You are descended from my first master." I look down quickly. I cannot bear it.

"How do you know? Why didn't you tell me?" Jered asks. I hear the hurt in his voice.

"I didn't know before. I mean, I knew your eyes. I just didn't connect it until I saw your father. He looks just like him. And now that we are certain he knows me, well, that confirms it."

"I thought he was looking at my ring a lot," Jered says, collapsing next to Gabe. I remain silent.

"Daddy wants you to stay with him forever, Jered," Sophie says, and I cringe inwardly at the truth in the statement. "He's afraid of Leela, not angry at her."

"Please go to Gabe's house. You will be safe there for a while. Let me talk to your father alone. I will...explain things." Jered cannot hear my heart speed up. I don't know what Achan has in the attic. Whatever it is, I am certain he's already retrieved it.

"I'll talk to him," Jered says.

I purse my lips and breathe deeply. "Please," I repeat. "Go."

"This doesn't make sense," Jered says, furrowing his brow like I am a particularly difficult puzzle. "What are you afraid he'll do to me? If anything, he wants to hurt you. I'm his son. He probably wants to warn me about you in private. He doesn't know what I know about you."

My chest feels heavy. Jered thinks he knows the real me. I have to think fast. I cannot tell him the truth. He would be devastated. Worse yet, if he does something stupid like confront Achan and lose, I will belong to my first master. And that will not happen. Not ever again.

What if Achan will have Jered free me so I will not impede his plans? If I were free, I could protect Jered from his father. I wouldn't have his restrictive commands getting in my way. And I'd have a chance at revenge.

"I wish to assess the situation. We need more information," I say, placing one hand against Jered's chest. His aura turns a deep purple and flows over my arm. My pulse quickens.

"I don't want you to get hurt," he says.

"I don't want you to get hurt either. Besides, I have more power than your father. I will be fine."

His aura recedes. He looks at me, biting his lower lip.

"I cannot hurt anyone, after all," I say, guessing what he might be thinking.

"I...I didn't think...I mean, you wouldn't on purpose," he says.

"I can't. On purpose or by accident, Jered. You've commanded it." I turn his face in my hand and force him to look me in the eye. He is still having trouble accepting the totality of his commands. This is dangerous, and he must be convinced. If kissing Gabe didn't do it, I don't know what will.

A knock on the door makes Sophie jump, and I shut my eyes tight with frustration. It may be too late. When I feel Jered's hand on mine, I realize I've clutched his shirt in my fist.

"Jered?" Achan calls.

"Can you make Gabe and Sophie disappear with you?" Jered asks softly.

I nod and do as he wishes, despite the absence of an actual command. Sophie slips her hand in mine, and I squeeze it reassuringly. I place my other hand on Gabe's shoulder, seeing the gaunt look on his face. Perhaps I should send him home. I promise myself I will if he is in danger.

"Hey, Dad." Jered pulls the door open and brushes a hand through the back of his hair.

"How are you doing?" Achan asks, gaze darting quickly around the room before coming to rest on his son.

"I've been better," Jered says.

I grimace, dropping Sophie's hand and clenching Gabe's shoulder until he nearly collapses. They both look at me, frightened. I want to tell them not to worry, but I find it difficult to get the words out through the pain, which is like a million tiny needles on my skin. Have I concealed our voices as well? I'm having trouble remembering...I concentrate with all I have, taking all sound from Sophie and Gabe, so they cannot give away our presence.

Sweat breaks out on my forehead from the exertion of doing magic through the prison of my skin. I know this pain—know it can get much worse. I manage to make eye contact with Gabe, who looks about as freaked out as I've ever seen him. I toss my arm forward like dead weight. I'm starting to lose motor control, but I must show him.

Understanding lights his eyes, and he wraps his arms around my waist as I collapse. He staggers and then lifts me up, heaving me over his shoulder. He moves us away from Achan and Jered, hesitating at the bed. I shake my head feebly, and he gets me all the way to the far wall. The only thing here is a window, and for a moment, I contemplate jumping out. But sense gets a hold of me, and I realize I cannot leave Jered. Literally or emotionally.

Gabe sets me down as gently as he can manage, and I crumple to the floor, knees to my chest. It is better here. I am farther from the source, and it fades rapidly from agony to mild discomfort. I smile as Gabe sinks to his knees beside me and puts a comforting hand on my shoulder. I mouth the words, "thank you."

Sophie slips into my lap, tears streaming down her little cheeks. I hug her to me, rocking us both back and forth, burying my face in her straw-colored hair.

"Why didn't you tell me about my powers?" Jered is asking.

"I didn't want to burden you with it until you were ready, son. I did plan on telling you though. Your mother was against it. She said she didn't want me to make you into a freak."

I lift my head enough to see Jered flinch like his father has hit him, and I feel a surge of hatred toward Achan. He is hurting us both, and that is most certainly his intent.

"She never said anything," Jered says. His voice is small.

"She wanted you to be normal. She didn't understand all the incredible possibilities. I hate to say it, but Corrie can be very small-minded at times."

"At least she didn't abandon me," Jered says, snapping to and making my heart lurch. "She worked double shifts, went back to school, and raised me on her own with no help from you."

"I wanted to help. I told you that. But she didn't want me near you. She didn't want me to make you a 'monster.' That's what she said, Jered. Her husband and son are monsters in her eyes. I know it hurts, but you have to hear the truth. You're old enough now."

Old enough for what? I lift a shaking hand to Gabe, who helps me to my feet.

Jered sits on the bed, and Achan moves to sit next to him. He's planted himself in the center of the room. I have about ten seconds to realize this before the pain falls over me like a shadow, and once again I crumple to the floor.

29

LESSONS FROM THE FATHER

GABE CLOSES HIS HANDS AROUND MY WRISTS; I NEARLY CRY OUT FROM THE pressure. I have to remind myself not to fight him because I know he's trying to help. I'm not heavy, but he isn't exactly Hercules either, so it takes him far too long to drag me around the side of the bed and toward the door. I know what's going to happen before he does though. As he passes through the doorway, I am stopped short by an invisible wall. Jered's command. I can't leave him.

Damn Achan. Damn him. Though I'm sure he is already damned. He's just too stubborn to die in the first place. I hate that I let him touch me only hours ago.

I want to scream at Gabe. Continuing to tug is not going to do anything but cause me more pain. Finally, he gets it and lets my arms drop, sinking to the floor next to me. I'm surprised to see his face swim into view, flushed and filled with sweat and concern.

I lick my lips, and he moves his ear to my mouth so I can whisper.

"He commanded I stay with him. Send Sophie." It's all I can manage before I am assaulted by another bout of intense stabbing. It is good that I haven't been around it for a hundred years because I know that my tolerance fades quickly. I should be able to manage one more spell, so I focus everything I have left and deposit them both at the foot of the steps, giving them back their voices and making them visible. The effort of this act has drained me, and I lie helpless and still.

"Show me now," Jered says.

What have they been talking about?

"Focus your energy. Open yourself up," Achan is saying. "Let the energy flow through you freely. Let down the walls."

No! I scream silently, meeting a wall of pain. *Don't let down the walls. Don't let him in.*

"Daddy! Jered!" Sophie's voice is above my head. She deftly avoids my body as she skips into the room. *Good girl.*

"Sophie. I thought you had homework," Achan says.

"All done. Jered, you have a visitor downstairs. You should go see him."

Confusion flickers over Jered's features for a moment.

"That must be Gabe. I texted him about Mom. I'd better go see him. Can we continue this later, Dad?"

"Of course, son. We have plenty of time."

I do not like the way Achan's aura clings to Jered's, stretching it as he pulls away.

Jered does not feel it. He beams at his father and follows Sophie out of the room. I have a momentary glimpse of Achan pulling his shirt up to smooth a hand over the lead vest beneath, before I am sucked out the door and down the stairs after Jered on my invisible leash.

"What's up?" Jered asks the second Gabe is in his sights.

"You dick! You commanded her to stay with you, so she couldn't get away." Gabe half yells, half whispers in Jered's face and then gives his shoulder a shove for good measure.

I materialize next to Jered, and he turns a worried face to mine.

"Couldn't get away from what?" he asks.

"Your father is wearing a vest made of lead beneath his clothes. He knows my weaknesses."

"Are you all right?" Jered asks in a husky voice that makes me quiver. I nod as he puts his hands on my arms and pulls me into an embrace. "He didn't know you were there."

I push away. "He knows."

"He was protecting himself," Jered says, turning to Gabe and Sophie for confirmation. "He thought you wanted to kill him. He probably still does, and you probably would have wanted to. To protect me." He adds this last part as if trying to cover his tracks.

"He deserves to die," I hiss.

"He's never done anything to you!" Jered says.

I clamp my mouth shut for fear of what might slip out. I was right not to trust him with the truth. He is too blinded by his father. I try to remind myself how easy it is to be blinded by Achan.

"Jer, calm down, okay? She was in pretty bad shape. You didn't see her. I'd feel the same way if someone did that to me, self-defense or no self-defense." Gabe intercedes as the voice of reason.

But I have already resolved to harden myself again. I must stop allowing my emotions to control me. I know better.

"I'm sorry, Leela," Jered says. "I'm sorry you were hurt. It was my fault. I don't even remember commanding you to stay with me."

"It was when you woke up. You were looking for me and told me not to leave you again." I cast my eyes downward, toward Jered's feet.

"Well, you don't have to stay near me. I rescind that command. Only do it if you want to." He sounds miserable.

"I do, Jered. Just not when it means I am in intolerable pain."

Jered opens his mouth to reply when we hear the front door and the sound of girls giggling.

"My sister's home. That means my brother will be here soon too." Sophie motions for us to follow, and we trail up the stairs behind her and into her room, a few doors down from the guest room. Gabe eases the door shut behind us.

"He's teaching me to use magic," Jered blurts out.

"I have already been teaching you. What he tells you is wrong," I say.

"He knows how to—"

"Knowing and teaching are two different things." I cannot stop my voice from rising.

"He's not the guy who hurt you, Leela. He's a descendant." Jered's voice alternates between anger and pity.

"He is just like him!" I stand nose to nose with him now, floating inches off the ground.

"Then so am I. He's my father!"

"Stop it, you guys," Gabe says. "Sophie's crying."

Indeed, Sophie sits at the edge of the bed, hugging her Djinni doll, sniffling with tears weaving down her red cheeks. We both rush to her side, and she lets out a loud wail.

"Don't fight! Please don't fight," she sobs.

"I'm sorry, Sophie," Jered says, running a hand over her back.

"I am not," I say. "I only want to protect you."

Sophie bawls louder. Jered glares at me. I cannot take this. Does he think I couldn't have let him die when Mira showed up? Then all my problems would be over.

I vanish with a cry of frustration, materializing in the hallway on the other side of the door.

"Leela." I snap my head toward Achan's voice. I am ready to vanish again, but he keeps his distance, lingering in the doorway to Jered's room.

"You murderous, treacherous—" I start.

"Abhorrent. Yes, I know. But look at it from my perspective, Leela. I have to protect myself. If I were you, I would want me dead as well."

"You think I cannot arrange for your death from a distance?" I ask through clenched teeth.

"I am beginning to wonder why you haven't, I admit. I also wonder how you managed to escape Jered's room. I know you had to have been there somewhere."

"I'm a Djinni. It's what I do."

"I meant what I said before. That I still love you."

"You never loved me. Not then and not now. I saw your magic lessons. You forgot to ask him to free me before you tried to take him over. I suppose it slipped your mind."

"I would have lost his trust if I brought you up. I would have done it afterward."

"I don't believe you."

"I can't blame you, Leela. But perhaps this will help." Slowly, very slowly, he raises his hands like a criminal with a gun pointed down his throat. He unbuttons his shirt and unfastens his vest. I can see now that it has smaller round pieces of lead attached by straps. Projectiles, I assume. Or perhaps meant to lay against a Djinni's skin. I shudder and tense, ready to flee, but he tosses the whole thing back inside Jered's room.

"I thought I needed protection from you, but I see I was wrong. You could have, should have killed me already, and you haven't. Now it's my turn to show you some good faith."

30

CONFESSIONS

I'VE HAD ENOUGH. WITH THE WAVE OF MY HAND, ACHAN AND I ARE transported to the master bedroom of his home. It's so big, it has its own sliding glass door that opens onto a balcony and a small sitting room arranged around a fireplace. One quick sweep with my senses, and I know his wife is downstairs in the kitchen feeding the two nonmagical children and their friends a snack. Sophie, Jered, and Gabe are still in Sophie's bedroom.

I lock the door with a wave, pleased to see that my gamble has paid off. That "not hurting anyone" does not extend to chaining them to the bed.

"That's better," I say, straddling Achan's helpless form on the king-size bed.

"You won't kill me," he says. He doesn't sound so sure.

"We'll see," I say, making the blinds snap closed with the flick of my finger. At the same moment, the fire roars to life in the fireplace. "Now, where should we start?" I watch as he swallows hard, and I smile. "If you are in a child's body, why do you look like you?"

"He was my son, and he happened to resemble me already. And over time, depending on my mood, I adjust my appearance using magic. I've grown tired of this look though. Now I think I'd like something a little different."

"Designer children," I say, unable to keep the disgust from my voice.

"Designer bodies," he agrees.

I wish I could slap him. Wish I could dig my nails into his tender human skin. Instead, I lean over him, letting my hair fall around us like a curtain. His chest moves against me with shallow, rapid breaths. Oh yes, he's scared.

"I cannot afford to think of them as children, Leela. It is more important to live."

"More important? For who? For you?"

"Yes. For me. For you. We're meant to be together, Leela."

"Ha!" I let a deep laugh escape into the air above.

"But it isn't just that!" he yells. "It's Kitra. She can't be left to take over. You think I am a monster? I am nothing compared to her. You know. You remember."

"Kitra?" Her name on my lips sounds like the hiss of a snake.

"She did it too, found out how to stay alive," he says. "And she kept her Djinni." *Mira. Taj.* My vision blurs with rage, but Achan takes no notice. I try to focus on his words. "I've kept careful track of her all this time. It wasn't easy staying out of her reach with a Djinni in her possession. She's never lost anything. And she still wants more. She won't stop until she owns it all. I had to call you."

"*What?*"

He shrinks at the sound of my voice.

"What do you mean *call* me?"

"You think it was coincidence my son found you?" he asks, desperation lacing his words.

"He's a Magician. I suppose I should have known he'd come from one of you," I say.

"True enough. I've been working for centuries on a summoning spell powerful enough to bring your stone within reach. It had to be you, Leela. Don't you see?" When I don't answer, he continues. "I finally managed it, and I've been hunting everywhere in a ten-mile radius. Every antique and jewelry store. Every yard and estate sale.

Imagine my surprise when my son showed up on my doorstep wearing the ring."

"You brought me closer through circumstance, but Jered found me first," I say, straightening.

"Yes, I couldn't have anticipated his magic being strong enough to wake you."

"You should not underestimate him," I say, aware of the edge of pride in my voice.

"You have feelings for the boy, don't you?" he asks. My answer is the glow of my eyes.

"You aren't killing me," he says.

"How observant of you."

"Nor are you hurting me," he adds, a smile playing at his lips. I feel him relax ever so slightly.

"Yet," I say.

"No. I think you would have already done so if you were able. You have every reason in the world to seek revenge."

"Times change," I say, but I fear the understanding in his eyes.

"I think my son has ordered you not to harm me." He laughs. Softly at first, and then harder, until his entire body is jiggling beneath me.

I snap my fingers, and his mouth is covered with a piece of silk. It won't hurt him, but it will bring a stop to that sound.

"Don't go anywhere," I say, patting him on the chest and disappearing.

Now that I've spent some time with Achan, my anger toward Jered has ebbed, and I am once again focused on telling him what I've learned about Kitra and convincing him of the danger he is in from his father. He is the innocent in all of this.

"I have news," I say, reappearing in Sophie's room to find her cuddled in Jered's lap, Gabe making silly faces for her amusement.

"So have I."

It isn't Jered who says it. Nor is it Gabe. Or Sophie. At the same time I appear, Taj and Mira do as well. It is Taj who has spoken.

My reaction is instantaneous. A wave of my arm through the air, and a wall of smoke appears between us. I look at Jered.

"Get everyone, uh, the humans, out of the house," he says.

I nod, and we are gathered in the lobby of Jered's college's intermural building. Fluorescent lights flicker above the gray tiled floor. The students and staff are all long gone for the day, and the quiet of the normally bustling place feels somehow disconcerting.

"Where's my father?" Jered screams.

"He is no longer in the house either. Just not here," I say. *Hope he likes being chained to his bed in the backyard.*

"Leela! I—" Jered starts.

"What is this? What's going on?" Jered's stepmother is clutching Sophie to her chest with one arm and has gathered her oldest two children to her side with the other.

I wave another hand, and they freeze in place. All except Sophie, who continues to stay still anyhow, watching us with wide eyes.

"Why did you do that?" Jered demands.

"Because they do not know about magic, and they should not," I say. "For their own safety. If you would listen to what I'm trying to tell you—"

"You seem to know what's best for everybody," Jered says. "Maybe that's why you need a strong master. Someone who can save you from yourself."

I recoil, feeling as though I've been hit. And for once, I have no words.

Jered draws a deep breath. "Look, I'm sorry. I can't help but feel like none of this would have ever happened if I hadn't bought this stupid ring." Jered holds up his hand with the large opal, and I stroke the choker around my neck, tears stinging the backs of my eyes.

"Jer, don't you think you're being kind of harsh?" Gabe says, pulling him off to the side. "She's only trying to help. I mean, do you really want their whole world turned upside down because of us?"

Jered's glances between Gabe, myself, and his extended family. He swallows. "You're right. I don't know what got into me. Leela, I...I'm sorry. It's just...my mom...I'm so scared."

"No need to apologize for the truth," I say. "I want permission to find Taj and Mira. I want to speak to them. Alone." If he is sorry, he can grant me my request.

"I don't know." Jered shifts his weight from one foot to another.

"I can put everyone back as soon as I know it is safe. And they won't remember any of it," I say, gesturing to the frozen family. I'm making an effort. Trying to be nice.

"All right, Leela," Jered says, folding his arms across his chest. "Let's do this your way. You have experience dealing with the other Djinn. But I want you to come back after you find out what we need to know."

I disappear without another word, and as soon as I am out of his sight, I allow the hurt that's been balled up in my stomach to wash over my body, claiming me.

31

THE BEGINNING

I HAVE NEVER CONSIDERED MYSELF TIMID. HOWEVER, SOMETHING ABOUT THIS situation has put me on edge. I am so afraid of disappointing Achan. Of not being able to prove my worth to the others on the Council. I try not to let these insecurities show as I enter the meeting place.

We are in a home in the village. It is made of adobe like the others, but the patterns in the carved stucco on the outside are far more intricate. The rounded arches of the doorways are higher. Clearly it is one of the nicer and better-maintained structures around, which leads me to believe the owner is wealthy. Perhaps the village leader? That would make sense if the Council is planning on taking charge of the others.

I gaze around at the colorful cushions scattered across the interior floor. All reds and golds, like the stains on the walls and the pottery on the tables. We stand in the rounded entry hall on a mosaic patterned out of varying geometric shapes. Achan leads me into this place with such an air of confidence and ease. He does not even announce our presence.

The strong smell of incense assaults my nose, and I press the back of one hand to it, trying to shut it out. My eyes water. Achan notices and nods encouragingly.

"A bit on the heavy side?" he asks, the corners of his eyes crinkling with

amusement. He is young, but the sun of the desert can be cruel to a frail human body. I would not change a single line or mark.

"I will get used to it," I say, not wanting to appear petty. Who am I to judge someone for liking the scent of incense?

"Ah! Achan. And you must be Leela."

I cannot believe who I see. The first thing I feel is betrayal. I smooth over my features so this does not show. I am sure Achan can sense me stiffen because he lays a hand on my shoulder. I believe it is less a gesture of familiarity and more one of restraint.

"Leela, this is Kitra. Kitra, Leela." Achan's introduction feels formal. I do not accept the hand she offers; instead, we all stare at it until she drops it to her side.

"Achan's told me so much about you," she says, a ridiculous smile plastered across her face. She is pretty. More so than I remember, with dark skin and eyes, long thick hair pulled back under a gold silken veil. And of course, her aura dances with color just as Achan's does, so there is no mistaking her role in the Council of three.

"He has told me little of the Council."

"We have been sworn to secrecy. You understand," she says. "These matters are of such importance and value, and well, we don't want anyone stealing the knowledge we have so carefully collected."

"Who else is on the Council?" I ask. I cannot take my eyes off her. Cannot stop wondering how Achan can bear to be near the woman who spurned him with such malice.

"That would be me," says a gruff voice from behind.

I spin to find a man filling the entire doorway to Kitra's home.

My eyebrows rise as I take him in. He is a giant of a man. His head is smooth, not one hair on his scalp. A carefully trimmed beard adorns his chin. And of course, there is the telltale swirl of color in the air around him. Impressive, but not in a good way.

"This is Cephas," Kitra says. "Now that we are all present, we can get down to business."

I tear my eyes away from Cephas, and the moment I turn back toward Kitra, I learn an invaluable lesson. Unfortunately, it is too late to be of use.

Never take your eyes off an enemy.

32

REUNION

TAJ AND MIRA ARE THERE, WAITING FOR ME. MIRA SITS ON THE EDGE OF Sophie's bed, legs and arms crossed, her foot tapping out an impatient rhythm against the mattress. Taj is examining the assortment of stuffed animals on a shelf in the corner. He barely looks up when I appear.

"That was completely unnecessary," Mira snaps.

"It's going to take me a week to get the smoke smell out of my hair," Taj says, running a hand through his mass of dark curls.

"Sorry," I say, though I doubt I'm fooling anyone. "I needed to speak to you both before you act."

"And your new pet let you?" Mira asks.

"He is far from a pet," I say, yanking a pillow from her hands and throwing it back on the bed.

"Well, I for one think he looks good enough to eat," says Taj. "Not bad in the personality department either. At least from the bit I saw the other night."

"How'd you find us?" I ask because I don't want to get to the real issue. And I certainly don't want to discuss the mess I've made of my relationship with Jered.

"It wasn't difficult now that we know who he is," Taj says. "I'm sure it would be simple enough to check the handful of places he might go to find him again."

"Then why are you still here?" I ask.

"We were waiting for you, idiot."

I choose to ignore Mira's insult. "Well, here I am. What command has she given you?"

"We are to bring the boy back to our master. Alive," Taj says.

"And you think I can let you do that?" I ask.

"It isn't like we want her to own you too." Mira rolls her eyes. "If I have to be saddled with your company for the rest of eternity, I'll go insane."

"And her whole determination to rule the world," Taj says, waving a hand dismissively. "I wouldn't mind your company though, Lee. It's been boring without you around."

I smile at my old friend, relieved that he doesn't blame me. For everything. "So what do we do?" I ask.

"You go kill her while we try to find your boy toy," Mira says.

"I can't," I say. I hold up a hand to stop Mira from berating me. "I've been commanded not to hurt anyone."

"That's the best one I've heard in...in a millennium!" Mira manages through snorts and giggles. "You know, I'm actually kind of glad I didn't kill him."

"That's what I was saying, Mir." Taj grins, shoulders shaking with each laugh. "He's priceless."

"Well, I'm so glad you all like him so much. But the question remains, what do we do?" I ask.

"You have to get him to retract the command," Mira says.

"I've tried," I say.

"Then someone else needs to kill him before we find him. But who would do that?" Taj is dead serious all of a sudden.

I glance out the window and back. Taj catches the gesture and moves to my side. I feel his arm around me, and a lump rises in my throat. Maybe I do want this to be over. Finally over.

"Achan is alive," I say.

"Alive?" Mira asks, springing to her feet.

"Your master did it too," I say. "She is Kitra."

"No. She's descended from Kitra. Believe me, they all act the same, but they are different people." Mira is in my face, examining my eyes as though she's looking for a hint of a joke.

"No," I say. "They inhabit the body of their descendants with magic. He told me. He's chained in the backyard right now."

"And you left him there?" she shrieks.

"Jered commanded I get everyone out. I couldn't bring him with us —he would have taken over Jered's body, and I will not allow him to own me."

Taj squeezes my shoulder. "We won't let that happen."

"Not that you don't deserve it," Mira says. "He won't want to kill Jered then anyway," she continues. "If what you say is true, he'll want to take over his body."

Taj tightens his grip.

"He'll rescind the hurt command," I say. My voice is strained. I'm not sure I could allow Achan to take Jered. It is more than having to protect my master. I couldn't live with myself. Still, I owe them, Taj and Mira. A debt that may never be repaid.

"Yes, but then they'll just war it out until only one is left standing, and we're all stuck together as slaves." Mira taps a finger against her lips and paces to the window. And I lean against Taj, feeling a rush of relief.

"Talk about complicated," Taj says. "I liked the good old days. 'Go kill that guy.' Or 'make me rich.' Humans are just as greedy, but they're getting more devious about the execution of it all."

"Well, let's go 'interview' Achan," Mira says. "Lee can't hurt him, but we certainly can."

For once, I can appreciate the mischievous twinkle in her eye.

33

BLIND

I STARE DUMBFOUNDED AT THE EMPTY BED. THE SHACKLES ARE OPEN AND empty on the mussed-up covers. How could I have been so stupid? So blind?

"Wonder where he went," Mira says to goad me.

"He doesn't know where they are," I say.

"He'll call his wife," Taj says.

"She's frozen. Which reminds me, will they be safe if I return them to this house?" I ask. "The family?"

"Why do you care?" Mira asks, genuinely intrigued. Perhaps she wants to know if I care for them because she'd like to hurt them to get back at me.

"It is part of my command," I lie. "I am to put them back if they will be safe. No memory of the magic, of course."

"We won't harm anyone in this house," Taj tells me.

I nod and transfer the family. I include Sophie, although I do not touch her memory. She should stay where it is safe, at least.

"I will come back here to meet with you, after I have moved Jered to a safe location," I say.

"Of course," Mira says.

I don't like the way she says it, but I don't have time to sit and ponder. I return the bed, minus restraints, to the bedroom and go back to my master.

He and Gabe wait on the cold tile floor, heads back against the glass showcase filled with trophies and books and all the things a normal college student should be concerned with.

"Your family is safely at the house." I start with this. I must keep him in a positive mood. I have to convince him to lift the command.

"And?" He leans forward, eyes wide.

"And the other Djinn have been commanded to bring you back alive."

"Well, that's good, right?" Gabe asks.

"No, Gabe. That is not good. That is so she can kill Jered herself and take the ring."

Gabe swallows.

"We must start by moving to a place they will not search," I say, glancing over my shoulder, afraid they may already be there.

"Take us to a hotel," Jered says.

I nod and sweep a hand through the air. We materialize in the living room of a penthouse suite overlooking Lake Michigan. It's the kind of place any of my past masters would have insisted on when traveling. My gaze shifts to the wall-sized window, at least twenty stories up. The view is incredible. Below, the water glints in the late afternoon sunlight. I stare at it, hypnotized by its beauty, not wanting to face Jered.

"My father could help me master my abilities," Jered says. "Maybe between the two of us—"

"No!" I say, spinning to face him. "He is gone, Jered."

"What do you mean 'he's gone'?"

"He is no longer where I left him," I say.

"Leela." Jered's voice is soft but strained. "You have to let me make the decision of whether to trust him or not."

"See? You just gave me a command, and again you didn't recognize it. Jered, of course you make the decision. You are the mas... mas...*arrgh*!" I snap with frustration. I am unable to speak the word master in relation to him because of another of his inadvertent commands.

He moves to lay a hand on my arm, and I flinch away. His eyes flash with hurt and frustration, but I cannot undo it. I fight back the tears that well behind my eyes, forcing myself to breathe.

"Jered, I must tell you everything."

"Tell me, Leela," he says, sitting on the plush brown sofa next to Gabe, who is now munching on some food from the snack bar.

I pinch my eyes shut because he's done it again. Given me yet another command. But I was going to tell him anyway.

"Your father is not who you think he is." I let this information sink in, but he does not react. "You see, the first Magicians are the ones who enslaved the Djinn. There were three of them. Two of them have found a path to immortality."

Jered leans forward now, drawn into the story. I think for a moment of how it felt to kiss him. How I've treated him. What it must be like to be him. These things do not help.

"They were able to do this by transferring their essence into the body of another Magician. Not any Magician. A relative makes it an easier transition." I wait for his reaction. Surely, he sees it now.

"So they transfer their souls into another human being?" His face is filled with disgust.

"Yes. Their children, who also have magic," I say, waiting for it to register.

"They kill their own kids?" Gabe asks, potato chip frozen in his grasp, forgotten.

"Yes. Their souls are displaced. They are forced out of their own bodies," I say.

"That's sick. And I mean that in the bad way," Gabe says.

But Jered's face is flushed. His nostrils flare, and he leaps to his feet. "You're accusing my own father of being a monster?" He's run his hands through his hair so much that it sticks up in odd places, giving him the look of a madman. "Of planning to kill me?"

"Jered, I am sorry." I fight back the tears and my fear of speaking the truth. My arms tremble, but I force my way through it, hugging myself. "I knew him—know him well. His real name is Achan. He fooled me once too." I look away from him to the water outside. It appears so calm from here, but I know it is always flowing. Always moving.

"I can't believe you, Leela. How can you lie to me like this?" Jered is right next to me now.

"I cannot lie to you. You commanded me to tell you," I point out, arms dropping helplessly at my sides.

"You actually fell for this?" he asks, his tone mocking. Harsh. "What? The other Djinn told you that, and you bought it?"

"No," I say, looking him straight in the eye. "I knew the moment I saw him who he was. He admitted it all to me." I am still determined to tell him everything. The rising anger inside me makes it easier to confront him.

"Then you lied to me before." He is directly over me now, red-faced and waving his arms. "You certainly omitted the information, if that's true. So which is it, Leela?" He grabs my arms, pulling me off-balance.

"Jer—" Gabe stands, and Jered spins around, letting go of me and lashing out with a hand as his bloodred aura flows across the room toward his friend.

I react without thinking, moving Gabe to my other side before the energy can strike. The cushions are torn off the sofa in a whirlwind. Chips fly everywhere.

We stand still and quiet for a minute, each unable to face the other.

"Perhaps I should go find your father after all," I say, gaze still cast downward.

"Go ahead. I...I need some space anyhow," Jered says.

"Gabe, do you want to go home?" I ask, peering up at him.

He looks from me to Jered and adjusts his glasses. "No. That's all right. I should stay with Jered."

I nod and disappear.

34

WHO WE ARE

Everything is a mess. What is happening? I have to find Achan because he has answers. I know he does. Maybe he's my best chance right now anyway. That thought sends my mind reeling.

I float through the wreckage. Mira did a thorough job. Yellow police tape flies in the breeze, secured only on one end. An unpleasant scent fills the air, perhaps spoiled food from a broken refrigerator. The damage appears confined to Jered's and the surrounding apartments. The neighbors on either side of the building remain an untouched picture of suburbia, complete with satellite dishes, minivans in carports, and tricycles askew on patios.

"Achan!" I call out. I know he will be close. This is what I would do.

The distant sound of traffic fills the evening, and the sun sinks behind large pink clouds that look just as raw as they did when we arrived this morning on Achan's doorstep. A sudden thought flits through my head. One more sunset, and there will be nothing stopping Jered from freeing me. Assuming, of course, that he would still want to. I laugh bitterly and settle on the crooked beam of what was once the overhang of Jered's back porch.

"Here to finish me off?" Achan's voice sends a shiver down my neck, and I wonder if it is from fear, the chill in the air, or old habit.

"No," I say without turning around. "We need to talk."

"How did you find me?" he asks.

"You thought he'd come back here. I know you."

"So you do, Little One." His fingers find my cheek, and I shrug away.

"I hate you," I say.

"I know." He slips down next to me, careful to keep his hands to himself.

"He doesn't deserve to die," I tell him, watching the last leaf struggling to fall free of the maple in the yard. Doesn't it know that as soon as it succeeds, its life will cease?

"Few mortals do, Leela. You didn't deserve what happened to you either."

I laugh at the way he makes it sound like there was no blame. It simply "happened."

I allow myself the luxury of examining his face. Soaking in his smell. His warmth. I see now that there are differences. Small ones. The curve of his nose, the shape of his lips. They are minor things, and his whole persona is so clearly Achan that those things are drowned out until insignificant.

I wonder if he remembers his original self as well as I do.

I place my palms on either side of his face, stroking his hair back like I used to. He closes his eyes, relieved, and a small smile plays at his mouth. I trace the shape of his face with my fingers, slowly, wondering what this man before me would be like if Achan hadn't stolen his body.

"And tell me, Achan, what would you do with me if you owned me again?" I whisper.

In answer, he closes the distance between us and presses his lips to mine, gathering me to him by my waist. My body responds as usual, but all I can think of is Jered, and all the hurt floods back.

I pull away.

"I see," he says.

"No. I don't think you do." I fly into the sky, but Achan follows me, taking hold of my hand.

"Bring me to him, Little One. It will be over quickly, I promise you. And he will feel no pain as long as he doesn't struggle."

A sickening sensation passes through my stomach. I must ask one more question. His answer will dictate my actions.

"Have you already done something to him?" I ask, tracing a casual path from his shoulder to his waist.

"I was almost in when we were interrupted earlier."

I recall Sophie's excellent timing. "And?" I press forward with both my words and my hands.

He answers with a ragged breath. "I left an opening in his aura. A place where I can climb inside quickly."

"What does that do to him?" I ask, lips pressed to his ear, slipping a hand beneath his shirt.

"It opens his emotions. Makes them powerful, less controllable." He tilts his head back, mouth parted.

"Can that harm him? Other than making him emotional?" I press.

"He will grow more and more unstable until I fill the hole, Leela. Only I can change it. There is nothing for you to do, so you will have to accept that."

I do not like this answer.

"I need you to kill Kitra," I say, withdrawing my hands and gazing back at the rubble that was Jered's home.

"Kill Kitra?" He laughs. "Don't you think I would have done it already if I were able?"

"The Djinn are on an assignment for her. You can get to her now."

"And what's in it for me?" he asks, though it doesn't take Sophie's mind-reading skills to know he plans on taking possession of them.

"Jered," I say. "And all three of us."

"I should collect some supplies at my house," he says at once.

I nod. I know what is waiting for us there. Know what the others will do when they see him. I don't actually expect him to kill Kitra.

Nor do I anticipate he will live through the night.

I spin in the air, still grasping his hand, and we materialize in the hallway of his home. I wonder why we are not greeted by the others. Instead, a shrill scream finds my ears—the sound of pure suffering. I know that sound well.

"That's Elle," Achan says, brow furrowing with confusion. He runs in the direction of the tortured voice, and I follow, invisible.

"Elle?" he asks at the doorway of Sophie's room.

"Peter! She's gone." Her strangled cries punctuate each word.

I fling my palm over my mouth in horror as the meaning sinks in. Once again, I was blind to the truth. Once again, my mistake costs too much.

I see the note that she holds up with a shaky hand. Achan reaches for it, and I read it over his shoulder. The magic makes words appear in scrawling handwriting.

If you want to see your daughter again, you will not call the police. I will contact you with my demands shortly.

But the note, the real one underneath, is fashioned from glowing green letters in ancient Aramaic. I know Achan sees them as well.

If what you say of your master is true, then he will come for his sister.

I read the words again and again, trying to make sense out of them, trying to fight the icy panic that threatens to overtake me. *Not Sophie.*

Achan lays an impatient hand on his wife's head, and her face grows blank and still. He looks up, hand trembling, sweat breaking out on his brow.

"We will get her back," I say, becoming visible.

"You can't bring them my son." He spits his words at me like venom, the muscles in his neck straining until they look as though they will pop.

"What?" I ask. Nothing should surprise me anymore. Still he's managed it.

"They are my only two safeguards right now. You will not cost me my immortality. You will not." His face is ugly and twisted. He glances toward the hall, and I know he is weighing his chances of getting to the lead vest, so I slam the door with a breath.

"You would sacrifice your daughter so that you can kill your son?" I ask. I need to hear it from his lips.

"You don't understand!" he says. He is all spit and fury. "It is difficult to start over. To have to deal with raising children until the right one comes along. The older this body gets, the more tenuous the situation."

When he sees my face, he tries a different tack, his old handsome features sliding back into place. "I'll do what you want, Leela. We'll wait until they realize it didn't work. When the Djinn come back for Jered, I'll go kill Kitra. It's perfect. And I'll free you, Leela. I won't need to keep you if I have them. Two is enough."

"Enough of your lies," I say.

"It is no lie! I will take a blood oath. Anything."

"Begging does not become you, Achan. Nor does it matter. It appears only one of us has grown a conscience over the past thousand years. I will not sacrifice another living soul for my own freedom."

"Then you are a fool."

"Perhaps. But you are a marked man. As soon as the command is lifted, I will find you. I promise you that. And if I don't, I'm sure Taj or Mira will."

I should anticipate Achan's next move. Perhaps I don't care enough to prevent it. He throws his hands in either direction, and his wife, Elle, is thrown through the window while he escapes in a burst of speed through the door.

I throw out my own hand, catching the woman in midair and laying her neatly on Sophie's bed. I cover her forehead with my palm. "Sleep," I say.

Achan will return with his vest. Of this I am sure. But it does not matter. Not really. What is important is that for once in the past several days, my head is clear. My purpose sure. It is time to face my real master.

35

THE BEGINNING

Cold and heavy, the chains surround my neck, cutting off my air supply and slicing into my skin like a hundred knives. I stumble to my knees, reaching toward Achan, grasping feebly at his robes. The colors swirl and flash before my eyes, making it hard to see.

"Put it in the cage," Kitra says.

Cephas yanks on the ends of the chain, and I grab at the front, desperate to put a finger's space between the lead and my throat. I am dragged across the floor, cushions scattering to the sides as I am pulled into a second room.

Enormous hands lift me, and I am thrust into a cage big enough for several sheep. It would be impossible to stand, however, as it is only about waist high. Not that I could stand if there were space. The pain is so horrible that I am barely conscious.

I lie on the ground, hands pressed against the bottom of the lead prison. The chain around my neck slides off, and Cephas pulls it out through the bars. I raise a shaky head to find a grin of pleasure on his face. His teeth are rotting stubs of brown and gray. I lean over and vomit.

"Put the blanket inside before it passes out," Kitra says. A gray woolen mass is shoved through the door, and Achan's face swims into view.

"Lie on top of it. It will be easier if you aren't in contact with the lead," he says.

I nod feebly and climb on top. The pain subsides slightly, and I lick my lips, trying to formulate words.

"Why?" I croak.

Achan refuses to look me in the face. Instead, he rises, and his place is taken by Kitra. Her expression alone makes me cower toward the far end of my blanket. I scoot backward, away from this horrible woman, until my hand slips through the bars where I touch something cold.

I swallow, realizing why the house was so filled with the scent of incense. It is meant to mask the smell of something far more foul. I turn toward the source, as though drawn by some unseen force.

The bodies are chained to the wall. They have been there long enough for the features to become bloated and gray. One is a man, human I think. Small and old. His flesh is already decomposing, a dark pool of congealed blood still staining the floor beneath him. The other's features are nearly unrecognizable, broken and marred as she is.

Rhada.

I recall Taj's words, "We are all connected." It was her death that brought such pain the other night.

I vomit again, retching to the sound of Kitra's laughter.

36

THE COMMAND

"Sophie's been taken," I say. There is no sense in sugarcoating it. Jered must be told. He must lift the command and allow me to find her so that I can make things right.

Jered's face grows pale. He sinks to the couch.

Gabe strides toward me, his long legs filling the gap in seconds.

"By who?"

"Taj and Mira. They are using her as bait to lure Jered to their master."

"I suppose you want me to stay here while you swoop in and rescue her?" Jered asks.

I dig my nails into my palm, reminding myself that he has been tampered with. "No," I say. "We have a better chance of saving her if we go together. But there is more you must understand."

"What's that?" he asks. It seems my answer has thrown him off-balance, so I take my best shot.

"Achan, your father, he did something to you when he was 'teaching' you magic. He opened a doorway in your aura. It affects your emotions. You are growing unstable, and this cannot be fixed without his help."

"That sounds nasty," Gabe says.

"It is," I agree. "But we must first take care of Sophie."

"I wish I knew if I could trust you." Jered's words sting, but he couldn't look more miserable. His sandy-blond hair is mussed and sticks out in all directions. Dark circles grow beneath his sunken eyes. Even his aura is flat, a mixture of varying shades of gray.

"What does your heart say?" I ask, crossing to face him and kneeling, both hands on his knees. He looks at me like a lost child. "I trust your heart, Jered."

He sinks to the floor before me, cupping my face in his hands. A tear escapes and flows down my cheek and over his fingers. Butterflies stir in my chest. Again, it is more than just my body responding to his touch. I do not try to hide my smile as he leans forward to kiss me.

"Um, little sister kidnapped by evil sorceress," Gabe calls.

Jered pulls away slowly, some of the color flooding back in his aura and his face.

"My heart tells me to trust you," he says, eyes locked on mine.

It is impossible to hold back the sigh of relief. I will not let him down. I will not fail again.

"I love you, Leela."

"You are experiencing stronger and stronger emotions," I say, brushing his hair back from his face.

"This is something I've known for a while."

"I will not hold you to it." I stand and help pull him to his feet. I won't even pretend to believe it. That would hurt far worse than admitting my own emotions to myself. At least I can prevent any illusory expectations that he could possibly feel the same.

"How do we find them?" Jered asks.

"We use the app," I say. "I can trace the source of the magic while it is in use. But as soon as we turn it on, they can also trace our location."

"Then we should do it while we're moving," Jered says.

"Of course!" I say. "That is perfect. Before we do it, you should remove the command. Allow me to hurt those holding Sophie. Be specific if you like."

Jered hesitates. "Leela, I don't think you should go."

"What?" Gabe and I ask in unison.

"You could be hurt. I'm already in trouble. If I am killed, you will be fr-fr..."

"Free?" Gabe finishes.

Jered nods. "I still can't say it."

I look outside at the moon reflecting on the surface of the lake, dancing like silver flames. Just a few short hours. If only we had time to wait.

"I want to go, Jered," I say. "I want to protect you. To save Sophie. Isn't her life the most important thing here?"

"It's what they are expecting. I've been practicing, Leela. I'm getting better at controlling it," Jered says, taking hold of my hand.

"It's true," Gabe says, chiming in. "He was, like, flying around the room and zapping things. Maybe whatever his dad did to him makes his powers stronger?"

"I don't think so," I say, considering this. "More likely, he is discovering his own powers. Achan would not have wanted him stronger. Quite the contrary. But, Jered, no matter what you can do, you must understand that Kitra is better. You've had days. She's had centuries."

"And there's the Djinn," Gabe says.

"Leela, if she gets ahold of you, the whole world could be at stake, isn't that right?" Jered asks.

"Yes," I say. "But you don't understand. You don't know what she's capable of."

"Leela, I'm sorry."

"Please—" I begin, desperate to make him listen.

"Leela," Jered says, touching a finger to my lips to silence me. "I command you to fly with me and use the app to locate Sophie. You will let me go on my own. You will return here and stay with Gabe." Tenderly, he wipes away some of the tears streaming down my face and kisses my forehead.

"Jer, I don't know. You should think this through," Gabe says.

"Let's go, Leela," Jered says, not taking his gaze off me.

I have no choice but to do as he wishes. I sweep us both out the window, opening my hand to catch Gabe's phone, which flies obediently into my palm.

37

STAYING WITH GABE

THE MOMENT THE APP IS ACTIVATED, TENDRILS OF LIGHT SHOOT FROM THE screen, wrapping around both Jered and me. I focus everything I have, and my own power glides along a beam, through the phone and out into space.

"Leela?"

Jered's voice gets my attention, and I realize I have been gripping his hand tightly. I loosen my grasp, continuing to pull us through the air.

"I found them. They are on an island in the Atlantic. It is invisible to human eyes."

"Can you get me there?" he asks.

I shut Gabe's phone down and bring us to a stop in midair. Miles below, the lake churns behind the mask of night. Above, the sky sparkles with a million stars.

"I can. But, Jered, please reconsider. I do not wish to lose you."

"I don't want to lose me either," he says with a grin.

I let out a sound between a laugh and a cry. "I need to tell you something before you go," I say.

"Don't," he says, and I draw my mouth into a tight line. "Save it for when I see you again. It will only make it harder."

Then he leans down and finds my lips, pulling me in close, and we float among the stars, bodies pressed together. I grip his shoulders, drinking in the taste of him. He kisses me like a dying man enjoys his last meal. His touch is far more urgent than our first such encounter. Less tentative. Less gentle.

He kissed His mouth finds my neck. As he works his way down, I tilt my head back, my eyes shut in ecstasy. I run my hands over his chest, his stomach. I want this. I want him.

"Leela," he whispers, his hot breath against my ear driving me mad.

"Jered," I answer, tempted to have my way with him right here in the sky. But my memory returns, even as he fumbles with the button on my jeans. This is not him. These are his emotions out of control. Passion, lust, fear of what he plans to face. I fear for him too.

"Jered. What about Sophie? Let me come with you." I push against his shoulders.

With a groan, he pulls away, and I see him work to bring his breathing under control. We both float for a minute, trapped between the brilliant sky and dark depths until he is able to speak.

"Do as I commanded, Leela." His face is all pain and longing. I feel so helpless. "Send me there. Now."

He disappears from view, on his way to an island in the Atlantic filled with more danger than I can fathom. And I reappear in the Chicago hotel room with Gabe, as promised. How I wish I'd never interrupted him. Now I may never know what it is like to be with him that way. I may never hear his voice again. Never feel his touch.

I run to Gabe and cling to his waist, crying into his chest. He stands motionless for a moment and then puts his arms around me, patting me awkwardly on the back.

"You really do care about him, don't you?" he asks.

"I do," I say. It comes out muffled into his shirt. I realize I'm getting him all wet.

"I wish I could fix it," he says.

I believe we both feel helpless now. Ashamed of my outburst, I separate from Gabe and straighten up.

An idea pops into my head. "Perhaps you can fix it."

"What are you talking about?" He takes a step back.

"I did what I was supposed to do. I came back here. Now I am supposed to stay with you. 'Go back and stay with Gabe.' You see?"

"No. I really don't," Gabe says, shaking his head.

"I came back. Now I must stay with you." I repeat it slower this time, remembering how dim the boy can sometimes be.

"So if I don't stay here, you have to come with me?"

"Exactly," I say as understanding floods Gabe's features. "If you decide to go after Jered and Sophie—"

"You'll have to come too!" he says. "Wait. I dunno. This is dangerous."

"You'll have me," I say, walking my fingers up his arm.

He pulls away. "Yeah, but you're one Djinni who can't hurt any of the bad guys."

"The other Djinn want us to succeed," I remind him.

"But they have to try to stop us if she tells them to."

"Gabe, are you going to help me save Jered and Sophie or not?" I ask.

"If I don't, you'll make my life miserable if something happens to him, won't you?"

"Yes," I say, folding my arms across my chest.

"Well..." He sighs. "I've always wanted to be a hero. And since you put it so sweetly...let's go."

38

FORTRESS

Because of the distance, and since I need to stay with Gabe, which in essence means I must follow him, we fly. Once I get him going in the right direction, he moves quickly. It's still not fast enough for me.

"Wahoo!" he yells, parting a cloud with his hands and spinning headfirst through the cotton-candy strands that remain.

"Gabe," I shout. "Please try to focus. Jered and Sophie could already be dead."

"You wouldn't know if Jered died?" he asks, turning and floating ahead.

"I suppose I would know that. But Sophie...and they could be torturing him."

Gabe squeezes my arm reassuringly and shoots off to the east. Below us, the water churns gray-blue and opaque. Every once in a while, the white-capped surface breaks and a dolphin leaps out.

"I think I found it."

Gabe's voice shatters my concentration. I did gift him the ability to see the island with his feeble human eyes. So I search ahead, and in the distance, I see what he means. Something enormous and foreboding reaches out from the depths. As I watch, this thing does not slip back beneath the waves. Instead, it grows larger and more menacing, the sea crashing around it, as though trying in vain to force it to budge.

"I believe this is it," I say.

"Genie GPS," Gabe says, cracking a smile.

I shake my head at him, aware of how he has grown on me. Funny how these things can sneak up on you.

"You should approach with caution," I tell him. "They will most likely have alarms set to warn them of intruders."

He nods, and we come to rest on the tip of some jagged rocks that shoot up around the perimeter of the island, like enormous stalagmites. The sound of the water thrusting against the protrusions roars in my ears, and I erase the noise so that we can talk.

Gabe shakes uncontrollably, and I realize he must be cold. I wave a hand, and his leather jacket appears.

"How are we even supposed to get in there, with or without alarms?" Gabe asks, pushing his glasses up to the bridge of his nose and scowling at the fortress. The rocks are the first and least of our problems. Before us stretches an enormous wall of pure iron. It shoots straight into the sky for what looks like a mile and curves far off into the distance in either direction.

"It surrounds the island," I say.

"It sure looks that way," he says.

"Well, it isn't lead," I say. "I can get us through. It's what's on the other side that worries me."

"How do we do it?" he asks, wiping the sea spray from his forehead.

"We send in a friend first. Then, while Kitra and her Djinn are distracted, we follow. We will remain invisible. It isn't foolproof, but it is helpful."

"Where are we going to find a friend willing to sacrifice himself?"

I nod toward the water where a seal is working its way onto one of the flatter rocks. Gabe still appears confused, so I wave a hand over the animal, which dissolves and reforms into the figure of a man.

The seal man is short and thin with shiny gray skin and whiskers. His head darts back and forth, arms shooting out to the sides.

"Whoa. That is just plain bizarre," Gabe says. "Can it...is it...?"

"No," I say. "It can't think like a human or speak." As if to prove my point, the creature lets out a loud bark, and Gabe jumps. "But it should be enough of a distraction to get us inside."

"Won't they figure out you're here when they find it?" he asks.

I wave an impatient hand, and Gabe flinches. "You'll see," I say. "If you ever decide to go inside, that is."

Gabe gulps some air and flies toward the wall. Seal man and I follow. I open a hole in the metal, and give my creation a little push inside. Gabe follows, and so do I.

The metal is so thick it feels like we are crawling through a tunnel into a mountain. About halfway through, natural rock seeps into the iron, creating a twisted, impossible mixture that sends a chill down my spine. The moment I step out of the tunnel, I realize the inner circle isn't much prettier. Everything is stone or metal, large enough for a giant to make himself at home. The fifty-foot walls open to what looks like empty sky. But I can see the reflective shimmer of a magical force field, no doubt meant to keep out the elements.

I close up the hole in the wall to cover any evidence of our arrival.

"Whoa." Gabe whistles, hanging back as the seal man wanders off toward one of several large passageways.

The uneven stone floors are covered with dirt and straw. The walls are lined with grotesque statues made of marble, men and women frozen wearing expressions of terror or sadness, as though the devil himself wished to commemorate each of his finest moments of torture.

"So the whole island is like a castle or something?" he whispers.

"So it would appear. Now do us both a favor and shut up."

Gabe looks ready to retort when I see something move in the shadows to the left of the seal man. I throw out an arm in caution, catching Gabe in the chest and pushing him up against the wall. I feel exposed despite my invisibility spell.

Apparently the animal senses the disturbance too, because it sniffs the air and darts back and forth like it's caught in a trap. Moments later, Taj appears at its side, shaking his head. I speak, my own lips moving, the words coming out of the seal's mouth.

"Taj, this is a warning. Release the child. Jered is not fool enough to risk his life or me."

I glance at Gabe, who mouths the word "creepy." Then I transform the seal back into his usual shiny self. Taj laughs and claps his hands as much in response to my performance as to return the seal to the rocks outside.

"Marvelous, Lee! Too bad we already know better. Jered got here hours ago. What took you so long?"

39

THE BEGINNING

"Let's try this again," Kitra says. She twists a handful of my hair around her hand and yanks my head back so that her lips graze my ear. My arms are stretched above my head, suspended from the ceiling by more lead chains.

For two days, I cowered in the cage, weeping, broken, and scared, certain I was either going to go mad or die in a pool of my own filth. I never before considered my own mortality. I have never known any Djinni who has actually died. Well, not until Rhada.

Rhada. I see her face every time I close my eyes. Swollen and lifeless. I imagine what my own face would look like if I were the soulless one chained to the wall.

The other body, it turns out, belongs to Kitra's father. I was right in assuming he was the village elder. Unfortunately for him, he also stood in her way. I gleaned this from the one-sided conversations she had with him while I wept and moaned near her feet.

When I finally quieted, emptied of every bit of emotion in my useless human body, when I lay down on the filthy wool blanket to die, they began questioning me. They being Kitra and Cephas. Achan has avoided me since shoving his last gift through the bars.

They have questions and demand answers that I do not know. They want secrets. Secrets to unlock hidden powers within themselves. But as far as I know, these things do not exist. I am what I am. I offer them everything to let me go. But they want more.

I thought the pain I felt when thrust into the cage was the worst of it. I was wrong. Each day, I am introduced to new horrors. Today, I hang from the ceiling while Kitra attempts to persuade me with a lead bar. Each place she pushes it into my skin sears like the brand Achan uses with his sheep. How I feel for those sheep now.

"Do you not think I would give it to you if I could?" I cry.

"Give me your powers? I wouldn't do it if our situations were reversed," she says, letting go of my hair. The next thing I know, she is slicing my side with a lead knife. This is not the first time, but I scream and scream as the blood spills out and drips on the floor.

Kitra laughs and licks at the wound with her tongue, sucking the warm crimson liquid into her mouth as my body shudders with silent sobs. When she is done, she seals the cut with magic and walks around until she faces me.

"It is not working," she says, teeth and lips stained red.

I wait, uncertain what she means.

"It was the blood of the other one that gave us our powers," Cephas says from the doorway. His mere presence elicits more tremors. My chains rattle with the movement.

"We drained your friend and shared her blood," Kitra says.

I feel dizzy.

"We thought perhaps if we did the same with you we would gain more power," Kitra says, running the flat of the lead blade against my cheek, causing steam to sizzle into the air. "You see, its blood wasn't enough. Our power still does not equal that of your kind."

I whimper as Cephas draws close and squeezes my face in one hand until I think my jaw will crack. He smiles, his rotten breath making my empty stomach squirm.

"But your blood isn't helping," he says. "Good thing Kitra was smart enough to test it first. You'd be little use to us dead."

"That's enough, Cephas," Kitra says. "Let us leave it, so that it may think about the wisdom of sharing its secrets."

"Please," I say as they turn their backs to leave. "Please, I will do anything. I will do whatever I can to help you increase your power."

Kitra pauses near the single oil lamp flickering against the wall. The light throws shadows across her skin, making me think of a tiger's stripes.

"If only we believed you." Her smile is the last thing I see before she blows out the flame.

40

MEMORIES

I PRESS GABE BACK AGAINST THE WALL BETWEEN TWO STATUES. HIS FACE is pale in the cold gray of the castle.

"Stay here. Do nothing unless I give the okay. No matter what you see. If I am taken, you must get out of here. If I still belong to Jered, I will be forced to follow you." I hand Gabe a small black disc with a red button in the center. "Push this. It will reopen the hole. I am leaving you invisible and with the ability to fly. Both will fade in twenty-four hours if I...if I am unavailable. Do you understand?"

He keeps staring at me, unable to speak. I sigh in frustration. Taj waits for me, leaning against the wall of the passage he came out of.

"Gabe. Do. You. Understand?"

"Y-Yes," he finally stammers.

I nod, satisfied. I'll have to take his word for it. Every moment I waste, Jered and Sophie could be in greater danger.

When I finally appear in front of Taj, he barely blinks. He presses his lovely mouth into an impatient line and narrows his eyes at me.

"Seriously, Lee. Are you dragging this out because you want to join us? I didn't think you liked Kitra much."

The mere mention of her name sets my blood boiling. How I would like to break each bone in her body, one at a time. I force myself to breathe.

"Where is he?" I ask.

"You can't save him," Taj says.

"I *will* save him," I say. I feel my eyes glow green, and the corners of his lips twist into a partial grin.

"Well, well, that's the Leela I remember. The one from before. The room is lined with lead. Just so you know."

"So you cannot enter either," I say.

"She doesn't need us there to break him." His eyes cloud for a moment, and I can't help but feel he is reliving his own punishments.

I know. "Have you been given a command regarding me?" I ask.

"Curiously, no. She believes you are trapped in that room, I think. She cannot fathom that the boy might not have kept you close. Frankly, it confuses me as well."

"He was protecting me." I cannot look Taj in the eyes.

"Smitten, eh? Poor fool. He'll be calling for you soon enough though. I'm impressed he's lasted this long." Taj confirms my worst fears.

My heart feels like it is being squeezed by a vise. I long to go to him but know I can't. I have to think.

"What about Sophie?" I ask.

"Mira is babysitting."

I look up, my pulse quickening. "What does that mean, Taj?" My voice is strong. Threatening.

"Don't worry so much. Mira only hates you, and Kitra is interested in the girl. She wants to use her. She uses anything with power."

"You mean enslave her?" I ask.

"Persuade her. At least that would be the first option. If that doesn't work, well..." He lets his voice trail off and sets a firm hand on my shoulder. "She's far too distracted with your boy right now."

"Sophie has nothing to do with this. She's a child," I say, shrugging his arm off.

"I have to follow my commands, Lee. I don't have the privilege of a master who cares what I think. You ought to know how that works. You're the one who did this to me."

I recoil, tears springing to my eyes. And all I can see is his face. His beautiful, terror-stricken face as I force the choker around his neck. I was a fool to think he could have ever forgiven me. I would never have forgiven myself. I haven't.

"Oh," is all I manage to get out.

"Her room is the last on the right. His is in the dungeon. Second cell on the left. The one *without* the skeleton."

Taj disappears in a flash of emerald light. I am left in the middle of the floor, one hand reaching for something I will never grasp.

I stand there, memories flashing before my eyes, blinding me, until Gabe squeezes my shoulder, bringing me back to reality. I swallow it all back and turn to face him.

"You heard?" I ask. I cannot pretend it didn't happen. And somehow, erasing his memory doesn't seem right.

"I'm sure it wasn't what it sounded like," Gabe says reassuringly. But his glasses don't hide the worry in his eyes.

"What if I tell you it is exactly what it sounded like?" I ask, looking toward the nearest statue—a woman, mouth twisted in a never-ending scream of pure terror.

"Then I'd say, knowing you, you had a really good reason."

"Does it matter?" I ask.

"Of course it does. It would to me. But right now, we have to get to the others. Can you focus?"

When did Gabe become the mature one here?

"Of course I can focus!" I snap, turning to face him.

"There's the Leela I know," he says in a bad imitation of Taj. "So what do you think? I go get Jer, and you get Sophie? You know, because of the lead?"

"I have to stay with you, remember?" I ask, rapping on his head.

"Oh. Yeah. Damn! Jered can really be an ass sometimes, can't he?"

"Let's start with Sophie. We have to get her out of here," I say, ignoring him. But inside I am relieved that someone else finally sees what a mess these commands can make.

41

FORESEEN

DESPITE THE MIDDAY SUN SPILLING THROUGH THE INVISIBLE CEILING, THE way is dark. The kind of dark that soaks up any color, any light, and swallows it whole. I swirl my fingers through the air, and a luminescent ball appears in my hand. Now three feet of stone floor are illuminated. A carpet runner of crimson and gold lines the hall. One thousand years hasn't changed Kitra's taste in decor.

Sophie's room, from the outside, looks like any of the others. A large metal door is set like a sentry toward the hallway with the symbol, an eye surrounded by sun, moon, and star, carved in the center. I hesitate.

"She should be in there," I say. I am trying to convince myself more than Gabe, who twitches at my shoulder. Taj gave me the information freely. Yet he still blames me. Is this a trap? Either way, Mira is waiting inside.

"Something wrong?" Gabe ventures.

"I can't go in until you do," I say. "But that's good. You will distract Mira while I rescue Sophie."

"Me? Distract a Djinni?" He wobbles a little on his feet, and I catch his elbow with my free hand.

"She probably won't kill you right away. She'll want to figure out what you are doing here." I smile, trying to encourage him, but I know I am not doing a very good job. All I want to do is find Jered and leave this horrible place.

Gabe readies himself by throwing his head back and shaking out his limbs. I try not to laugh. He licks his lips and pulls at the door, which creaks open with an ear-piercing screech.

Mira is on him in a heartbeat. He is thrust up against the wall by his throat. Inside the room, Sophie sits straight up on a small cot. She looks frightened but unharmed. Her eyes are red from crying, and I see Little Leela in her hands.

"Who dares disturb my master's domicile?" Mira demands. It isn't like Gabe can answer, since she's crushing his windpipe. She waits, examining his face as strangled sounds escape him and a deep shade of purple creeps up his cheeks.

I motion for Sophie to run behind me. Just as the Djinni senses me, I pull my arms up into the air, and Mira is lifted from the ground. Gabe slides to the floor and then scrambles up and to the doorway next to Sophie.

"Put me down, you bitch!" Mira screams.

It takes almost all my power to keep her still. The moment I let go, she will be free to retaliate. The only thing I could possibly do is conjure lead restraints. I cannot bring myself to do it.

Gabe pauses at the threshold, waiting with wide eyes. Sophie hovers behind him, still clutching her doll. He knows if he leaves, I will have to do so too. I do not know what to do.

In my mind, I see Mira cowering in the corner, unable to rip her gaze from what remains of her lover. I see Taj crying like a child at Cephas's feet. See my own fingers holding the thing that remains to this day around Mira's neck.

My hands tremble. Mira has grown silent and remains pressed against the ceiling, staring at me. What does she see? Does she see a monster? A murderer? A traitor?

"I will hold her here." Taj's voice in my ear startles me.

"But—"

"Yes, I have a lovely butt," says Taj. "No need to thank me, it looks ever so much fun. Now, go save that handsome master of yours."

"But—"

"Yes, he also has a nice ass. Too nice to get beat to a pulp. Now go." Taj raises his hands toward the ceiling, and I feel the burden lifted from my own. He refuses to make eye contact with me.

I lean in and kiss him on the cheek. Gabe's face is white when I rejoin them, but I focus my attention on Sophie.

"Let's get your brother and get out of this horrid place."

"It's going to be hard," Sophie says, tugging on my hand.

I scoop her into my arms and follow Gabe back down the passage. "Not with all of us working together," I tell her.

"No. I mean, I've seen it. It was all in my dream. The mean person."

Gabe stops between two statues that reach toward us blindly, as though we can save them from some horrible fate.

"You said I saved you in your dream," I say, stroking some stray hair from her face.

"That's right. And you did. Just now."

"Sophie, what else did you see in your dream?" Gabe asks, taking her into his arms.

A tear rolls down her chubby cheek as she looks back and forth between us. "Maybe if I don't say it—"

"On the contrary, Little One. If you warn us, we may be able to prevent it," I say.

She shakes her head, her little mouth working as she mulls something over in her mind.

"Jered. He's hurt real bad," she says, no longer able to hold back.

"I won't let that happen," I say, though I'm sure she can hear the urgency in my voice.

"It's going to be too late," she whispers, dissolving into hysterics, muffled only by the sound of my pounding heart.

42

THE BEGINNING

My head hangs limp; my throat is raw from screaming. The pain has not subsided. If anything, it has grown worse. Yet I cannot manage to react outwardly any longer. I stopped begging to die ages ago.

Cephas stands at my back, his enormous body pressed against mine. The remaining rags I had on, he ripped away when he started. He runs his giant hands over the front of my chest. The lead rings he wears on every finger leave trails of red, raw flesh in their wake.

"If you gave me your magic, I could make you enjoy it," he says.

I do not answer. Do not try to explain that even I do not have that kind of power.

"Get away from her!" Achan's voice cuts through the room like a sword. My heart dares leap to life, my gaze rising just enough to see him framed in the doorway, aura glowing orange like a flame.

"Look who's decided to join us," Cephas says. He presses his hands back over my body, eliciting an involuntary groan from my lips.

Somehow my voice has returned. Weak but present. I thought I could handle no more. Now I die another death, worse because of Achan's presence.

"I said, take your hands off her," Achan says. He takes several strides into the room, eyes locked somewhere behind me. I see that his robes are no longer those of a shepherd but golden silk, those of a king. Yes, as far as I have fallen,

he has risen out of my sight. And I would have given it all to him freely had he only asked. Instead, he murdered my friend, drank her blood, and gave me over for the same.

"You want a turn? She's all yours. I'm bored anyhow. Maybe I'll watch you for a while." Cephas pushes me away, and I swing from my chains. He spits on me and walks past Achan to the other side of the room.

In a single fluid movement, Achan reaches out, flattening him on the head with a heavy sword conjured from nothing. Cephas clutches his skull in one massive hand and turns growling toward Achan. He swings. Achan darts to the side, bringing his sword's hilt up hard into Cephas's chin. Blood spurts from his mouth as he staggers backward, reaching for anything in range, but Achan is faster and uses magic. Within moments, Cephas lies unconscious on the floor.

As soon as it is over, I once again drop my head, unable and unwilling to look Achan in the eye. I hear the heavy clang of the sword hitting the ground and then movement. I pay little heed until a cup of water is pressed to my cracked lips. I can barely swallow, so he tilts my head back and tips it slowly down my throat. Some slips over the edges of my mouth and down my skin, making me more aware of the stinging fire everywhere else.

When the cup is emptied twice, Achan runs a hand down my cheek. I squeeze my eyes shut so I cannot see him. Then the impossible happens. He is lifting me, untangling my bonds. Pulling them from my wrists with magic.

I collapse into his arms, familiar and comforting despite the pain. I have not the ability to protest. I simply lie back as he sits on the floor, cradling me to him like a baby. He presses his lips to my forehead, and I feel his aura running over my body, healing me. Cleaning me. Caring for me.

"It is still there. It is just hidden," I say. My own voice sounds foreign.

"That's because this room still has so much lead. The longer you are here, the worse the reaction. At least that's how it was with the other."

I fall silent again, drifting away to the sound of his heart.

"I can get you out of here," he says, and my eyes snap open again. "I've found a way."

"But you brought me here," I say. I have been avoiding the very thought all this time. Focused only on what was happening in the moment.

"I know, Little One. I am so sorry. So sorry. I didn't know. I thought they'd

let me explain. If they knew you were harmless, they wouldn't treat you this way. You aren't savage like the other one."

I do not think he understands Kitra at all. But I remain quiet.

"Take me out of this room, Achan. I can stop this."

"It isn't that simple, Little One. I'm sure you want to hurt us for what's been done. I can't let you do that either."

"I won't, Achan," I cry. "I will leave if that is what you want."

He rocks me tighter. "That is what you say now. But when you heal, you will see things differently. Do not cry. I know a way..."

43

WILLPOWER

WE RACE DOWN THE CORRIDORS, MY SENSES STRETCHED BEFORE US, searching for a way into the dungeons. I wish with a pang that I could send Sophie home with Gabe. But he has to stay, or I will be drawn away with him.

"To the right!" I yell, and Gabe switches course. "Behind that door."

I open it this time to avoid the telltale scrape of metal on stone. It disappears, showing the way to a winding staircase where the walls are lit with gas torches. I pause, remembering Kitra's face as she blew out a flame a thousand years ago.

"Are you okay?" Gabe asks. "Is there lead or something?"

"No. Not yet. But there will be." I set Sophie down on the ground and focus on Gabe. He is my best hope. "You will need to be strong."

"Haven't I proved that yet?" he asks. I decide his eyes look older than they did when we first met.

"Yes. Do not underestimate Kitra. She is powerful, Gabe, and evil. Truly evil." I did not realize I was crushing his sleeve. He gently pries my hand off, holding it in the air between us.

"I'll try to keep it in mind."

"We already know there is lead in the room, so I will not have long before I am unable to perform magic. I'll have one spell at best."

"Can you transport Jer out of there?" Gabe asks.

"It is likely protected by the magic of the other Djinn, so I won't be able to unless he commands it," I say. "We can't risk it. He could be confused or...or incapacitated."

"Can you remove the lead since you know it's there?"

"I'm sure she has safeguards to prevent it. If not, it would be no good against her own Djinn."

"Right."

"We need to get her to leave," Sophie says, tugging on my arm.

I spin around, shocked. "Yes! Yes, that's it. Good work, Sophie." I ruffle her hair.

"I'll do it," Gabe says. "I saw something like this in Zombie Squasher 4000."

"Your video game?" I cannot keep the skepticism out of my question.

"Hey, video games can come in handy."

I follow him down the steps. Sophie's hand is clasped firmly in my own, Little Leela trailing behind in her other.

The first door is smaller than those above but still made of heavy iron. Above the symbol is a rectangular window about the width of a face, striped with bars. I peer over the opening and see a mound of dirt and hay punctuated by gray bones. Shackles hang from the ceiling with disembodied skeletal hands still dangling within.

"You're shaking," Gabe reports.

"It's nothing," I say, turning toward the passageway. One more door. I can do this.

We stop outside, and I hold up a hand to halt our group. The silence is broken moments later by a faint sound. The single moan carries with it such misery that my vision is flooded with red. My throat closes up, and I cannot say it. But Gabe does.

"Jered." Gabe's face is ashen.

I place a hand on his arm, feeding him strength just as I've seen Jered do. His shoulders square in determination, and he fishes in his pocket before pulling out the small black disc I'd given him. Is he thinking of escape? My heart races. I'll be dragged along with him.

But instead of pressing the button, he takes aim at some far-off point and throws with all his might. The disc flies like a Frisbee and meets the center of one of the torch brackets down the hall. The button depresses against the metal with a loud *clank,* and a giant hole opens in the wall. The torch, left with nothing to support it, falls to the ground. Instantly, fire rises along the dry hay in the hall.

Our trio stands there for a moment, staring at the glowing inferno that takes off with abandon. Alarms blaze, and I pull us all back against the wall.

"You will have to show me this zombie game," I say.

Gabe blushes. "Well, um, to be honest, that went a little better than I was hoping."

The door to Jered's cell is thrown open, and a young woman steps out. She is dressed in a crimson bodysuit, her gold emblem etched on the back. Her long auburn hair is pulled back in a braid, and I hesitate, forgetting she is using a different body now. She has not been as careful as Achan. Or perhaps she has searched for anonymity, afraid of being found. She looks no older than Jered or Gabe, but I know the soul that lurks within.

Power builds in my hands. She cannot hear the crackle over the roar of the fire and the blare of the sirens. She isn't even looking in my direction. I am about to let go when I remember my command, and my hands fall uselessly to my sides. I could have ruined my one opportunity to save Jered if I'd let go and gotten her attention. I have to get control of myself.

Gabe darts into the room the second Kitra is out of earshot. I follow with Sophie, but not before adding magic to the flames and opening another hole in the ceiling to make it look like the intruder has gone that way. It is the best I can do to give us a chance to free my master.

My gaze falls on Jered as I round the corner, and a gasp escapes my lips. His arms are stretched above his body so that the toes of his sneakers graze the ground. A leather whip lies discarded nearby. His limp form twists, and I see his bare chest glistens with sweat. The angry red lashes that decorate his back stretch across his stomach. His face is gaunt, eyes half-open and unfocused, and his hair is matted with blood.

The reality of what I see hits me full force at the same time as the stinging pain of the lead.

44

UNEXPECTED

I HAVE SECONDS TO MAKE UP MY MIND BEFORE THE LEAD IN THE CELL overwhelms me. Seconds to decide what one spell I can cast, but I see no options. There is only one choice.

As I sink to my knees inside the door, I will Jered to heal. Some part of me knows that this is not smart. That Kitra will just re-inflict the wounds if she returns before Gabe can manage to get us all out. I should have granted him superstrength instead...

"Leela!"

Jered's voice is like a slap in the face. My eyes snap open to the sound of my name, and I see with relief that he is all right. Perhaps he can use his magic to help.

As I begin to slip back into the blurred world of torment, the pain is parted like a curtain. I lift my head to find Sophie standing before me, her small arms raised, her eyes closed in concentration. The rainbow aura that normally pulses around her has stretched out to cover me instead.

"Jered," I say. "Sophie is protecting me from the lead, but she cannot hold it long."

"Get us out of here, Leela."

I wave an arm. I cannot get us far with all this lead, but I have been given a command, and I manage to make it upstairs to the kitchen. It is a long room with steel counters running for what seems like miles and an enormous open-flame oven built into the rock at the far end. The smattering of servants is the first sign I've seen of other life inside the fortress.

Sophie opens her eyes, and I watch them roll back into her head. I catch her as she falls, gathering her to me.

"Sophie." Jered's voice is filled with pain.

"She'll be all right," I say. "She's just exhausted all her energy."

"She saved us," he says.

"I think I did a pretty good job too," says Gabe. "Tell him about my kick-ass ninja move, Leela."

"Don't congratulate anyone yet," I say. "We aren't out." I gesture around at the handful of human servants who have stopped their preparations to stare at us. "I can only get us so far, and now that she knows we are here, she will order Taj and Mira to reinforce all the magic she already has in place to prevent us from escaping. It will be near impossible."

"How did you even get here?" Jered asks. "I told you to stay with Gabe at the hotel."

"No. You told me to go back to the hotel. And to stay with Gabe. I did both."

"God, I can't get anything right. This is all my fault. All of it. My mom, Sophie, and now you guys are in danger too," Jered wails. He sinks to the ground beside me, head buried in his hands.

Then I realize he is not wearing the ring.

"What...what have you done?" I ask, grabbing his hand.

"We're here because of me. Because I was stupid enough to think I could handle this on my own. I should have let you go. I should have—"

"No. I mean the stone," I say, unable to take my eyes from his naked hand. I finger the cold opal in my choker. Surely I would have felt it if he'd transferred ownership.

"Oh," he says, lifting his head. "Oh, it's still there. I hid it. I hid it so that she couldn't take it from me. I remembered that if she killed me without my giving it to her or her taking it, you'd be okay. I knew there was nothing she could do to convince me to hand it over. She tried pretty hard, though." His aura grows dark, making my heart leap. I know firsthand the kind of pain Kitra inflicts.

"So I did this to keep her from stealing it," he continues. "Since I knew I couldn't free you myself."

I lick my lips. Clear my throat. "You said it."

Sophie stirs in my lap.

"Said what?" Jered asks.

"Said 'free' me," I say. "And you didn't choke."

We all stare at each other for a moment while Sophie sits up, rubbing her eyes with her fists.

"Don't worry," I say, casting my eyes downward. "I don't expect you to do it. Not now anyway. I never really did." After all, I should know better. Even Jered can't be expected to go that far.

Before he can answer, the door to the kitchen bursts open, and Kitra rushes in, flanked on either side by a Djinni with glowing green eyes.

"Get us out again!" Jered shouts.

I wave, and we are back down in the dungeons. It seems the least likely place for us to go. The fire still blazes, thanks to my assistance, but it has been quartered off.

"Leela." Jered places a hand on each of my arms. I desperately want to cling to him but force myself to focus. "Can you get Gabe and Sophie out of here? Back home? They want us. Not them."

"You have to rescind your command to stay with Gabe," I say. "Then I can get them outside the fortress."

"I can fly us home," Gabe says, sounding more like himself.

"Then I rescind the command to stay with Gabe," Jered says. "Leela, help them out."

I nod once and open a new hole to the outside. The alarms are already set off and they know we are here, so there is no further harm in it.

Before climbing through, Gabe leans and whispers in my ear. I glance hurriedly at Jered, who is busy hugging Sophie good-bye. I nod after a moment and hand Gabe his request.

Gabe goes first, followed by Sophie. She hesitates on her hands and knees, looking over her shoulder in anguish. I smile at her, meeting her eyes.

"It is okay, Little One. We will be fine. You must go home with Gabe." A thought comes unbidden to my mind. Achan will use her instead. If Jered and I don't make it out, he will take her body instead.

We will just have to make it out.

"Close this side, so they won't be able to follow them," Jered says.

I do as I am commanded, sealing off Sophie's face from view. Jered's shoulders relax, and the colors in his aura swirl more freely.

"She'll be all right," I say, laying a hand on his back. By the way his body trembles, I know he is crying. Achan's handiwork. His emotions grow more and more unstable. I have to get us out of here, have to find Achan and force him to reverse it.

But how can I do that when I'm still not allowed to cause anyone harm?

45

THE BEGINNING

A<small>CHAN</small> <small>SETS</small> <small>ME</small> <small>GENTLY</small> <small>ON</small> <small>THE</small> <small>FLOOR</small> <small>NEXT</small> <small>TO</small> <small>HIM</small> <small>AND</small> <small>REMOVES</small> *something from his pockets. He holds out his closed fist and opens it to reveal a length of black velvet ribbon with a stone set in the center. The stone is a large, rounded opal that gleams beautifully in the firelight from the wall.*

"Jewelry?" I ask, stunned.

He grins, eyes dancing with the same magical light as the stone in his palm. "If you put this on, you will be tied to me forever."

"Forever?" I ask, hand fluttering to my neck.

"That's right, Little One. It is something that Kitra has been working on since discovering she cannot increase her own powers beyond what she already has."

I withdraw from him. If it is something that woman has created, it cannot be good. I will not use it.

"It binds you to a matching stone," Achan continues, seeming not to notice my reaction. He pulls the matching stone from his other pocket and holds it out. "The idea is that you will give the owner of the stone whatever he wishes for."

"Achan, you need no stone for that. Do you not know that I love you? That I would do anything you ask?"

His eyes meet mine, and the pain is worse than that of the lead in the room.

"Then it won't be a problem," he says. "If what you say is true, this will change nothing between us. And if I use it on you before Kitra does—"

"Then I will belong to you and not to her?" I ask.

"That's right," he says.

I stare at the thing in his hand, wondering what I should do. "Why can't we go?" I ask. "I want to leave this awful place, Achan. Now that you know the truth about me, we can do whatever you want. Go wherever you like. Perhaps to see the pyramids and the great wall we have heard about." I place my hands on his wrists, pleading, cajoling him.

Cephas's large form shifts on the floor to the right.

"We don't have much time," Achan says. "Put it on, Little One."

"Why?" I cry, trying to pull him up by his wrists. He remains firm. "I do not understand, Achan. If you care for me, why are you doing this?"

"I do care for you. I am also afraid. You hid your true nature from me, Leela. You are the one who lied, not I. You set fire to my tent that night. If I hadn't learned of your kind from Kitra, I might never have known. Never have read the signs."

"But I would never hurt you," I say, sobs racking my chest.

"Then trust me and put it on."

"Why hasn't Kitra put it on me if she made it?"

"Because you have to agree to it!" he says in a harsh whisper. "Your magic is stronger, but she will figure out a way around it; it's only a matter of time."

Cephas grunts and rolls over, pushing up dazedly from the floor. I scuttle back farther, nearly hitting the lead bars of the cage.

"Leela, put it on and this will all be over. You do want it to be over, right? Who would you rather be with? Me? Or Kitra? Or perhaps Cephas here?"

On cue, Cephas lets out a bellow of rage, as though the memory of their fight is coming back to him. His black eyes, filled with hatred and rage, meet mine. His aura glows bloodred as he works his way slowly to his feet. He is coming for me, not Achan. This much is clear.

"Please," I say, unable to tear my eyes from the monster.

"I'm offering you a way out," Achan says.

Cephas reaches up and pulls a long lead stick from the air above, grinning at me. The flames on the wall dance in his obsidian eyes.

I reach for the ribbon in Achan's hands and thrust it around my neck. The moment the ends meet, they fuse together until it grasps my throat like a serpent. I gasp, my hand pulling at the stone in the center. It does not budge.

Achan stands, throwing out his arm as Cephas reaches me, raising the stick in the air, ready to bash it down on my helpless body.

"It is done," Achan says. "She is mine."

Cephas growls but lets the stick clatter to the ground. Achan helps me up.

"I do not understand," I cry.

"I must test it before I can let you out," he says.

"Achan—"

"From now on, you will refer to me as Master."

I shake my head, not comprehending what he has just told me. "But, A... A...A..." My throat closes, choking on the word. My heart races, panic setting in. What have I done?

"Say it," Achan says, clutching the other stone in his fist.

"Master." I hear the word burst from my lips without my willing it. I press my hand to my mouth, as though trying to push it back inside. But it is done. And there is no going back.

46

A PROMISE KEPT

"Come on," I say. "We have to go. If we don't keep moving, they'll find us."

Jered takes a great shuddering breath and turns to grasp my hand in his. We are about to run back down the passageway, but it's blocked by Kitra, Mira, and Taj. Their long shadows stretch so far, they almost touch our feet. We take a step backward.

"Don't bother trying to run again," Kitra says. Her voice is different from what I remember but has a similar cold quality to it. It is her smile that is the same. No one else could look like that. Not ever. It's as though I can still see my own blood coloring her lips.

"You are encased in a bubble of power that you cannot penetrate. Both of my Djinn have created it."

Taj and Mira step in front of her protectively as she strides toward us. I do the same to Jered, though he has given me no orders. She cannot have him. Cannot.

"So it *is* you, is it? My, my, my, what a small world this is, Leela. I will finally have you after you were so rudely stolen from me."

I steel myself to take whatever is to come, wishing I could find a way to save Jered. To get him out of here.

"You will not have Leela." Jered steps out from behind me and rests a hand on my shoulder.

I see his aura pulse and bleed, churning patches of indigo and silver.

Kitra laughs, the sound echoing off the stone walls into the distance. "Very brave. But I think you will change your mind very soon, child." She taps Mira and Taj on the shoulders, and moving as one, they fly forward, wresting me away from Jered's side, pulling me down the hall, and slamming me into the rock so hard the breath is knocked from my chest. Mira's hand is around my throat, not completely choking me, but preventing me from moving my head. She holds one wrist firmly; Taj holds the other.

I watch helplessly as Kitra saunters toward Jered. I struggle against the others, though I know there is little I can do. *Please make it quick*, I think. I cannot bear to have him suffer any more.

"I'll give you one more chance to do this the easy way," Kitra says.

I see his right hand flex, the hand that bears the invisible ring. He looks past Kitra to me, and I struggle to nod. To let him know that it is all right.

"Give me the stone, and I will give you your freedom."

Her words shock something inside Jered, and I see his eyes grow sharp. Sharp like Achan's. He actually smiles.

"All right," he says.

Kitra beams at him. I stop struggling. I can only hope she is true to her word and lets him go.

"Leela," Jered says, looking me straight in the eye. "You are free."

The stone in my choker cracks down the center and falls to the ground. Kitra's face falls with it. Taj and Mira loosen their grips, stunned. We all stand motionless until Kitra screams.

I am in shock. I cannot believe what has just happened. I am free. I burst from the arms of the other Djinn with an insane laugh. We are still trapped with a powerful Magician and two Djinn under her control on an island in the middle of the Atlantic Ocean.

But I am free!

47

CAGED

"You idiot! What have you done? Now no one has her." Kitra strikes out at Jered.

I throw my power out in front of her, blocking the attack, and she is blown backward onto the ground.

I send a blast of power meant to incinerate Kitra, but Mira blocks me with a gust of wind that repels my power. Part of the wall crumbles into a mixture of dust and melted metal.

"Stop her!" Kitra shrieks, and the others take to the air after me.

We are a whirlwind of movement, so fast that it would be impossible for human eyes to follow. If I can find a way to take out Kitra without being stopped, then Taj and Mira will be free as well. The way Mira strikes at me, though, I cannot help wondering if that is such a good idea.

I risk a glance at Jered and see that he is wielding his magic against Kitra. Blocking her attacks, throwing some of his own at her. As I see a blast of blue lightning fly from his fingers and scrape Kitra's cheek, Taj catches up to me. He grabs a handful of my hair and yanks me backward into the wall.

I cry out in pain as Mira does what I could not bring myself to do. Lead hands reach from the wall and pull my arms and legs against it, burning right through my pants and searing my skin. Images flash before my eyes once more. I see myself a prisoner in Kitra's original home. Rhada hanging dead on the wall. Masters locking me in rooms painted with lead, flogging me with lead pipes.

Screams scrape at the inside of my throat as I thrash around like a caged animal. Taj and Mira back away. Taj's face is a mask, though his eyes glimmer with moisture. Mira looks on with a satisfied sneer.

"Leela!" Jered calls. His voice breaks through to my consciousness, and my tirade slows.

I see it happen as if in slow motion. Kitra is on the floor; Jered has gathered his power into his hands as I taught him the night he made a milkshake. His miniature sun glows between his palms.

He has the power to finish her in his hands. But he's stopped. He's seen me. Watched me thrash against my bonds in pain and terror. I want to take it back. Take back my reaction so that it never happened. But I cannot rewind time.

The ball of blue flame flows from Jered's hands over Kitra's head and right at me. The lead hands pinning me down disintegrate into dust. Then several things happen at once.

Kitra sees her opportunity and strikes, knocking Jered to the ground along with her. Mira's teeth clench, her eyes narrow, and she flies at me, Taj in her wake. Behind them, I see a hole opening in the wall, and I know what I must do.

"Jealous much?" I ask Mira, holding her off with one raised hand. Inside I wave the ruined ribbon that has choked me for a thousand years.

Her eyes blaze with fire, and she attacks with a war cry. She is off-balance. Angry. I duck downward, thrusting her into the wall with all my strength. But Taj is on top of me, and no matter what his real feelings are, he must obey his master.

We clash in midair, tumbling downward in a tangle of arms and legs. Our magic collides at the same moment, and we are each repelled across the passageway, backsides scraping the dirt and hay. Taj crashes into Mira, who has righted herself. I hurtle past Kitra and Jered, who struggle on the ground. I see fresh claw marks scratched across his cheek.

I skid to a stop by the two crouching figures I had aimed for. Sophie and Gabe have just dropped from the hole. Gabe looks like a frightened mouse, head skittering in every direction at once while Sophie is calm.

"You have to get their stones from Kitra," I say.

Gabe steps forward, but I stop him with a hand.

"Only a Magician can control them. You have to get it to Jered."

"Right." He nods in a determined way and scrambles off to the ground scuffle.

I've made it just in time. Taj and Mira have come for me again, and this time, they combine their efforts. I doubt I can win, but I have to last as long as I can or all is lost.

Thrusting my hands out, I charge. They do not expect this brash action. They know as well as I do that I cannot succeed. So I have taken them by surprise, and they are momentarily divided as I hurtle through their center, parting them with my magic as I pass.

But Mira is not thrown for long; she reaches out her own fist and clenches the air before her. Invisible hands constrict my throat, and I am yanked backward in the air. I dangle, digging at my neck for release. Strong arms catch me from behind and spin me around. Taj.

He wrestles me to the wall, pressing me between himself and the stone wall until I cannot move. Mira's fingers continue to squeeze. Stars dance before my eyes as I gasp for air. I make a strangled noise. Taj follows my gaze.

"Mira. Our command was to stop. Not to kill, you naughty girl," he says.

"Killing her would stop her," she says.

"No! I want her alive," screams Kitra.

Instantly the fingers relax, and I suck in air with a greedy wheeze. How is it Kitra is able to give the command? I struggle to see over Taj, which is not an easy task given the hold he has me in.

As I feared, Jered is on the ground, head in Gabe's hands. His friend holds him as he coughs blood onto the ground.

"No," I rasp.

Kitra smiles. "You actually care for him, don't you?" she says, striding closer, so that she is below our feet. "Perhaps I ought to wait to kill him. Maybe even have you do it. Slowly. Once you are mine, of course."

"I am free," I manage to say.

"Enjoy your five minutes, Leela. That's all you get."

48

THE BEGINNING

I AM A SLAVE TO THE MAN I LOVED.

Since putting on the choker, Achan has commanded several things. First, I will not harm the members of the Council. In fact, I must protect them from danger. The moment Cephas approached me outside my cell, I tried to strike him down, but the burst of power rebounded on me, causing excruciating pain.

Second, I am to obey all Kitra and Cephas's commands as well, as long as they do not harm Achan in any way or usurp his authority. His word is law. I fought harder than I have ever done in my life when Kitra commanded me to kneel and kiss her feet. Yet seconds later, my lips grazed her slippers.

And third, I will not tell Kitra or Cephas about the second half of command number two. It is only a safeguard, after all. I have not bothered to test this one. I learned quickly enough that the magic of the binding stone is thorough. Even my attempts to set traps for my new masters have resulted only in harm to myself.

"Stop crying," Kitra says, and at once my tears cease.

She was not happy that Achan took me for himself. She planned this as a last resort and wanted to find a way to make me her own. But Achan is not one to miss an opportunity. Or so I am learning.

"Kneel."

I find myself on my knees before her. She is seated in a velvet high-backed chair I fashioned. I wait, knowing she looks for a chance to punish me. And now that I must obey, I am even more at her mercy than before.

"You will bring us two other Djinn. You will not warn them in any way about what awaits. You will lure them here. Can you think of a way to do this?" She pauses, waiting to see if I am able to follow her uncomplicated orders.

"Yes."

"Yes?"

"Yes, Master." I grit my teeth but choke out the word she seeks.

"Well, what are you waiting for? Go!"

Not knowing how else to obey, I end up searching for Taj and Mira. They are far too easy to find in the treetops where we always meet. Both jump to their feet at the sight of me.

"You must come with me," I say, concentrating on the way the leaves flutter in the breeze. I want to say so much more, but the words catch in my throat.

"Slow down, Lee. Where are we going?" Taj asks, his impish grin painful and beautiful at the same time.

"And where have you been?" Mira asks, folding her arms across her chest.

"I...it is Rhada," I say, and I hate myself for it. "You must come with me."

I disappear, knowing Mira will follow. Will Taj do the same? He hadn't the feelings for Rhada that Mira had.

But he does follow. Perhaps he is worried about me.

I stop outside Kitra's front door, Mira and Taj in my wake.

"What is this, Lee?" Mira asks.

I cannot look her in the face. "She is inside. They have her trapped." How I wish I could still cry.

Mira and Taj burst through the door. Cephas is ready for them. He tosses the heavy chains across their necks and drags them kicking into that awful room.

I move to follow, but Kitra's voice stops me short.

"No. They must be weakened first. Then you will put these on them." She holds out two black velvet ribbons. One has a tiger's eye in the center, the other a ruby.

I take them both with shaking hands. Everything inside me is fighting the command, but it is useless. I must obey.

"*I thought they had to agree,*" *I say weakly.*

Kitra considers me, head tilted to the side. I suppose she is deciding what to do about my speaking out of turn, but when she responds, she simply answers my question.

"*You have been free of the lead for a while. They will be bound by it. I will also be protecting you with my own magic like a shield. Your power will be far stronger than either of theirs. Something I could never accomplish. You should be able to force it around their necks.*"

Kitra rises from her throne and circles me. She pulls me in by the back of my neck, her touch sending tremors of fear down my body. "Once all of you wear them, you will be unable to take each other's stones off unless commanded. I wouldn't want you to have any false hope, now would I?" She releases me, and I fall back onto the floor.

I feel ill. I want to rise and run the other way, to tear at her face. Anything but wait for her command and enter the room. Yet this is exactly what I do a mere hour later.

I wonder where Achan is. Perhaps that is why they are rushing to proceed. Kitra may be afraid that he will stop it, so she cannot have her own slave. Achan, where are you?

Taj's face is a picture of terror as he cowers and cries against the wall. Mira's misty gaze is fixed unblinkingly on the decomposing corpse to her left. They are both naked and wrapped in lead chains from their chests down to their feet.

Kitra's hot breath tingles on my neck. She is shielding me as promised, since I feel nothing amiss.

"*Do it,*" *she commands, and I move forward, kneeling before Taj.*

His skin is clammy and yellow, his eyes sunken and round. I wonder how I looked the day Achan burst in and presented me with a choice. Taj has no such choice. Just a friend sent to betray him.

With trembling hands, I reach forward and clasp the ribbon around his throat. I feel it pull away from my hands and tighten around his neck. The tiger's eye in the center gleams for a moment.

"*Now the other,*" *Kitra says.*

I slide over to Mira, who barely glances my way. I hear heavy chains hitting the floor and turn to find Taj sobbing at Cephas's feet. The ogre holds the end of the unraveled chain above him in one hand and clutches the matching stone in the other.

I swallow and turn to Mira, who whimpers slightly. When I pull my hand away, the ruby tightens about her neck, glowing like a flame.

"Why?" Mira whispers.

I open my mouth to respond, but Kitra has dropped her shield now that I have done her bidding, and I collapse forward, writhing on the ground. I hear the bonds being removed from Mira's body, see a flash of red in Kitra's hand.

"You will soon see she had no choice," Kitra says. "None of you do anymore."

49

DÉJÀ VU

"Don't you remember, Leela?" Kitra calls, her voice light. "I have Djinn under my control. I don't need your consent."

Taj's face is like stone. My heart aches. It is happening all over again. I suppose I deserve this. I have waited quite some time for karma to find me. I glance at Mira and am surprised to find tears in her eyes.

Kitra lifts a hand. Beneath her scarlet sleeve, two bracelets glint. One has a red stone, the other golden and brown. I know there is nothing in this world that can stop Mira and Taj obeying her command.

I lay my cheek against the cold stone. She will make me torture and kill Jered. I do not doubt it for a moment. And once more, I am helpless to prevent it. The evil bitch wins again.

A stone materializes in her hand. An emerald. A length of black flutters from her fingers, a matching stone glimmering at its center. My body shakes uncontrollably as she swings it lightly back and forth with a chuckle.

"I will do it willingly, if you let them go," I say.

"How touching. But I don't think so. It will be far more fun to make you hurt them. Besides, we have to learn a lesson somehow, don't we?" she asks.

"Please," I say. "There must be something I can offer."

"You have nothing to offer that I don't already possess."

I sob into Taj's shoulder and feel his lips brush the top of my head.

"So the question is," says Kitra. "Which one is going to do it. Any volunteers?"

Taj's grasp tightens even more. He freezes in place, and I think I know how he feels. If our positions were reversed, I would want to blend into the stone. Anything not to be noticed. But I doubt he has anything to worry about: I'm surprised Mira isn't jumping for joy at the prospect of revenge. Perhaps she is afraid if she volunteers, Kitra won't pick her, just for punishment's sake.

"No?" Kitra asks, her voice light. "Hmm. Let me see. Eeny meeny miny moe. Taj."

I watch as his head snaps upward to receive the command. Our eyes lock.

"It's okay," I mouth. "I know."

His brows knit together, heart pounding out a sporadic rhythm against my own. It feels good in some strange way to be this close to him. Comforting.

"Mira. Put the restraints on her again. Taj, you come down here."

They move to obey. The lead hands shoot out of the wall behind me, pinning me down. One grabs my head this time, forcing it back and up so my neck is exposed.

"Now, Taj," Kitra says. "Take this and put it around her pretty little neck."

Taj takes the ribbon in his own trembling hand and floats toward me.

"No!" Gabe's voice rings across the passage. Taj pauses and then continues on his path. Kitra does not even glance back.

But I can see.

Jered has grabbed Gabe's hand, quieting him. Tiny little Sophie has escaped all attention as she creeps near Kitra's side. I hold my breath, not even meeting Taj's gaze as he draws close. He reaches his arms around my throat, and I feel him hesitate as the cool surface of the stone touches my skin.

"This has dragged on quite enough," Kitra says. Taj squeezes his eyes shut tight, anticipating her next words.

"Do it *now*," Kitra commands.

But Taj does not.

His hands snap away from me, and in one swift move, he crushes the emerald in his fist. I stare openmouthed as a rain of fine green dust falls at Kitra's feet. The corner of Taj's mouth quirks upward as his eyes light up.

"What?" Kitra asks. "How is this possible? Was I not clear?"

"Oh, you were crystal clear," Taj says, landing neatly in front of her. "It's just that you forgot to say 'please.' Isn't that right, darling Little Master?"

Kitra spins on her heels to find Sophie holding the tiger's eye stone.

"That's right," Sophie agrees. "She ought to learn some manners, don't you think?"

Kitra lunges for the child, and I pull against the restraints that bind me, causing them to cut painfully into my arms. It isn't necessary. Taj blasts Kitra backward with the flick of his fingers, and she is thrown hard across the room, her shoulder skidding across the ground.

"Mira, protect me," Kitra screams.

Instantly, Mira stands ready before her. Sophie runs to Jered.

"Taj, help him please," she says.

"I believe I am going to enjoy being your Djinni," Taj says. This earns him an adoring smile while he heals Jered.

"Get me out of here," Kitra hisses, grasping at her scraped and bloody arm.

Before disappearing, Mira glances my way, misery written all over her face.

It is the last thing I see before all goes black.

50

THE BEGINNING

I AM NOT CERTAIN WHICH ONE I HATE MORE: KITRA, CEPHAS, OR ACHAN.

Kitra has had us arranging her new palace right over the top of her old home. Her new symbol decorates the doors. She says that it is the Council. She is the sun with an ever-watchful eye, while Achan and Cephas are the moon and star, circling. Together, they are the universe.

Kitra enjoys humiliating me rather than Mira, whom she has claimed for herself. She asks me to do ridiculous and meaningless things. Or things she knows I will detest.

"Leela," she coos from the arm of a handsome but frightened villager. "Niv here does not believe you will do whatever I say." She laughs. "Wash his feet and feed him without using your hands or your magic to aid you."

Achan has all but withdrawn completely, perhaps afraid to face me. Inside I cry for him to come to my rescue as he did in the lead-lined room.

Cephas finds pleasure in torture. Whenever he is able to get me alone, he enjoys picking up where he left off before the choker was in place. If my wounds lasted, I would be covered in bruises and welts. Luckily, it is rare that he and I should be alone together.

But nothing is as agonizing as watching my friends suffer because of me. Achan's absence bothers no one but me as Kitra and Cephas chain me up by my wrists in the center of the dining hall. A punishment for not obeying a command quickly enough, or so they claim.

I have learned to escape into my mind when tortured, but this time is different. It is different because they have called Taj to put on a show for them.

His eyes are wet, his face scarlet as he strains against the command to swing a lead rod at me. My strong, clever Taj cannot control it. None of us can. I do not blame him, but I cannot say this through the pain or before my masters. They would surely only make things worse.

And so when he beats me, his own screams are louder than my own.

51

ROOFTOP

WHEN MY EYES SNAP OPEN, LIGHT FLOODS IN, AND I WINCE. I automatically feel for the stone at my throat. I find nothing but skin. I blink rapidly, pulling myself into a sitting position on the bed. The window facing me is covered in streams of flowing water, the sky beyond a solid mass of gray. A sudden wave of perfume hits me full on. The scent of iris.

"What happened?" I ask, looking around.

I am surrounded by friendly faces. Gabe sits in the armchair in the corner, with Sophie perched at the arm. Taj stands behind her, arms folded across his chest. Jered is by my side, stroking my hair back from my face, his own face streaked with tears.

"We're in the hotel, Leela," he says.

"How did we get here? Why was I unconscious? What time is it?" I can't stop the questions long enough to get a single answer. Taj points a finger at me, and I find I cannot speak.

"Settle down there, Lee," Taj says. "I did it. You were saying things in your sleep, and I wasn't sure you wanted them public."

I flush with this information. I feel at the base of my throat again to make sure it is truly gone.

"Jered asked me ever so nicely to get us out, and since it was partially my own magic that was keeping him there, well, I decided to comply." Taj grins and continues. "And it is Tuesday afternoon at about three thirty Chicago time. Or so the clock claims." He lifts his finger, and my voice returns.

"Then...it really happened?" I ask. "I'm free?"

Jered squeezes my hand, speaking through his sobs. "I told you I would do it. I love you, Leela."

I glance around me on the bed and find the source of the perfume smell. There must be a hundred iris blooms scattered over the covers near my feet. I look back to Jered and his tortured face. Oh no. The tear in his aura. Would he have freed me if he had been in better control of his emotions?

Should it matter?

"Jered—" I take his hands in mine and hold them down in my lap. "Did you do this?" I ask, nodding at the flowers.

"Taj told me they're your favorite," he answers.

"After he pestered me for about an hour. It was either that or kill him, and Little Master wouldn't allow it," says Taj.

I swallow. "Jered, you aren't quite yourself."

"Yes, I am!" he shouts, his aura bubbling and glowing in shades of yellow and pink. "And if you don't believe that I love you, I'll prove it!"

He yanks his hands away from me and runs for the window, throwing it open with his magic. The sounds of storm and city flood the room. "I'll throw myself out into the night if you reject my love."

"Oh, for shit's sake, Romeo, settle down." Taj claps, and the window snaps shut in Jered's face.

I slip a hand to my forehead and breathe out slowly.

"Okay, we have a problem," I say. "Achan is the only one who can fix the hole in Jered's aura. But if he gets his hands on him, he will take over his body. Thoughts?"

"Who's Achan?" Sophie asks. I see that though she lost her doll somewhere along our escape, Taj has supplied her with a new one—a Little Taj this time.

"I think Lee and I should have a chat. Would you mind, Little Master?"

"Okay." Sophie beams up at Taj. His eyes twinkle back at her and then shoot over to me before he pops into nothingness.

I smile reassuringly at Jered and pop off after Taj. I meet him on the roof of the hotel beneath the pouring rain and thunder. A flash of lightning streaks across the sky, and I shake my head at the chaos.

"Shall we?" Taj yells above the tumult.

I take his hands in mine, and moments later, the storm clouds above our heads lift and separate, revealing a patch of blue beyond. Rays of sunlight spill down and over the top of the building, bathing the old brick hotel in a warm glow.

"That's better," he says. "Now, as I said inside, we need to chat."

"I shouldn't have said that in front of her," I say. "I can't be the one to tell her that her father is a monster."

"That isn't why we're here. If her father is a monster, it is better she figure it out now. Don't you wish you'd done so sooner?"

"Of course, but that's different." Taj raises an eyebrow at me. "Why are we here?" I ask.

"A better question is why are *you* here? Shouldn't you be gone by now?" He runs his thumbs back and forth over my fingers, soothingly.

"Where else would I be?" I ask, looking away toward the now-breaking storm.

"Lee."

"I know," I whisper. "I'm free. But, Taj, it isn't fair."

"Fair? Who cares, Lee? You have your life back. Don't concern yourself with the little people. Cross back over. You can do it now; there is nothing standing in your way."

"Is that what you would do?" I ask.

"In a heartbeat."

We stare at each other for a while, the sun warming our skin. I realize there is something I have to say.

"I'm sorry. I should have been stronger. I should have just died like Rhada."

"Lee—"

"I know. She didn't have a choice. Somehow I think if it had been any of you, you would have done the right thing."

"Lee—"

"She commanded me not to cry, Taj. Of all the things they did to me, that was the worst. I couldn't even mourn. I couldn't show you the devastation inside. It killed me every day," I say, reaching up to touch the stone around his neck.

His eyes press closed, and he takes a deep breath.

"Lee, will you stop for two seconds, or do I have to take your voice again?"

I mash my lips into a thin line and wait.

"It wasn't your fault."

I stare. He sighs deeply and continues.

"It could have been any of us, and we would have made exactly the same decision. Even Mira. There is a point when a Djinni will do anything to stop the pain. We were there for what, two hours? I would have put the stupid thing on myself if she'd asked. You were gone for days, Lee. And if what you were saying back there is any indication..." He shudders.

"What did I say?" I ask. My voice sounds tiny even to my own ears.

"You spoke of Cephas, Lee. You were pleading with Jered to save you from my old master. I think you thought Jered was Achan."

My face twists in anguish, but I cannot help it. I don't know what to say.

"I'm the one who should apologize," says Taj.

"What?" What could Taj possibly have to apologize for?

"There was a moment," he says, voice choked with emotion, "when they made me hurt you, when they told me to swing...I stopped it, Lee. I held it back, but then I couldn't...I couldn't..."

"There was nothing you could do." I squeeze Taj's shoulder. "There is no way to break a command, no matter how much you want to."

"I should have done something to stop it in the first place. I should have seen what was happening with you, instead of indulging my new senses. I should have protected—"

"I guess we both have a lot to be sorry about," I say. "But I don't want to feel that way again, Taj. This time I want to do what's right. Jered freed me. He was willing to die, hole in his aura or not."

"And your feelings have nothing to do with it?"

"My feelings are irrelevant. Well, except for revenge. I admit getting even with Achan would feel very good."

"Now that I can understand."

52

LOSING BATTLE

By the time we arrive back in the hotel room, all hell has broken loose. Sophie stands before Gabe, a shield of energy in front of them. Jered paces like a caged lion, scarlet electricity sizzling at his fingertips. Every muscle in his body is strained and tensed.

"Move aside!" he bellows.

"Oh no, you didn't," Taj says, landing protectively between them.

I grab hold of Jered's arms before he can let loose at Taj. He would never survive the encounter.

"Jered," I say, spinning him to face me. "What happened?"

His pupils are dilated, his nostrils flared. Breath comes ragged and uneven from his mouth. He's having trouble focusing on me, so I hold his face between my hands, letting my magic calm him. I am vaguely aware of Sophie crying in Taj's arms, Gabe white-faced behind them.

"Gabe was saying bad things. I had to stop him from spouting those lies," Jered says under his breath, pleading with me to understand the rage that burns inside him. I do not release my hold on his face.

"Shh," I soothe.

"He called my father an asshole," Jered says.

I bite my tongue to keep from laughing. Though I do shoot a look at

Gabe. He should not be talking about Sophie's father like that in front of her.

"It's okay." Sophie sniffs, as though reading my thoughts. "Daddy hurt Jered, didn't he? And...and you?"

All words are lost in a jumble in my head, and all I can do is nod and swallow.

"He hurt you?" Jered asks. He's looking feverish now, and I smooth a hand over his forehead. "Is this about that lead vest again? Because... because I already told you, he was just protecting himself."

Taj is by my side in a flash, prying Jered from my arms. "No, Jered. This is not about the lead vest. This is about a thousand years of torture, degradation, and enslavement for which your father is responsible."

I wish I could somehow prevent the look on Jered's face. The kind of pain no one should have to experience. Ever. Except maybe Kitra. And Achan. But not his son. Not his children.

Jered collapses against Taj's chest, sobbing and wailing until I have to cover my ears. I cannot stand this another moment.

"I will find him." I tug Jered gently away from Taj. "If I don't do it soon..."

"You should take him," Taj says, cutting off the sound of Jered's lament with a finger. "I can't be responsible for what might happen, and I hate to kill someone you care about."

I nod. I should be able to protect him, now that I am free. I gather Jered into my arms awkwardly, unsure how to handle him when he is so unstable.

"It seems to me," Taj says thoughtfully, "that the emotion is strong but adjusts depending on how we interact with him." He winks.

I find Jered's face again, wet with tears, and press my lips to his. The change is immediate. He pushes back with abandon, knocking me onto the floor in his haste to return my kiss. I would laugh if I could catch my breath. But, I don't want re-start his faucet of tears.

"Jered," I say, as he trails his lips down my neck. "Not here. Sophie. Gabe."

He pulls away from me, clasping a hand to his mouth. Embarrassment. Good. This is more manageable.

"Let's go," I say, offering a hand to help him up. He complies, and I transport us to his father's house.

It appears at first that no one is home. I stretch out my senses before us, searching. And just as I am about to give up and move on somewhere else, I find the hint of a heartbeat, upstairs in the master bedroom.

I squeeze Jered's hand and lead him up the steps and down the hall. I thrust my palm against the door, flinging it open to find Achan sitting on the edge of the bed, head buried in his hands.

"Get up," I say.

His fingers slip down his face, and he looks at me.

"Are you going to let your Djinni speak to me that way, Jered?" Achan asks.

Jered looks pained again, and I sigh. "I am no longer his Djinni."

"What?" Achan stands.

I pull Jered behind me. "That's right. Don't you notice anything different?"

His gaze falls on my neck, and he quakes with fear.

With one hand, I grasp the air in front of me, lifting him from the bed by his neck. Jered claws at my arms, pleading with me, but I silence him.

"Leela," Achan chokes. "Leela, please."

"Yes. Beg." I drop him to the floor, and he crawls to me like the coward he is, tugging at the bottom of my shirt. "Don't touch me," I say, flicking a finger at him. He flies back across the room, crashing into the nightstand and knocking over the lamp on top.

He's crying now. How pathetic. Unfortunately, Jered is doing the same, clinging to my leg. I have to fix him.

"You will repair his aura. NOW." I backhand the space in front of me, and Achan, who is trying to work his way to his feet, is flung back to the floor.

"Okay! Okay!" he says with arms raised protectively over his head.

I watch wearily as he stands and slowly makes his way toward us.

"That's far enough," I say. "You will not touch him directly."

"How do you expect me to repair the damage if I can't touch him?" Achan asks.

"Do you think I am a fool? You will not take his body," I say.

"We both have reason not to trust each other," Achan says. "I want a guarantee. A guarantee that you will leave me alone if I fix him."

"You are in no position—" I begin, lifting my hand to strike.

"He will die soon," Achan says, some of the cold, calculating gleam back in his eyes. I pause. "If I don't do something, the stress on his heart will kill him."

I lick my lips. "What do you propose?" I ask.

"What I propose is a deal. You can have him. Whole and unblemished if he means that much to you."

"And?" I ask.

"And you put this on." Achan pulls a black ribbon from the air. A second opal gleams in the center.

"I see," I say.

But all I really see—is red.

53

TRAP

"It isn't what you think," he says quickly. "It is a fake. In fact, you can make your own if you like."

"How considerate," I say, snatching the thing from his grip and crushing it.

"What I want to do is make it look like you are mine," he says. "You see, I can bargain with Kitra. I can make her think I am willing to join her along with you."

"Just like the good old days?" I ask, folding my arms.

"Then you kill her," Achan says with a grin.

"And what makes you think I will be able to do that?" I ask.

"She only has one Djinni. It should be easy if she lets her guard down."

Something is not right.

"Then you can have Jered," he continues.

"And what do you get?" I ask.

"Revenge. And of course, the other Djinni."

I squeeze the space in front of me again and lift him into the air. Jered tugs on my elbow urgently, but I pay him no attention. I will find a way to fix him myself. Achan needs to die.

"D-Don't you want him to live?" Achan squeaks out.

"How did you know she has one Djinni left?" I ask, shaking him.

Before he can answer, I am pulled to my knees from pain. *No.* Jered catches me in his arms, holding me tight. His shirt is soaked with tears. I can see how he tries to gather his aura around me protectively, but he is too hysterical to manage.

"You should listen to your boyfriend," Kitra says from behind me. "He was trying to warn you."

"I want my reward," Achan says, standing and rubbing his bruised neck.

"For nearly blowing the whole thing?" Kitra asks. "I don't know."

I turn my head toward Kitra. I am not surprised to see Achan's vest over her clothes or Mira, her shadow, cowering in the background. Kitra kneels beside us on the floor, smiling down at me. I wince from the pain.

"You are so predictable, Leela," she whispers in my ear.

My chest is heavy. I've been exposed to a lot of lead in the past few days. The effects are sharper and more immediate than ever. "Take him, Achan. He is in my way."

I feel Jered dragged from beneath me, and I scream in frustration, tears welling in my eyes. Kitra kicks me hard in the ribs before fishing two of the round weights from a pocket in her vest. I hear a body falling to the ground and then footsteps. I strain to turn my head.

The last thing I see before she places the weights upon my eyes is Jered's face staring at me, calm and collected. I scream his name, feel his hand against my cheek, but I know it is not he who touches me.

"No," I sob. "No."

"He is gone, Leela," Jered's voice answers me. "Still struggling, but that will stop soon enough."

"*No!*"

More lead discs are placed on my lips, so I can no longer call out. The weight of the vest itself falls across my chest.

"Mira," Kitra purrs. "Don't look at me like that. I am protecting you from the lead. Now, give our friend here her welcome-home gift."

I hear rustling as I struggle against the pain, both physical and mental. But there is nothing I can do. My motor function is already failing, and the best I manage is a series of twitches. *Jered*, I call in my mind, *I've let you down.* It seems I always let down the people I care about.

Mira's hands are at my throat. The ribbon stretches for my skin like a hungry snake. It is over. I am bound to her again. Just as she promised.

"Go home," she tells Mira.

Hands on my mouth, my eyes, lifting the burden from my body. The pain subsides, and my vision returns. I wish it hadn't. Then I wouldn't see Achan's lifeless body on the floor, Jered watching me hungrily from the bed.

"Kneel." Of course this is her first command. I do it, still unable to tear my gaze from Jered's face. Taj was right. I should have gone.

"Did you really think I'd let you live, Achan?"

Achan freezes in fear. "We have a deal, Kitra."

I know what is coming next before it happens, but I cannot prevent Kitra's command.

"Now, Leela, kill your lover."

54

THE BEGINNING

"AGAIN," KITRA CALLS.

The Council members are dressed in matching red robes with the gold embossed symbol of Kitra's design, seated in their favorite spot, at the grand table in the dining hall. A banquet has been called in honor of their new positions as leaders of the surrounding four villages. The guests of honor are those whose position of power they have usurped. The guests sit, like frightened lambs, forcing down the food before them. Any merchants or others with wealth or power of their own have also been gathered.

Human servants rush around, cleaning spills and filling goblets. They refuse to meet the eyes of their masters. I have no such luxury.

Kitra makes a show of us at every meeting she attends. Sometimes Cephas joins in. Achan stands back, watching from the shadows. But here in their palace, he laughs and drinks, enjoying his bounty. Hardly ever meeting my eyes.

"Dance!" she yells at us, clapping her hands as we move faster in our red-and-gold harem uniforms.

"You think you are gods?" A man pushes away from one side of the table, unable to stand it any longer. "Because of this black magic you've found?"

"Oh, we are far more than gods," says Kitra.

Cephas smiles, and those around the brave man recoil, scooting their own *seats away and leaving him as alone as I am. I study his lined face, the proud brace of his shoulders.*

"We have found the gods and brought them to their knees," Cephas *bellows.* "Watch as they bow before us. Kneel." *He gestures at us, and we stop dancing to fall to the ground, prostrating ourselves before him.*

Achan glances at me, but I fix my gaze on the man now standing at the table.

"Well, I will not worship you." *The man spits at Cephas's feet.*

"Then we must make an example of you," Kitra says. "Stand on the stage here with my Djinn." *Her voice is pleasant but commanding. Perhaps she thinks all these people wear collars.*

The man turns his back to her and walks toward the doors.

"Mira, bring him on stage," Kitra barks, *and the man stands beside us, stumbling in confusion.*

"Apologize," *she says.*

"What?" *he asks.*

"To show I am a forgiving queen, I give you a second chance. Now, apologize."

The man stands firm, staring her down.

"Leela," *she calls. I step forward.* "Make him apologize."

I focus on the man's hands, pressing down on the air with my fingers until the bones crack. He shouts out in pain but does not apologize. Poor stubborn fool.

I continue on to his hands, then his arms. By the time I get to his shoulders, he is crying on his knees, elbows bent at odd angles from his body. Kitra's aura shines a bright pink. Finally he has enough sense to scream, "I'm sorry!" *And I stop.*

"I'm afraid I cannot accept an apology under duress," Kitra purrs. "Kill him."

I picture Kitra's neck being crushed beneath my hands as I strangle the air before me. And though it is the man who falls, eyes staring blankly at the sky, it is her face I see, all life drained forever from her body.

The crowd clears the moment Kitra allows it. She tells us to chain the man's remains to the front gates as a warning to those who would challenge her.

One of the servant girls screams, letting a plate crash at her feet as Cephas gathers her in his arms, planting wet kisses on her face. I tense for fear this night may become even worse. "Taj," he calls to his Djinni. "Make her love me."

"I cannot," Taj says, chin jutted proudly in the air.

"What?" Cephas bellows, throwing the girl to the ground.

"It is not within his power to do what you have asked," I say, stepping forward.

"Then you do it," Cephas says, moving closer to me.

I shuffle backward slightly and shake my head. "I do not think you understand," I say. "No Djinni can do this. My power is limited as well."

He lifts a massive hand to hit me, but Achan materializes, catching it midswing with the help of his own magic.

"She is mine. If you want to strike someone, strike your own. Obviously she tells the truth, or it would have been done."

But Kitra is smart. She sees the discomfort on my face and pushes forward. "Is there no way, Leela? Tell me."

Mira glares at me as I speak. "If we combine our powers, we can do more. The more of us there are, the more we can do."

"And how many more Djinn are there? Out there?" she asks, waving a hand vaguely.

"I...I do not know," I say. "Several that have crossed over the veil into this world."

"And can you do as Cephas asks, if you work together?" Kitra asks, her warm breath on my face.

My gaze falls, and I nod.

"Then do it. I wish to see."

I glance at the girl, who has backed frightfully into the corner, and my heart catches in my throat. But my hands are already joining in a circle with the others, our power blooming between our arms, wrapping itself around the servant. We drop our hands to our sides. The girl rises.

She runs to Cephas's arms. He lifts her, and she covers his face with kisses, hands clasped behind his neck.

Kitra's eyes are alight with possibility.

55

INSOLENCE

"He is not my lover," I spit back.

Kitra's hand answers me, and I sprawl on the floor laughing, even though inside I am dying.

"And what exactly do you think you gain through such insolence?" she asks. "Don't you remember what I do to those who talk back?"

"How could I ever forget?" I ask with my palm pressed to my cheek.

But I've done it. I've distracted her long enough for him to escape. Not that I do not wish to crush Achan. But I cannot do it while Jered still struggles inside his body. *As long as he is in there*, I tell myself, *there is hope.* I try to ignore the voice inside, screaming that it is too late. My heart twists into a knot.

"You will pay for this," Kitra says. "I thought you would have hated him as much as I do. But apparently you still have a soft spot for your former love."

I do not answer. I do not need to explain myself. Do not need to explain that, as impossible as it seems, trying to help Jered means even more to me than revenge.

"We have more important matters to address," she says, dismissing my emotions with a wave. "I am missing a Djinni, thanks to you. We must get him back. It should be simple enough to wrest him from the child. You will take me to him and incapacitate him upon first sight. Do you understand?"

"Yes."

"Yes?" she asks.

I stare hard at her. I know she will force it, but I want her to know I am not the same Djinni she had a thousand years ago.

"You will acknowledge my every command with 'yes, Master' before implementing it. Is that understood?" she asks. She digs her fingers into my skin as she takes hold of my arm and shakes me.

"Yes, Master," I say.

She smiles, relaxing her shoulders back, satisfied she is in control. "Then let's go."

"Yes, Master."

I wave a hand, and we materialize inside the hotel room where I keep my eyes shut tight. She said, 'upon first sight.' If I do not see him, I do not have to incapacitate him. The scent of iris is still strong.

I hear the frightened murmurs of my friends, and I shout out. "Go! Achan is in Jered. She has me!"

"Both of my Djinn, on your knees!" Kitra screams.

I fall to the ground and risk opening my eyes. I am surprised to find Mira kneeling next to me at Kitra's feet. But the others are gone. Taj is fast and strong. He will help Jered. He has to.

"What is the meaning of this?" Kitra's normally calm voice is shrill. Her fists clenched in rage. "How is it possible you have disobeyed me?"

"I did not," we both answer at the same time. Mira and I look at each other, both openmouthed.

"Explain," Kitra says, hand on her forehead.

"Yes, Master. You said to incapacitate at first sight. I closed my eyes," I say.

"You ordered me to go home. The closest thing I have to a home is wherever Taj is," Mira says, miserably.

"You will both be punished for this insolence. But not until we have rectified the situation." Kitra paces back and forth before us. "What did you tell them?" she asks Mira.

"Everything of importance," Mira spits.

Kitra kicks at Mira's face. I use my magic to move Mira out of range. "Enough!" Kitra screams. Red hair flying out in all directions. Eyes wild. She pulls a large lead pipe from the air. "You will take your punishments without interference," she breathes, and raises the pipe to swing.

I lie coughing on the floor, bloody and bruised. Mira is unconscious next to me. Kitra seems oblivious to this, as she continues to bash her body with the pipe. I raise a weak hand.

"You'll kill her," I manage.

Kitra stops, glaring at me. She knows I am right. She needs her Djinn. Kitra straightens, and the lead pipe vanishes into nothing. Our wounds heal right away.

"You have lost me valuable time," Kitra says, smoothing back her flyaway hair.

Mira's eyes flutter open. I feel bad for her after she tried to help us. But this is good. It gave the others enough time to find Jered. Maybe to help him. Achan said Jered would only have about an hour before he was expelled from his body completely. How long has it been? My heart races, and I push away the panic as best I can.

"We must find them," Kitra says. "Do either of you know where they went? Either Achan, or Taj and the brat? Tell me."

"Yes, Master. I do not know," I say automatically. I have suspicions, but no verifiable knowledge.

"Neither do I." Mira coughs.

"Where would you go if you were them? Tell me."

"Yes, Master." I wonder if Kitra will grow as tired with me saying this as I am. "I would be looking for Jered if I were Taj and Sophie. If I were Achan, I would be finding a hole to hide in."

Mira smirks. "If it were me, I would be long gone by now. But since Taj still has a master, well, he'll have to do her bidding."

"And she will search for her brother?" Kitra asks me. I do not respond, enjoying how this frustrates her. "Tell me!"

"Yes, Master. I believe she would."

"I will break you, Leela," she promises, leaning over me menacingly.

"You already have. Long ago," I say.

"You will take us where you believe they will search for Achan," Kitra says. "And this time, the moment Taj is within striking range, you will incapacitate him."

56

QUIET PLEASE

ACHAN IS A COWARD. IT WILL BE NEARLY IMPOSSIBLE TO FIND HIM IF TAJ has not already succeeded. So I hope with all my being that he has. And if he has, where would they take him? *Of course.* Assuming that Gabe is smart enough to think of it. Because if there is one thing Achan does not understand, it is love. And perhaps he underestimates its power as well.

We appear, unnoticed in the hospital hallway. Three women in skirts and red shirts. Kitra's idea of fashion sense. I tolerate it because I have to.

"Where are we?" she whispers. "This better not be another attempt of yours to—"

"Jered's mother is here," I say. "Thanks to Mira. She's hanging on to life by a thread."

"How touching."

I ignore Kitra and continue. "I would bring Jered here to try to reach him."

Her eyebrows lift with surprise. "So where is she?"

I motion for them to follow and lead the way through the bright-white halls, past a nurses' station and empty stretchers to the room I remember being hers. The door is ajar, and voices filter through the opening. Kitra motions for us to wait, and we cock our heads to listen.

"Jered, you have to fight. You have to try." Gabe's voice is filled with more emotion than I've ever heard come from his lips.

My heart speeds up. I was right. But it sounds as though it hasn't worked. I have to give them more time. But how? I glance at Kitra. She remains still, listening.

"I've already told you, he cannot hear you. Now, will you please let me go?" Achan, using Jered's voice, asks.

"Hold him steady," Sophie says.

Kitra pushes forward, nudging the door in, and we see the back of Jered's head. He is seated in a chair near his mother's bed. Sophie holds her hands out to him, her aura flooding into his, so that the colors mix and swirl in a breathtaking way. Gabe stands on the other side of the bed. The concern on his face is clear, but he hasn't seen us. He only has eyes for his friend. And Taj. Taj holds Jered by the shoulders, keeping Jered firmly in the seat.

My hand twitches. I've been given a command. Taj is thrown backward into the wall, where lead shackles bind his wrists and ankles. Gabe lets out a yelp, but Sophie is so focused on whatever is going on between her and Jered that she does not even see.

Oh, this is bad.

Kitra strides confidently into the room, and we follow behind. My gaze meets Taj's, and he smiles through the pain.

"Round and round we go," he says through his torment.

"Find the stone, and give it to me," Kitra says.

"Yes, Master," I reply, frustration in every word.

Mira moves toward Sophie. I have to do something. Then it hits me. Kitra has made a mistake, and I must obey.

"Allow me, Master," I say, flying at Mira and knocking her away from the little girl.

"What—" Kitra begins.

But I've already tackled Mira and wrested my fingers around her throat. After all, I was given a command. It just might work.

"I command you—" Kitra says.

But no one has paid attention to the one conscious human in the room. Gabe has sneaked up behind Kitra and brings a hospital tray down on top of her head, cutting her off in midsentence. Mashed potatoes and green beans fly everywhere.

"Command this!" he shouts as the stone comes off in my hand. Mira grasps at her throat, and I fling it at Kitra.

"You asked for the stone!" I scream. "Be more specific next time."

The door thrusts open, and a nurse rushes in, followed by two men in security uniforms.

"What on earth is going on in here?" the nurse exclaims, exasperated.

I wave a hand, and they freeze.

"Find the stone, Gabe. Mine," I plead. He is already searching through Kitra's pockets. "Mira, release Taj!" I shout. But when I turn, she is gone.

I cry as Kitra stirs beneath Gabe's nervous fingers.

"I can't find it," he says.

"Check her wrists," I say, recalling the location of Taj's stone. But as he pulls at her sleeve, she regains her voice.

"Get off me!" she shrieks, throwing Gabe across the room with a burst of power.

"You," she says, venom dripping from the word. "Take me to my island, and bring only Taj and the girl with us. Do it NOW."

My gaze flickers helplessly to Gabe as I say the words. "Yes, Master." And we disappear with a wave of my hand.

57

THE BEGINNING

"I hate humans," Taj says. The ferocity of his words causes me to flinch. I am so afraid we will be overheard.

"Best not let them hear you say that," Mira says. She is lying across the chairs arranged around the empty dining hall table, head upside down and long hair sweeping the floor. "They aren't mere humans, remember? They are Magicians." The contempt in her voice is crystal clear.

It is so rare that the three of us are left to our own devices. At first, I thought it a blessing in disguise. So afraid that they would hate me for what I'd done. Mira mostly ignores me, at best tolerating my presence. Taj, though, still speaks to me. And for this, I am grateful.

"How long do you suppose before they all kill each other off?" Mira asks, righting herself and gnawing at a crust of bread she has conjured.

"Not soon enough," Taj says, pacing the length of the massive table. "We are going to have to do something."

"Do something?" I ask, breaking my silence. "What do you mean?"

"Don't tell her," Mira says. "She'll probably go blab it all right back to them."

"I had no choice," I say. "You were there. You know what happened."

"It doesn't matter," Taj says, and I fall quiet once again, picking at the

fabric of my skirts. "What's done is done. And now they will be searching for more of us."

"But how can we do anything?" I cry. "How?"

"We have to be smarter than they are, Lee." Taj halts his stride and places a hand on my shoulder.

"Well, it isn't hard to be smarter than that master of yours," Mira says in his ear.

"Precisely," says Taj. "And that is what we will use against them. You'll have to do your part too, Lee. I need to know you are strong enough."

I draw in a deep, shuddering breath and nod. I owe them this much.

"We have to play on their mistrust of each other," Taj continues. "Each of us has to work on our master when we are alone."

"Make them want to split up?" Mira asks. "Then we will no longer be together either."

"But look at the damage we did today, making that girl love the monster," I say. "As soon as Kitra figures it out, she will have us do much worse."

"Who cares about the stupid humans?" Mira hisses in my face.

Taj pulls us apart, leaving a hand on each of us. "Forget the humans. This is for our own kind. We cannot let them take us all. And if we are apart, they will be much harder to find and trap. Lee, do you think you can go to Achan?"

"Now?" I ask.

"Yes. He already mistrusts the others. He tricked you into wearing your stone to steal you away from Kitra."

"Yes, but—"

"He still has feelings for you," Mira says.

I look up, wanting to hit her for saying such cruel things.

"I'm serious. Did you see how he protected you from Cephas today?"

"He can barely look at you," Taj says. "Has he asked for you to share his bed since this happened?"

I shift uncomfortably on my seat. "No," I say, casting my gaze downward. "But why should he? He has Kitra now. It is what he always wanted."

"I think you underestimate your power over men, my dear." Taj tsks softly. "Go see for yourself."

I chew on my tongue, thinking. How would it feel to have him touch me again? He did save me from Cephas. Twice now. Though the first time, he could have come so much sooner. Was it all an orchestrated plan, with Cephas's complicity? I have avoided dwelling on this for quite some time. When the monster awoke from their fight, he never once tried to strike at Achan. Does that not speak volumes? Still, what could have been in it for him?

"You still with us, Lee?" Mira asks, rapping on my head.

I glare at her before popping into my master's bedroom. He is alone at least. His chest rises and falls with great snores in the center of his enormous bed decorated with crimson sheets of satin and about a thousand cushions as well. My heart aches as I watch him. Hate and betrayal battle with the love I cannot deny.

I must do this for the others, I think, crawling over his sleeping form. I dip my mouth to his, inhaling his scent, so familiar and sweet. My body moves against his, beneath the sheets. His eyes flutter open. Shock. Fear. Then passion, as I continue to kiss him hungrily.

He wraps his arms around me, flipping me over onto my back, running his hands along my side. I tangle my legs around his as he freely reacquaints himself with my body. We are as familiar to each other as the sun is to the sand.

When we finish, he holds me against him, murmuring in my hair. "Little One," he says, over and over again.

I cannot return the favor. For the only name that will come from my lips is "Master."

58

TURNING TABLES

Apparently we missed the throne room on our first tour of Kitra's island. It is perhaps the one bright room in the palace, large and open with marble floors and pillars around the perimeter. The only furniture is the throne itself, which sits on the dais in the center of the room. The chair is solid gold, decorated with every gaudy jewel known to man. She hurries to sit in it the moment we arrive, running a hand along the armrest like it is a long-lost friend.

Sophie lies in my arms unconscious, though I'm not sure I understand why. Perhaps she expended too much energy trying to help Jered. Taj appears on the floor next to me, hands pressed to the ground, biceps straining to push himself up. Of course I neglected to bring along the restraints. She said only Taj and Sophie.

"Restrain him!" Kitra shouts.

But in the time it takes me to say, "Yes, Master," Taj has risen and disappeared with Sophie.

"Reinforce the shields so they cannot escape!" She barks through clenched teeth.

"Yes, Master." I bow slightly and wave my arm out in a circle. Hopefully, I am too late. But I doubt it. I'm sure Kitra has things set up to prevent any Djinni from getting too far on his own.

She is seething now. She grips the sides of her throne so tightly, I expect pieces of gold to break off in her hands. I smile.

"Do not waste time saying 'yes, Master' again. You will obey me at once."

I incline my head. She stands. I know I will pay. But I would not change a thing I have done so far. I meet her gaze head on as she strides toward me. I've lost my freedom, but she's lost two Djinn.

Mira is free. I have finally repaid that debt. Though how I wish she had stayed to help. I suppose I didn't really expect her to.

Taj is in danger. From me. And so is Sophie. I swear that if she makes me harm that child, I will spend the rest of eternity finding a way to kill her. And then there's Jered. My heart breaks, thinking he is gone. But I cannot afford the luxury of grief. Not yet. What will Gabe do now? Will Achan harm him? I don't think so. He is more interested in saving his hide than in revenge.

Kitra pulls me up by the hair. "You have always been a thorn in my side." She shakes me. I do not react. "But you will not succeed. You have already lost. Hear this command: if you are aware of any threat to my person by human or Djinn, you will stop it. Right now, you will find the girl and her Djinni. You are to immediately incapacitate them both, but do not kill them. Bring them back to me, bound in lead chains, to await further instructions." She lets me go. I pop out of the room without another word.

I sweep the rooms with my senses as I pass, allowing the tears to slide freely down my face. I do not attempt to hide my presence. In fact, I make as much noise as I dare, hoping they will find me first. I would not mind if they killed me. I have nothing left to live for, except to see my friend freed.

"Where are you?" I ask the nearest marble statue. The man, whose face is contorted with fear, remains immobile, arms thrown protectively over his head. I don't blame him; I bring disaster to the innocent wherever I go.

I sigh. I haven't tried the dungeons. So I race down the stairs on human feet. The passageway is clear, though the area where the fire burned out of control is charred and crumbling.

A sound, like a whimper, comes from the second room. The one where Jered was tortured by Kitra's hands. I step inside. Pain sizzles along every inch of my skin, and I crash to the ground. The lead-lined cell. Had I honestly forgotten? Or had some part of me remembered what was here?

"Oh, Taj. We can't leave her like this." Sophie appears, standing over me, her blond hair tangled, eyes full of concern.

"No," I try to mouth.

"How do you wish me to leave her?" Taj asks from somewhere behind. Somewhere at a safe distance from the lead.

"Can we get that thing off her neck?" Sophie asks.

"Judging by how Leela freed Mira, if you command it, it is possible. But I can't go near her while she's in there and hope to have the strength to take it off," Taj says.

"I can protect you," she says.

"You are still too weak, Little Master. I can see your aura."

"This is horrible!" Sophie yells.

"I believe we have to leave her there until you are stronger," Taj says.

"Will she be okay?" Sophie asks.

"I hope so," says Taj. "I can't get us out of here alone."

59

DREAMING

I DON'T KNOW HOW LONG WE WAIT. I PASS IN AND OUT OF CONSCIOUSNESS on the floor of the cell, alternating between the horror of the present and the agony of the past. The pain washes over me with stronger and stronger waves until I'm no longer certain I know the difference. Finally, I hear Sophie's voice again.

"Taj, you can't get us out. But can you bring someone here?"

"'Fraid not, Little Master."

"Why hasn't she come for us herself?" Sophie asks.

"She is afraid of me," Taj says.

Sophie giggles. The sound echoes around the walls.

"You don't think I am intimidating?" Taj asks, sounding hurt.

"I think you're the strongest Djinni in the world," Sophie says. "Except for Leela."

I don't feel very strong right now.

"You are the brightest master I have ever had," Taj says. "Stand back!" he yells.

I struggle to turn my head and manage to flop around enough to see a large hole opening in the wall. Seconds later, out tumble Gabe and Jered. Or is it Achan? I feel as though I'm in the ocean, bobbing above and then below the waves. Perhaps this whole thing is some dream induced by the lead poisoning.

"It's us," Gabe yells.

"Jered?" Sophie asks.

"Yes. It's me."

My heart turns over, and I manage a groan. If it's a dream, at least it's a good one.

Jered runs to me, and his face swims hazily in and out of view. I can't tell by looking at him who is inside, and that makes me feel even worse.

"You have to leave her there," Taj says in warning.

Jered sits beside me and lifts my head into his lap, stroking my hair back from my face. A gesture, I realize, that both men have used with affection. I move my lips, but nothing comes out.

"What happened?" Sophie asks.

"He woke up a few minutes after you left," says Gabe. "As far as I can tell, it's him. I mean he knows stuff the real Jered would know."

"Achan would have run with his tail between his legs," Taj says.

"What did you do to him, Sophie?" Gabe asks.

"I gave him some energy, so he wouldn't disappear. But I'm still little, and Daddy says it won't last." Her chin falls down, and she shuffles her foot in the dirt.

"He was just upset because you are smarter than him," Taj says, and she looks up with a smile.

"Anyway," Gabe says, "I told Jered what happened, and he wanted to come by himself, but I kind of insisted. I mean, you guys really need my help, you know?" I can visualize the goofy grin on his face all too well. "So call me crazy, but why isn't Taj killing Her Royal Pain in the Ass?"

"Little Master has forbid me from trying," Taj says. "Apparently she has a thing against killing people too."

"It's bad to murder people when it's not in self-defense," says Sophie. "Even the evil ones."

"Oh God, I'm so sorry, Leela." Jered hugs me to him, rocking me back and forth. I want so badly to tell him it's okay. It wasn't his fault, but my own. Also that he's hurting me.

"Can you put a shield around Taj so he can get in there and take the necklace off?" Sophie asks from above.

"Of course I can," Jered says.

He lays me gently on the ground and backs up enough to let Taj in. Taj reaches down over my throat and tugs at the stone. Just as I feel it give, Taj jerks wildly and collapses on top of me.

"Taj!" Sophie screams.

Jered looks up, smiling. "I'm back. Now give me the stone, Soph." He extends his hand and moves from view.

"Daddy?" she whispers.

"That's right, sweetie. Now give me the stone. Daddy isn't happy that you tried to kill him. But I forgive you. You were confused. Confused about where your loyalties lie because you've been hanging out with the wrong crowd."

A loud crash, and Sophie screams. "Gabe!"

Jered's voice. "Give it to me, or Daddy will have to take it from you."

I want to yell at her to run. But I can't even open my mouth. Taj's body is suffocating me. How could everything have gone so wrong? The sounds of struggling fill my ears, and Jered's body comes back into view, dragging Sophie with him.

"Where is it?" he asks, dropping her to the ground beside us.

Above me, Taj's hand flexes, but all he can do is grab Jered's ankle. Then something happens. Jered's face twists in pain. He raises his fingers to his head, and he stumbles backward.

Moments later he freezes, breathing hard and staring at me wide-eyed.

"He's still in there," he says, and I believe it is Jered talking. "I'm trying, but I don't know what to do."

I have to get up. Have to get to him. But how can I? Even if I succeed, my command is to bring Sophie and Taj back in chains of lead. How can I help Jered if I hand them over to Kitra?

My forehead pounds against my skull. Pins and needles prickle through my skin. My vision fogs again. Jered drops down next to me, pulling Taj off and shoving him out the door as best he can. I can see the strain in his eyes, though. See that Achan might take control again at any moment.

"What do I do?" he asks, leaning over me.

I have to help them. I try to move my lips. Then I feel his aura wash over me, protecting me. But it is weak, and I'm sure it is costing him in his fight with Achan. My hands jerk to fulfill their command, but I am not strong enough. I force words from my mouth while I have the chance.

"Sophie." It is all I can manage before Jered pulls away again, yanking at his hair like it is on fire.

"Sophie, come out of the room so I can protect you!" Taj calls, and I feel her sweep by.

"I know what to do now," she says excitedly. "Taj, you have to let her out."

60

THE BEGINNING

"*I worry for you so,*" *I say.*

Achan sweeps the hair from my face, cupping my cheek in his hand.

"There is nothing to fear, Little One."

"Oh, but there is, Master. Please, I did not tell Kitra everything about the Djinn. But I will tell you. I trust you." I bat my eyes at him, letting the satin sheet fall away from my body.

"Tell me," he says, eyes drinking me in.

"So you have commanded. We are very powerful in numbers."

"This much you have told us," he says.

"But if Kitra manages to get more than one Djinni under her control, she will be strong enough to take us away from you, one by one," I say, climbing to my knees and sliding my hands over his shoulders.

Achan looks away, licking his lips. I see the fear flit across his face as the reality hits him.

"But she would never—"

"Wouldn't she?" I ask, tilting his head to look into his eyes. "Is it not she who controls the Council? Is it not she who commands us all? She has grown comfortable in this position. Power seduces all."

"What would you have me do?" he asks.

I drape my arms around him, pressing my chest against his. "We must leave. And Cephas should leave as well, with Taj."

"Since when do you care what happens to Cephas?" he asks, pulling back enough to search my face.

"I do not, Master. But I do care about Taj. And I worry about the kind of power Kitra can take for herself."

"Well, well, well." Kitra has appeared in the door. Achan swings around, and I cling to his back with a gasp. "Trying to poison Achan's ears?"

"Worried that I will listen?" Achan asks, smoothly.

"Never."

"Then why are you here, Kitra?" he asks.

"I thought I heard my name," she says.

"All the way in your room? Were we that loud?"

They stare at each other for a long time, neither wanting to back down. I stay cowered behind my master's back.

"I think you had better come here for your punishment, Little One." Kitra mocks my nickname as she says it.

I rise, but Achan holds out a hand.

"You do not have to go," he says. "She is mine to punish if and how I see fit."

"Very well, Achan." Kitra leaves, spine straight, slamming the door behind her.

"She has been listening. Perhaps you are right about the situation," he says, pulling me around into his lap. "You have done well."

"Thank you," I say.

"I think perhaps it is time we take our leave of the Council and its ways."

My heart leaps in my chest. Does this mean what I think it does? Will he finally see that he does not need this collar in order to have what he wants?

He kisses me deeply, and I return his passion with equal fervor. I only hope Taj is having as much luck with Cephas.

61

STONE

THE SECOND TAJ FREES ME FROM MY LEAD PRISON, I LEAP UP AND WAVE A hand, fulfilling my command. Kitra sits upon her throne at once, glee filling her eyes when she sees what I have laid at her feet on the scarlet carpet.

I hate that she forced me to bind Sophie in chains. I've made sure they are as loose as possible.

"That took quite some time," Kitra says. "I was beginning to wonder if you'd found yet another way to disobey me."

I say nothing as she steps between the two figures on the ground. My fingers twitch as she leans over Sophie, who lets out an involuntary whimper.

"Give me the stone, and I won't kill you," Kitra says.

Sophie looks at me with wide eyes. Inside, I rage at Kitra; outside, I am careful to keep my expression impassive. I can only hope the child has come up with a solution, though I cannot see it.

"Okay," Sophie says.

Kitra straightens, satisfied. "Take off her chains."

I snap at once, and the chains are removed. Sophie stands awkwardly.

"Hand it over," Kitra says.

I hold my breath. Sophie's gaze darts around the room, searching for help. But she is on her own. Finally, she reaches into the air above her head and pulls out a large round tiger's eye.

I glance at Taj. His eyes are wide. He shakes his head feebly back and forth, making me want to cry.

Kitra snatches the stone from Sophie's hands, licking her lips hungrily. She pulls up her sleeve, and on her wrist, I see a golden bracelet with an emerald set inside. I touch my throat. I hadn't even thought to look. I didn't care what color it was.

Securing the stone to the same bracelet, Kitra allows herself a smile. "Let him out," she says.

Again, I obey at once. Taj stands. His eyes focus on me, the intensity of his gaze making me sway. This can't be happening.

"Now, I think *this* needs to pay a price." Kitra gestures to Sophie.

My heart speeds up as the girl staggers backward. *Please don't,* I beg inside. I know doing so outwardly will only light fire to Kitra's cruelty.

"Taj, you seemed to enjoy her company. Kill her."

Taj turns to Sophie, his face as frightening as I've ever seen it. He stalks forward, coming to rest inches from her. She reaches for her throat, eyes rolling back in her head. I flinch as she falls to the ground, eyes shut, unmoving.

"Good," Kitra says. "Now it's time to punish our friend here." She indicates me. "But what can I do that will be bad enough? Flogging made little impact on her." She taps her lip with her index finger as she circles around me.

I stand stock-still, unable to pry my gaze from Sophie's body.

"I would kill someone you care about, but it seems they are all already dead." She flicks a strand of my hair over my shoulder, toying with me. "As I recall, there was only one thing that ever truly frightened you." She comes to a stop behind me, lips grazing my ear.

I continue my statue-like stand. Whatever frightened me a thousand years ago cannot touch me now. What is the worst she can do? She's already taken Sophie.

"I have someone I want you to meet," she says, clapping me on the shoulders. "Don't move from this spot, Leela. Taj? I think you might be interested in this as well."

Kitra leaves the throne room, and Taj runs to Sophie. He scoops her into his arms and hugs her to him, laughing. She giggles right back.

The world tilts with shock and relief despite my frozen stance. How can this be?

"I gave her a fake tiger's eye," Sophie says with a wink.

Taj turns to me, ready for Sophie's command. Desperate to remove the choker now that Kitra is not present to complicate the situation. But we hear footsteps, and he freezes. Sophie jumps from his arms and runs back to the ground, pretending to be dead. Taj remains at my side.

"I'll keep up this little charade for your sake, Lee. But only until you give the signal."

I cannot risk another misstep. As long as Kitra controls me, he must not attack her. I would see it coming and be forced to protect her. And I will not lose him too. "Get Sophie out," I whisper. "Listen to me, Taj. She commanded I make it so 'they' can't get out. One at a time you could do it."

Before he can respond, Kitra reappears at the door, smiling. "Ever wonder what happened to your first master, Taj?" she asks. "Well, let me tell you. After he lost you, I was a tad angry, as you can imagine. So I asked Mira to turn him into a statue for the foyer."

She moves aside, and two human servants wheel in an enormous slab of marble. My vision blurs. Inside I am shaking. The sight of him elicits tremors that threaten to send me into hysterics.

I feel Taj's fingers entwine with mine.

"You may move now," Kitra says, sweetly.

My muscles relax, and I fall against Taj for support.

"Come here, Leela."

I walk forward until I am before Kitra. I glance at the thing next to her, and she waves the humans away. He looks exactly the same as I remember. Every bulging muscle frozen in time. Even his stubby teeth are marbleized. Now I know why the statues in the hallways wear such expressions of terror.

"Leela," Kitra says, unable to disguise her glee. "Turn Cephas back to flesh and blood."

62

DEMON FROM MY PAST

I WAVE A TREMBLING HAND THROUGH THE AIR, WANTING TO RUN BUT unable to do so. The marble statue in front of me cracks. Chunks of rock fall to the ground at my feet, revealing the person trapped inside.

He steps from the rubble, coughing up a fine cloud of dust. The first thing his gaze falls on is Kitra.

"Do not let him hurt me." She stretches out an arm to examine her nails beneath the torchlight. "He may be a tad upset."

He stops his progression, turning to face me. Recognition lights in his eyes. A deep rumble grows in his chest.

"Cephas, have you enjoyed your nap? I trust you will not disappoint me again?" Kitra asks in an ancient yet familiar tongue.

I want to back away.

"You remember Leela? And Taj, of course? They are mine now, in case you are wondering. And if you are a very good boy, I shall let you have some time alone with Leela here."

I could signal Taj. No. I cannot risk it. Not in front of Kitra. I cannot blow this. I order myself to get control.

"So tell me, Cephas. Are you ready to accept me as your queen?" Kitra asks.

Say "no," I think.

"Kitra?" he asks in an ancient language. "Is that you?" His voice is hoarse yet painfully familiar.

"The one and only," she says.

"Yes," he answers, dipping his head in a bow.

I shut my eyes tight.

"Good. I shall take you to a cell down in the dungeons, which is lined with lead. She needs punishment badly, Cephas, and I know you are the best."

He watches me eagerly, licking his lips.

"There's no rush," I say. "Take care of your friend's needs first, Master. Surely Cephas is hungry after a thousand years."

This earns me a slap from Kitra. Cephas laughs.

"Punishing you will be enough to quench his thirst. Now come."

Taj follows, but she stops him with a hand.

"Stay here and wait for me."

He looks at me, jaw working quickly. I meet his gaze but do not move to signal him. *Get the others out of here*, I try to tell him with my eyes. It does not matter what happens to me, I keep reminding myself. If he escapes with the others, then Kitra is one Djinni down, and the people I care about are safe.

I repeat this like a mantra as we descend toward the dungeon. My gaze flitters around the passage and through the orange glow spackling the stone walls. I search the shadowed corners to make sure Jered, whether as himself or Achan, was smart enough to get out. I breathe a little easier, seeing that Gabe's body is gone as well. I hope this means he's recovered and safe.

Kitra pushes me into the cell. I stumble forward, collapsing onto the coarse hay. I watch the enormous shadow engulf me as Cephas reaches down, pulls me up by my wrists, and secures me in the same shackles that held Jered in place.

Panic sets in. I'm once again hanging from the ceiling in a small dirty room, surrounded by Cephas and Kitra. I'm not sure, but I think I may be hyperventilating. The air is suddenly thick. No. It's the smell. The overpowering scent of incense.

I snap my head toward Kitra, who laughs delightedly.

"For old time's sake," she says. She takes a knife from the air, and my eyes grow wide. "Perhaps a little drink?" She slices my arm, and blood spurts out and down my shirt. She presses her mouth over my stinging skin and draws deeply from the cut. After a long minute filled with the sound of my sobs, she wipes her mouth on the back of her hand, offering the knife to Cephas.

He takes it and strikes without hesitation at my collarbone just above my chest. His beard prickles as his mouth works against my skin. I cannot help the violent shaking in my body. It isn't just the pain. It's the memory becoming real.

"I think I will leave you to it," Kitra says. "I have another Djinni to punish. Leela, you will obey his commands so long as they do not harm me. Remember, Cephas, don't kill her. Just make her wish you had."

Cephas turns me to face him, forcing my head down with one hand to look into his ugly maw. My blood still runs down his chin. He lifts his other hand and flexes it while two rows of lead rings circle his fingers. I squeeze my eyes shut.

"Nuh-uh," he says. "Keep your eyes open."

63

THE BEGINNING

*K*ITRA DOES NOT LET ME OUT OF HER SIGHT, BUT *I* BEHAVE AT MY BEST, GOING *about my business, doing what I am told. I have no wish to offer her any excuse. Of course I have not had a moment to let Taj and Mira know what I have accomplished either.*

Achan pulls me to his side after lunch. Kitra is distracted by her guests who have arrived from the West. They are exotic-looking people. A woman and a man, with smooth faces and straight, glossy hair. They seem apprehensive but perhaps more confident than those who are used to the strange Council that has taken root here.

"I have a plan," Achan whispers, pressing me against the wall and pretending to nibble at my ear. "Act like I am kissing you while we talk. I want you to steal the stone from Cephas. The tiger's eye." I tense at his words but continue to behave as he commands. "Once I have two Djinn, Kitra will not be able to use the others against me, even if she were to find another."

I nod and busy myself with kissing him. I turn his words over in my head. I have been commanded to steal Taj's stone. But he never told me to give it to him. Just assumed that I would. My heart nearly skips a beat.

"Yes," I hear the strangers telling Kitra. "We do know of some of these daemons you speak of. If you share with us how to control them, we will help you get more."

"Leela, come here," Kitra calls. Achan's eyes light like liquid fire, but he does not stop me from ducking beneath his arm to obey. "This is one of the creatures that I own. I will share incredible powers with you right now, if you tell me where to have my other slaves find some more."

The two exchange looks, like they do not believe her. "She does have the eyes," one whispers in a foreign language. I wonder if Kitra can understand them like I can.

"Very well," says the man. It is impossible to miss the hunger in his eyes as he drinks me in from head to toe.

"Splendid," says Kitra. She takes out a leaden knife and grabs my wrist. I cry out as she slices the inside of my arm. "Drink."

"Is this a joke?" the woman asks, hand on the hilt of what looks like a dagger.

Kitra holds my arm firmly in her grasp. "No," she says evenly, staring at the strangers without blinking. "Do it if you want power like mine. Stay still, Leela."

I freeze. The man steps forward and leans down over my arm. He sucks at the wound tentatively and then more greedily. His jaw works as he takes in my blood. My heart races. What if Kitra allows them to drain me, as she did Rhada?

Finally the man pulls away, wiping at his mouth. Around him, a dim aura swirls with color. I grow dizzy.

"How does it feel?" Kitra asks.

The man flexes his fingers. "Good. I need more." He lunges at me.

"Ah, but that is all I can give," Kitra says, pulling me behind her and stopping him with the palm of her hand against his chest.

"What about me?" asks the woman.

"Tell me where to find them," Kitra says.

The woman swallows and glances at the man. "You will find some in our homeland. They walk among us humans, but you can always tell by their eyes. Bright green like hers. If you follow our route back through the desert and up north to the sea, you will find some. They live near the water. Our legends say they like the water—it attracts them, as nectar does bees."

Kitra smiles. She pulls me back over and slices at my arm again, as the cut has already begun to heal. She offers me to the woman, who drinks hungrily.

I stagger after a few minutes, unable to hold my balance. Achan pulls me from them.

"That's enough," he says and stalks away with me in tow.

He scoops me into his arms and lays me on his bed, shutting the door carefully behind us.

"Are you all right?" he asks.

"Yes, I think so," I say.

"She was trying to weaken you. She will no doubt send the other two after these new Djinn, if she hasn't done so already. We must move quickly. I will distract Kitra tonight. You get that stone. My life depends on it."

64

DEATH AND PAIN

CEPHAS CIRCLES ME UNTIL HIS HOT BREATH INCHES DOWN MY NECK. MY own breath speeds up. He grips the back of my shirt, and he rips it.

"The last thing I remember," he says, "is Kitra telling Mira to freeze me in stone because I let you trick me out of my own Djinni. Then here we are, Leela. It took me a minute to understand that girl was actually Kitra. Obviously it's true even though she looks different. But your face I recognize. And you know what?" he asks, drawing his hands down my shoulders and back, causing me to arch in pain. "I blame you for everything. So this is going to be fun."

He tugs at the remainder of my shirt, and it flutters to the ground. All I can think is, *I must deserve this because of the mess I've made.* He comes around to the front of me and grins. "What is this thing? Some strange body armor?" he asks, pulling at the shoulder strap of my bra.

"Get away from her."

Jered? I dare a glance. He stands in the doorway, staring at Cephas.

"Who is this?" Cephas asks. "And what gibberish is he speaking?"

"I said get away from her," Jered repeats.

No. Not Jered. It has to be Achan. Doesn't it? Sorrow, fear, and memories flow over and through me. They mingle with the searing sting of the lead, threatening to drown me in pain.

Cephas rolls his head back on his shoulders as he cracks his neck. He turns back to the figure in the door, only the figure has stepped farther inside the cell. Closer to Cephas. I see the power building in his hands. My eyes grow large.

"Who are you supposed to be?" Cephas bellows.

Jered lets fly a blast of blue lightning that knocks Cephas off his feet. He lands with a thud against the stone wall, and Jered runs to my side, opening the shackles with a wave of his hand. I collapse into his arms, and he carries me from the room, setting me gently on the floor.

"I couldn't understand a word he said, but I didn't have to," Jered tells me, stroking my forehead. "Are you all right, Leela?"

"It is you," I say.

"For now. I keep blacking out when he takes over."

I throw my arms around his neck, burying my head in his chest. "You have to go," I say, through my sobs.

"Not without you," he says, pressing his cheek to my head. "I won't leave you here with them. I see now why you couldn't trust me right away. Leela, I'm so sorry that I didn't trust you either."

"You couldn't have known, but you have to go now, Jered. Please." I tug at his shirt with my fists, trying to make him listen. "When he wakes up...oh, Jered, he can give me commands."

Before he can answer, Jered is plucked from my grasp. Cephas punches a massive fist into his stomach. I watch as he crumples to the floor, and Cephas pulls him up by a fistful of hair, drawing back for a second round.

"Stop!" I cry, and Cephas turns his eyes on me. He drops Jered in a heap on the floor, and I scoot away from him, toward the steps.

"Get over here," he commands. His face is cast in shadow except for the torchlight, which reflects off his eyes like two burning orbs.

I stand, wondering how my feet can actually support me, but as I take a step forward, Cephas's fiery eyes roll back in his head, and he crumples to a heap on the floor. Behind him, Gabe is left standing, silhouetted in the glow from the hall and clutching an unlit torch in his hands.

I rush forward and throw my arms around him. He lets the torch fall and pats me on the back. "Wow, I should hit people over the head more often."

"We have to go before he wakes up," I say. "I must obey him."

Jered climbs to his feet. "You can understand his commands?"

"Yes, I understand all spoken languages. His is an ancient form of Aramaic."

Gabe takes one of Jered's arms and circles it about his shoulder. I take the other side, and we hurry up the stairs.

"Who is that freak?" Jered huffs.

"He was Taj's original master," I say. "Cephas."

Some kind of dark recognition passes over Jered's face, and I recall Taj's report of my earlier babblings. I look away, at Gabe.

"Um, Leela, you might want to put, you know, a shirt on," Gabe says.

I glance down and conjure a new one.

"Okay," I say. "Kitra's probably figured out by now that Sophie tricked her and Taj is not hers. I hope they were able to get away before she got back."

"I don't," Gabe says.

"What?" I ask, bringing us to a stop.

Jered backs into the wall between two marble people, clutching his head, and it is all I can do not to break down and sob. Achan appears to win the battle as his eyes widen at the sight of me, and the coward turns and runs.

I place a hand on Gabe's chest, stopping him from pursuing his friend. "Let him go. He is safer away from me so long as I'm controlled by Kitra." It hurts to say it, but I know it is true.

Gabe pounds a fist into his palm. "Maybe Taj is still around," he says. "He could probably kick that bitch's ass, and this whole thing would be over."

"I would know if I'd been freed. Or if my keep were transferred to someone else," I say.

"Oh." Gabe's face falls.

"I'm sorry, Gabe. I wish Jered never found me," I say, touching his arm.

"I don't," Gabe says. "Leela, this is the most exciting thing that's ever happened to me. You make me feel like a real superhero, you know? Taking on the bad guys, well, it feels pretty damn good."

I smile and hug him once again. When I pull away, he's blushing so deeply, his skin matches the carpet below.

"You better be careful," Gabe jokes. "First that kiss, now all this hugging and shit. I might start thinking you like me or something."

I am about to answer when Gabe's entire body shudders. His mouth forms an *O* of surprise, and a strangled sound escapes his lips. I reach for him as he falls, blood trickling from the corner of his mouth. I lower him to the floor, confused until I see him clutching the hilt of a dagger now protruding from his side.

"Gabe!" I grasp his leather jacket in my fists and will him to heal. "Breathe!" I sob, shaking him. But he doesn't comply.

"He's dead," Kitra says from behind me. "I don't miss."

65

TAJ'S CHOICE

KITRA BENDS OVER ME, YANKING ME UP BY MY WRIST. I WRESTLE AWAY from her grasp and throw myself on Gabe's lifeless body, holding on with all my might as more tears splash down on his shirt.

"How touching," Kitra says. "But we don't have time for this."

I quake with rage, standing slowly because I know I must face her. At least Jered got away. Maybe he'll listen to me and leave. Find a way to push Achan from his body.

"I thought I left you with Cephas," she says. "But then again, I thought I had a second Djinni as well."

If only I could strike her dead.

"He is gone and does not answer my calls. And the body of the child is gone too. Tell me what it is that weakens my hold over my Djinn."

I pause, considering the best way to fulfill this command. "Perhaps I've grown more cunning over the centuries," I say at last. "You've always underestimated others."

"I see." Her face is nearly purple with fury. "And where will I find Cephas?"

"Unconscious on the dungeon floor," I say.

She raises her eyebrows. "And this human helped you escape?"

My gaze falls on Gabe's lifeless body, and the tears threaten to choke me all over again. "Yes." He did. Just not alone.

"Then it is just as well he is dead."

"I hate you," I cry, and my voice echoes down the massive walls.

A smile spreads slowly across Kitra's face. "Good. You can dwell on that while you serve me for the rest of eternity. Now get back in the dungeon. Cephas and I are going to have some fun."

I spot them both crouching in a dark corner alcove as we descend the dungeon steps. They appear deep in conversation. I say nothing, hoping not to attract Kitra's attention, but stare wide-eyed as Sophie hands Taj something that catches the light and makes me squint. A large brown-and-gold stone. His eyes meet mine as he crushes it in his fist. My fingers flex involuntarily, ready to protect my master.

Kitra spots them as Taj's collar falls from his neck. She hides behind my back, whispering, "Protect me."

It wasn't necessary, though. Because, with the flick of his wrist, Sophie disappears, followed immediately by Taj. Something inside my chest squeezes.

He's gone.

At least he took Sophie with him. At least she is safe.

Kitra relaxes at my shoulder and shoves me forward, causing me to stumble into the wall and down the remaining steps. "You obviously can't depend on friends, Leela. They always leave you one way or another. So tell me, was it worth your sacrifice?" She does not pause for a response. "Wait here while I wake Cephas." Her body and voice both shake with barely controlled fury.

I stand obediently at the bottom of the stairs as she helps the giant to his feet. The hate burning in his eyes should send a chill down my spine the same as it did minutes ago. But what does the pain matter when Gabe is dead because he wanted to help me? It is good Taj left me. I don't want him to die for me too.

"You will pay," Cephas says, stalking toward me. "I will see your skin peeled from your body."

"No killing, Cephas," Kitra says. "But all else is fair game. She's cost me two Djinn."

Kitra's words free something inside me. Let them do what they want with my body, I decide. I've succeeded in saving both Taj and Mira. I am absolved. I am untouchable.

Cephas reaches out a hand for the back of my neck and throws me forward toward the cell. I crash down on my knees just short of the lead. He raises a foot to kick me forward, and I turn away, when Kitra shrieks.

Both Cephas and I look over to find her and Jered struggling at the base of the stairs. She was wrong. Not everyone leaves. Jered hasn't. He has his hands on her arm, and I can see golden light swirling around her wrist. She repels him with a burst of her own power. As he flies to the floor, her bracelet breaks, and I stare in disbelief as a gleaming emerald skids to a stop directly between myself and Cephas. But Kitra isn't done. She has pulled out another dagger, aiming it at Jered's heart.

Time slows. I can reach the stone before Cephas, but if I do, I will be unable to help Jered. Again, memories flitter before my eyes. They are new memories, though. Different pictures that have wiped away some of the old.

I watch Jered gather me to him as I cry. Feel the touch of his lips on mine as we float in the night sky. See him laughing with Gabe. See the light in his eyes and the flush of his cheek as he thinks of new ways to help the unfortunate in the world. See him glowing gold as he watches his sister play.

The choice is made before I have time to blink. Kitra's dagger comes crashing down on my force field, and she is thrown backward, striking her head on the hard stone wall. Jered stops, one hand reaching for me as Cephas retrieves the stone.

"Go," I tell him, my voice thick with emotion.

The wounded look on his face is more than I can take, and I cry. He collapses backward, clutching his head. Fighting internally with Achan no doubt. I wait, crouched on the floor for Cephas's command. But it is not his voice that speaks next.

"Well, well, well. If it isn't my old master. Has anyone ever told you that you have a nasty habit of trying to take things that don't belong to you?"

Taj stands, arms folded, breathing down Cephas's neck. I laugh through the tears, and Taj throws me a smile. Cephas turns, the veins in his massive throat strained and pulsing. Taj plucks the stone from his hand and tosses it to me.

"What do you want?" Cephas asks.

"I want you to die," Taj says.

Cephas tries to throw a punch, but Taj catches his fist in midair and squeezes, bringing him to his knees with a scream.

"You see, I owe you," says Taj, circling Cephas's crouching figure. "This is for me." He strangles the air in front of him, and Cephas claws at his own neck as he turns blue.

"And this is for Lee."

Cephas chokes out a sound somewhere between a gurgle and a cry, and falls to the floor, eyes open but blind.

I feel the sharp cold emerald in my fist as it disintegrates into glitter, but my gaze is cemented on Taj. He came back too. For me. My heart swells.

I am about to speak when behind him, Jered reaches up in the air with a deadly smile, pulling a long lead rod from nothing. I try to call out, but it is over before I can. As soon as he raises the weapon to strike, it vanishes, and Mira appears at his back.

"No, you don't, Achan," she says, laying a hand on his shoulder.

"I didn't mean—" he begins.

"Oh, shut up," she says, pushing him aside, so that he lands next to Kitra, who has come to and cowers on the ground.

Mira helps me to my feet. When our eyes meet, she smiles.

"Thank you," I say.

"What should we do with the skank?" Taj asks, eyeing Kitra's cringing figure.

"Mira," I say. "Her fate is yours to decide."

Mira stares hard into her old master's face, raises her hands, and Kitra flies into the lead-lined cell. The door swings shut behind her, and her screams are drowned out as the gaps at the edges fuse to the surrounding metal, sparks flying like fireworks.

"The walls and door are sealed," Mira says. "Let her die alone, thinking about her crimes. If she's taught me anything, it's that slow and painful is always better."

We all turn toward Jered. Taj moves to strike, but I hold out a hand. "He is still in there. We have to find a way to get Achan out."

66

THE BEGINNING

KITRA'S MOOD IS GOOD. SHE HAS SENT BOTH TAJ AND MIRA TO RETRIEVE A new Djinni for her from the visitors' homeland. So I entertain the guests alone. They eye me eagerly as I dance, and my heart beats faster.

When all the humans have drunk themselves to staggering, Kitra announces that they will retire for the night. Reluctantly, the strangers allow the servants to lead them to their rooms.

Achan stops Kitra with a hand on her arm. She pauses, and he pulls her into his arms, kissing her fiercely. I find it impossible to look away as she runs her hands through his hair and he lifts her into his arms.

"What about your pet?" she asks.

"Let Cephas have her for the night," Achan says. Kitra is delighted by this turn of events and continues to kiss him as he carries her to his room.

I feel Cephas at my shoulder. "You heard him. You're mine tonight," he says. "Come."

I follow obediently as he leads me through the stark gray halls to his room, barely waiting for me to get through the door before groping me like a hungry lion. I pull at his clothing, desperate to find the stone. He grins, pleased that I seem interested.

"Take yours off first," he commands. "No magic."

I fumble with shaky hands to remove my dancing outfit. But when I move toward him again, he stops me with his arm thrown out.

"Dance," he says.

I want to cry in frustration. But I dance about the room for him, my hair swinging loose around me. After a few minutes, he removes his own clothing, and I scan his body for the treasure. I need not have panicked. It hangs around his neck on a piece of black cord. I know what I have to do.

"Stop," he says. "Now come here."

He pulls me into his arms, kissing me. I try not to gag and offer him a goblet filled with wine when he pulls away. My gaze remains on the stone the entire time. I continue to conjure more spirits throughout the night, practically pouring them down his throat. Finally, he passes out. I wait to make sure he will not wake, and I take the stone.

I wonder how something so small and lovely can be so foul. I am about to destroy it when I hear a sound behind me. I turn to find the female stranger, who throws one of Cephas's own heavy lead chains on me before I can react.

"I have to have your power," she says, pulling out the dagger from her belt.

"You will get no more power that way," I say, desperate. "They tried. But it did not work. That is why they enslaved us."

"How do I know you tell the truth?" she asks, jamming her knee into my stomach and leaning down over my head. "Your kind twists truth to trick humans."

"No!" I cry. "Why else would they keep us? Why would Kitra not have taken such power for herself?"

She considers me, holds the knife to my throat. "How do they enslave you?" she asks.

"It is the stone," I say, "In our collars. They have matching stones that we are tied to. We must obey the owner."

"What are you holding?" she asks.

I clamp my mouth shut.

"Give it to me," she says, pressing the lead into my skin. She pries the stone from my hand and examines it. "I command you to kneel before me," she says.

"It is not mine," I wail.

But before I can try to explain, Taj appears on his knees at her feet. He looks as surprised as I feel. The stranger smiles and releases her pressure on the chains.

"Kitra will kill you," I say, desperate to protect Taj. To fix it.

"Then we will have to leave tonight," she says. "Come, slave." Taj follows helplessly as she leaves the room.

I remain trapped beneath the chains on Cephas's bed. I am certain that when he awakens, he will kill me for losing his Djinni.

Worse, he may force Achan to give him my stone so he may reap his revenge the more painful way.

67

FREEDOM'S PRICE

"I AM GOING BACK," MIRA SAYS.

"What?" I ask. "But you came—"

"Taj asked me to. He convinced me I owed you for freeing me. So I'm here. I helped you, but I owe the human nothing. Now we are even, and I am leaving. I will not stay for another minute in a place crawling with these evil creatures, always looking over my shoulder."

I open my mouth to speak and then snap it shut. I nod instead, feeling Taj's hand on my shoulder.

"Good-bye, Mir," he says.

"Good-bye," I say. "And thank you. For coming back."

She nods before disappearing from our lives. Forever.

"Are you going too?" I ask. I am unable to look him in the eye. Afraid of his answer.

"No," he says, lifting my chin so I can see his smirk.

"But on the roof you said—"

"I lied. As it turns out, I have a lot of living to do as a free Djinni. And I don't plan on ever getting caught by another Magician," Taj says.

"Where is Sophie?" I ask. "I thought when you both left..."

"That I deserted you? I can't blame you, but no. I merely needed to retrieve Mira to make sure we could overpower you while Kitra was in control. And as for Sophie, she is home. Safe. I've erased her memories, Lee."

"It's for the best," Achan says.

We both turn to glare at him, our eyes glowing green. He cowers back into the shadows of the dungeon corner.

"She won't remember ever meeting us," Taj says gently, turning his attention back to me.

I feel a pang of sadness but have to agree that this is best. She's witnessed too much horror for someone so young. "She was wonderful."

"The best master I ever had," Taj says. "Smart too. And powerful."

"I believe she will use her powers for good," I say.

"She just may break the mold," Taj says, approaching Achan once again.

"I'll do anything," Achan says.

Taj squats beside him and pokes a finger at his forehead. "The question is, how do we get you out of there?"

"You can't," Achan says. "Not without killing Jered."

"If I found you another body, could you transfer to it?" I ask.

"I won't," he says. "Even if you find one that would work."

"Work?" I press.

"A Magician related to me by blood. Anyone else would be too strong to take control of."

I swallow, thinking.

"You will not use Sophie," Taj says.

"No," I agree. "What if the Magician is no longer occupying his body?" I ask Achan.

"Where would I find a fresh Magician's bod—" He stops cold, following my gaze to Cephas's lifeless form. "No! I won't leave this body." He grasps his head with a moan, falling to his side. Then with deep breaths, he looks up at me.

"Jered?" I ask.

"Leela, I can't hold him long. You have to hurt me. I don't think he can stand the physical pain. I think he'll move to the other body just to get away."

"I don't want to hurt you, Jered," I say.

"Please," he says, and then falls into his hands yet again.

"You won't do it," Achan says. "You won't hurt him."

"She doesn't have to," says Taj. "I have no particular emotional attachment to the guy." He twists his hands together, and Achan shrieks, doubling over in pain and clutching his leg.

"Jered!" I cry.

Taj twists again. More shrieks. And again.

"Stop," I sob, tugging at Taj's arm. "Please, Taj."

"Please," echoes Achan.

"Hmm." Taj taps a fingertip against his lip, considering. "No." He twists again. "Leave."

"Wait!" I scream. "It isn't working. I think I know another way."

Taj holds with hands raised at the ready. I nod, grateful, and rush forward all at once, diving and squeezing into Jered's body, just as I had with Gabe the day that I met them.

Jered is a crowded place. I feel around, finding his thoughts, which now fade dimly into the background. He's expended so much energy trying to save me. *Don't leave me, Jered,* I beg.

Achan's mind is the one that answers. Loud and frightened.

Leela, how can you? I didn't know you could...

I force myself on him, prying into his thoughts, digging for the answers I need while I have this chance. I find old memories buried deep within. Things seen from his own eyes.

I see him making love to Kitra. Promising to bring me to her as a prize. I see myself being dragged into the lead cage by Cephas's chain. I feel the sick twisting in his stomach when I ask "why," and he has to turn away from my sunken eyes, unable to face me. I see him wince from the shadows, where I never even knew he'd been, as Kitra and Cephas drink my blood—as the inhuman screams scrape my throat raw.

Then comes the moment I have been searching for. A conversation between him and Cephas.

"If you can wear her down," Achan says. "I can come to the rescue. We can make it look like I best you, though of course I never could."

Cephas grins, flattered. "We'd have to make it look good."

"I'm not sure she'd be able to tell at this point. But we have to make sure. Make absolutely sure she will do it. She must feel that there is no alternative. And that I am the safe choice."

"You will share her with me?" Cephas asks, taking a long swig of ale.

"Of course I will." Achan claps him on the shoulder.

Cephas grunts in acceptance and rises from his chair. "Give me some time."

"Not too much, Cephas." Achan is nervous now, contemplating how to convince Cephas to take it easy on me. "She has to be conscious."

"I can arrange that."

"And...and Kitra won't be gone long; we must do this before she returns from the neighboring village."

"You do your part; let me do mine. I want time with her. A good hour at least, or you can wait and do it Kitra's way," Cephas says.

Then I am there, inside, while Achan waits in the shadows as Cephas tortures me. Pain. His pain. But it is not enough to force him to move early. He does not come into the light until I seem ready to lose consciousness. He needs me awake.

I've had enough. I have my answers.

You will leave now, Achan. I have already lost someone I care about; I am not losing Jered too.

I move Jered's body forward. Achan fights. I am far stronger. I press our fingers to Cephas's temples.

Leela, wait. No! I can explain...you don't know what it was like.

Actually, now I do.

I push with all the force of my power, wrapping around Achan's essence and catapulting us both outside Jered's body.

I tumble onto the floor to find Jered collapsed on top of Cephas.

We wait, Taj's hand on my shoulder. My own on my mouth. Jered's fingers twitch at the same time Cephas's do. I scramble forward, pulling him away and into my lap. Healing his wounds.

His eyes open, drinking me in.

"Jered?" I whisper.

"I don't know how to prove it," he says, sitting up.

"Kiss me," I say.

He reaches out tentatively, drawing my face to his. I close my eyes as his lips brush mine. So soft, so gentle, that the kiss is that of a phantom. I breathe in sharply and press forward, kissing and crying and laughing all at once.

"I take it he passes the test," Taj says, watching Cephas's body rise from the floor.

I cannot remember ever seeing Cephas frightened. It is an interesting sight.

"Lee? I got mine. Mir got hers. Your call."

I rise, Jered's hands locked with mine. He holds me tight, and I lean my head against his chest for strength as his aura, a deep purple, enfolds me like a blanket.

"What should I do with you?" I ask, facing Achan.

"Let me go. Being in this body is punishment enough," Achan says.

"Jered?" I ask, turning back to him. "He tried to kill you."

"That doesn't mean murdering him is right," he says, mouth on my hair.

"Even after all you've seen?" I ask. "All you've been through. You don't want him dead?"

Jered takes my shoulders in his hands and holds me at arm's length, looking me in the eyes. "I'd be lying if I said I thought he didn't deserve it. But if you kill him, his blood will be on your hands."

"Do you know how many people's blood is on my hands because of him?" I ask.

"Whatever you decide, I will stand by you, Leela. But you don't have to do this. You don't have to murder. This is your own choice," Jered says.

"He made me what I am," I say.

Images flash through my mind. Achan and I making love on the desert sand. Rhada's bloated body on the wall. Cephas's hands burning tracks in my skin. Kitra's mouth covered with my blood. Achan saying, "From now on you will refer to me as Master."

"I really did do it for us," Achan says, pulling my attention away. "It was the only way."

Grinding my teeth, I turn back to Jered and lay my head on his chest. I want to scream so many things. That he was not the one who had to pay the price. That he never had to turn me over in the first place. That he could have actually let me go. But I know that no matter what I say, he will never understand.

"I'm sorry," I say to Jered instead, grasping his shirt in my hand. Achan crumples behind me, writhing on the floor. As I let go of Jered's shirt, Achan stops and retches in the dirt.

I wave an arm behind me, and Achan vanishes from view.

"Where did he go?" Jered asks.

"He can spend eternity with his true love," I say. "Or at least the rest of his miserable life. If it was good enough for Mira, it is good enough for me."

I feel Taj's hand on my back. "Let's get out of here."

"Wait," Jered says, looking around. "Where's Gabe?"

"Jered," I say, reaching up to stroke his face, tears streaming down my cheeks. "He's gone. I'm so sorry. It was Kitra."

Jered stumbles back, and I grab onto his hands, steadying him. His Adam's apple works up and down in his throat as he stares off into space.

"I'm sorry," Taj says.

Jered jerks to life. "No. No, you have to bring him back."

Taj and I exchange a glance.

"Jered," I say, reaching for him. "He's gone. There is nothing we can do."

Jered shakes his head, nearly backing into the stone wall. "There are two of you. You can. Right? I mean he can't...he can't be gone."

"Jered, I'm sorry," I say. I wouldn't have thought there could be more tears in me, but here they are, falling freely once again.

Jered looks desperately to Taj, who nods to confirm what I've said.

"I want to see him. Where is he?" Jered searches wildly around for his best friend.

I wave an arm, and Gabe's body appears at our feet. Seeing him there again, so pale and still, clothes matted with blood, I fall to my knees by his side, crying.

Jered freezes at the sight of him and turns away, vomiting onto the straw. When he finishes, he turns back to us, clutching his stomach.

Silently, I arrange Gabe's hands to rest across his chest and fix his glasses, askew on his face. Taj claps, and Gabe rests on a satin sheet in clean clothes. The dagger is gone.

"Thank you," Jered says, unable to tear his gaze from the body. "I...he...I should have listened to you, Leela. I shouldn't have told him about you in the first place."

"This is all my fault," I say. "I did this. Please believe I would give anything in the world to change it."

Jered pulls me into his arms, rocking me. "This isn't your fault, Leela. This was Kitra's fault. And my dad's. I'm so sorry I ever doubted you."

"You had every right to, Jered. I'd give all my power to get him back." My throat is too tight to say any more.

We stand in silence for quite some time, each of us remembering our friend with the glasses and the goofy grin.

"Let's get you home," I say, finally.

"Aren't you coming?" he asks, voice still laced with pain.

"Coming?" I repeat.

"Home? I mean, I thought that you felt the same way I...but I guess you don't." He looks away embarrassed, but not before I see more tears escape down his cheeks.

"How is it you feel?" I ask, turning his face to mine and stroking the moisture away with my thumbs.

"You know how I feel, Leela. I told you before," he whispers.

"But Achan tampered with your emotions."

"He couldn't change how I felt, Leela. Just how strongly I reacted. Leela, I really do love you."

Of course Achan could not change his actual feelings. It would take several Djinn to accomplish that. I am such a fool.

Jered swallows, waiting with wide eyes for me to respond. I glance over at Taj, who rolls his eyes, placing a hand on his hip, and I laugh.

Jered's face falls, and I realize he thinks I am laughing at him, so I grab hold of his shirt, pull him to me, and press my mouth to his. He goes rigid for a moment and then relaxes into the kiss.

"Home it is, then," Taj says behind us, and we are still kissing when he deposits us on the hotel roof.

68

THE BEGINNING

CEPHAS DISCOVERED MY TREACHERY THE MOMENT HE WOKE, AND NOW HE *presses the chain against my throat, watching me struggle to breathe.*

"Leela!" Achan calls, having tracked me down once I did not arrive with the stone. "Let go of her, Cephas."

"Your little whore stole my stone," Cephas roars.

"Let her up, we'll get it back," Achan says.

"It's gone," Cephas says. "One of those visitors took it. They left her here covered with these chains. Very thoughtful, to leave something for me to use to kill her."

My vision turns black.

Achan throws out his aura, and Cephas is torn off me. The chains are lifted from my chest, and I scramble to hide behind Achan.

"Leela, we have to leave. Now."

I take us to the desert, because I do not know where else to go. Achan is furious with me.

"How could you be so stupid? So careless?" he shrieks. Never have I seen such hate in his eyes.

For the first time, he strikes me with his own hand, and I fall to the dirt, crying.

I hear scuffling and look up. The male stranger has appeared and attacked

Achan, jumping on his back and bringing them both to the ground. I rise, ready to throw him off when he stands on his own, holding up the opal. I rest my hand on my neck as I let out a gasp.

"The woman," I say.

"She's gone. She left me. So I started on the road away from here and that insane Kitra. But then I saw you. A gift from the gods. Now as soon as we kill your previous master..." He turns to the spot where he struggled with Achan, but Achan is gone. Slithered away like the serpent he is.

"No matter," the stranger says. "You are mine now. Hajima told me how it works before she left. She told me I should try to find a stone that matches your necklace. But she refused to take me home with her."

I stand in the sand, unsure what to do. What to expect.

"You belong to me now," he says, stroking the stone.

I stare.

"Kneel and call me Master."

I do.

69

LIFE

Done with classes for the day, I hike my satchel onto my shoulder and open the heavy door, allowing the cold air and sunshine through. The steps have been cleared by a light salting and heavy foot traffic, but soft white powder lines the edges and blankets the grass.

I see Jered, leaning casually against his car, watching me with those eyes. I smile and sigh, pulling a hand through my new short-cropped haircut. I felt it was time for something a bit more modern. A bit more me.

"We have to get to the house; Mom's having a heart attack about all the guests."

"No worries. I'll help," I say, hugging him tight.

"This is going to be weird without Gabe there." I can tell Jered fights tears, even though it has been some time.

I hold him tighter. There are no words of comfort I can offer. At least his mother has recovered. I do not know what he would have done if she had not.

When his mother awoke, Jered was hesitant to tell her anything. But I insisted she must know the truth. I suspected that she knew something. That she spent all those years afraid of Achan. And I was right.

Corrie listened to the story, unable to tear her eyes from her son.

And when I finished, she gathered us both to her in a tight, and wet, embrace. She wept, telling us that she knew Jered's father had powers and that Jered did as well. She sensed the evil in Peter—as she referred to Achan—and ran, doing everything in her power to keep Jered safe and oblivious to his abilities. This was the reason for her inability to let go when Jered flew from the nest.

"Wow," Jered says, as we walk up the path to her new house. "Are you sure this is okay? You didn't, you know, take it from anyone?"

"It is fine. No one had purchased it yet. I used some of Kitra's billions."

Taj used some as well. He removed Achan's body from Sophie's home, altering the family's memories so that they believed he ran off with another woman. He was adamant that Sophie be taken care of and deposited a large sum in her mother's bank account. Thus far, she seems to be adjusting well. I do have to be careful about guarding Jered's thoughts around her.

They are already inside. Jered's half brother and sisters. And Corrie and Elle, who chat in the gleaming gourmet kitchen.

"How was class?" Corrie asks, catching sight of us. She'd encouraged me to go for an actual history degree, and I couldn't be happier with the decision.

"Good. Are you ready for the housewarming party?" I ask, hopping up on a barstool.

"Yes!" Corrie's gray eyes crinkle with a smile so wide, I have to return it.

"We're starting a club," Elle says, nibbling on a cracker and cheese.

"Oh?" I raise my eyebrows.

"The ex-wives of Peter Archer club," she says.

"Let's hope there are no more members lurking about," Corrie adds, giving me a wink. She knows that I am the charter member.

I eye the glass of wine held casually in Elle's hand, and she passes one over to me so we can toast. The liquid's cool, fruity flavor bites my tongue as it passes over.

I squeeze Corrie's hand with genuine affection. I've never experienced a mother before. She is the only one with whom I have ever shared the pain of my past. Bit by bit, in tears on her sofa each night while Jered sleeps at our apartment from which I teleport. It's not that he hasn't offered to listen, but he will not push me to tell him all, and for that I am grateful.

"No way!"

Jered's siblings huddle together in the living room. Amanda leans over Chris's shoulder. I join them on the arm of the sofa to see Chris concentrating on the phone in his hand. His fingers fly across the screen.

"What are you doing?" I ask.

"Just a game," Chris says, catching sight of me and blushing.

"Zombie Squasher 4000?" I ask.

"Um, yeah. Do you know it?" he asks, pausing to glance up from the screen, eyes wide.

"It was my friend's favorite game. I've been practicing." My stomach clenches with the still raw pain of losing Gabe. "I believe I'm getting pretty good."

My gaze slides across the room to Jered, who is deep in discussion with Gabe's parents and sister. The official story of his death was that Gabe fell during a hike with Jered. Far less than the heroic reality he deserves. I haven't been able to speak to his family since the funeral. After all, they might not know it, but I am actually responsible for their son's death.

The doorbell rings, and I jog to answer, Sophie fast at my heels. I find Taj's impish grin on the other side. Sophie's jaw drops open.

"You look like my doll," she says.

Taj squats down before her with a twinkle in his eye. "Then he must be an unbelievably handsome fellow."

Sophie laughs, delighted. I place a hand on my hip and glare at Taj. So he left his Little Master with a gift. I shake my head.

"What's your name?" Sophie asks.

"Sophie," I interrupt, gaze fixed on Taj so as to convey a warning to watch what he says, "this is my brother, Taj."

Sophie giggles again. "That's a funny name."

Once the crowd thins to family, and Sophie cannot stifle another yawn, Elle and Jered's half brother and sisters say their good-byes.

"I better get to this mess. I'm getting awfully tired," Corrie says, stifling a yawn.

I wave a hand, and the house is spotless. "Get some sleep."

"Thank you, Leela dear. Get some rest as well, you two." His mother smiles and then stalks up the winding steps.

"I ought to be going too," Taj says, leaning down to give me a peck on the cheek.

"Where are you going?" I ask, hand on hip once again.

"It's nine o'clock on a Friday night. I have a hot date. And from the looks of it, so do you."

Jered has come up behind me. His arms wind around me along with his deep-burgundy aura, and I lean back against his chest. Taj winks and disappears. I turn around, linking my hands behind Jered's neck.

"Alone at last," I say.

"Want to kick back and watch a movie?" he asks, drawing me in closer so that our bodies mesh.

"That's it?" I lean in, grazing his neck with my lips. I enjoy the shudder that works its way down his body.

"What did you have in mind?" he asks, and I transport us back to our studio apartment, clothes conveniently removed on the way.

Our bodies are now familiar to one another. We've been unable to keep our hands off each other since returning. For me, it is to remind myself that this life—my new, free life—is real. That Jered is real and has chosen to love me for myself and not my service.

I shove him down on the bed with one palm splayed across his chest and climb over him, nipping and licking my way toward his mouth. His breath quickens and grows more sporadic with each flick of my tongue until our lips meet.

Jered flips me onto my back and caresses my breast before pulling away long enough to say, "My turn."

I spread my arms lazily across the rumpled bedsheets as he works his way down my stomach, over my navel, and finally between my legs, where he finds me wet and ready to receive him. Still, he takes his time, using his own mouth masterfully until I am reduced to a writhing mass beneath him.

The fire in my belly builds until its flaming tendrils reach through every inch of my body, and I scream out his name with my release.

Without a moment's break, he slides inside me, driving deep and hard as he carries me beyond the point of satisfaction until wave after wave of euphoria quake through my body. Only then does he find release as well, rolling off me so I can snuggle into his arms, my head nestled against his shoulder as I run my finger through the soft blond dusting of hair on his chest.

"I want to make you come all night long." His husky tone melts me like butter.

"You've been doing that for weeks now, Jered," I tease, resting my chin on his pecs.

"My goal is to give you more memories of pleasure than pain. It might take an eternity though, and I don't mind one bit."

"It's good to have goals," I agree, letting a hand slip down to test if my resilient man has recovered so quickly.

His laugh is cut short by a sharp intake of breath, followed by a groan of longing.

"So, Jered, shall we get to work on that?"

"That, Leela, is up to you," he says, rolling over the top of me. "Your wish is my command."

EPILOGUE

TAJ

"Hello, Tom," I say, greeting the unsuspecting human. He would be hot had I not known about the disgusting files he kept on his computer in the bedroom. Also, that shocked look on his face does nothing for me. I suppose I can't blame him. I did just pop into his luxury apartment overlooking Lake Michigan without warning. "Oh yes, I know way too much about you and your dirty little secret."

The color rushes back into his cheeks, and his gaze betrays his intentions by darting toward the bedroom where, aside from the evidence still open on his desktop screen, there's a safe with a gun inside. I could have a bit of fun and let him overreact, but then again, I don't want any bullet holes in my new walls. I do rather like the way he's decorated despite his despicable behavior. I think I shall keep most of it as is after cleaning out the filth.

I sit on the leather sectional and wave a hand so that the electronic footrest rises, and then conjure myself a whiskey from his personal stash. "So you're going to have to leave, Tom. I'm still deciding whether to kill you, hand you over to the human authorities, or mmm...I don't know, maybe turn you into a dog." I pause, letting the idea filter into my thoughts. "Nah, that would be cruel to dogs everywhere." I raise the glass in salute as he makes a run for his silly weapon.

Automatically, he covers his heart with one shaking hand when I pop in front of his face, and he leans dramatically against the bed. Too bad the picture on the screen behind him is of an underage girl provocatively posed. Too bad for him, that is, because I feel my eyes glow green as my powers rise to the surface along with my anger and impatience.

It's the perfect trade, really. I do a favor for humanity by ridding them of this scum, and in return, I get the apartment.

He shakes his head back and forth, turning as white as the satin sheets currently on his—my—king-size bed. The corner of my mouth turns up in a smile as my eyes glow brighter. He shrinks back.

"I'll give you anything. Please don't hurt me."

"Oh dear, Tom, I didn't know pedophiles were such sensitive souls. I don't suppose you care whether you're hurting your victims?" I tower over his cowering form.

"It's just a few videos. I never touched anyone in person."

"We both know that's not true, nor does it matter. How do you suppose those videos you support are made? On the backs of slaves." Okay, so maybe this is a bit personal.

Before he can snivel at me again, I snap my fingers, and he is hand-cuffed at the local police station along with a nice, neat little manila file containing tons of evidence against not only him, but also everyone involved in the ring he dabbled in. Hope he has fun in jail. I hear the other inmates don't typically take kindly to guys like him. Oh well.

Lucky that I happened to like this apartment so close to the water. The things I uncover when I snoop.

I pop back onto the sofa and snap to turn on the giant flat-screen on the wall. Settling into my seat, I take a sip of my drink as the ice cubes clank against the crystal.

Yes, I think I'm going to like being a free Djinni.

Thank you for reading! Did you enjoy? Please add your review because nothing helps an author more and encourages readers to take a chance on a book than a review.

And don't miss more in the The Djinn series from Lizzy Gayle coming soon!

Until then discover CURSE OF THE AMBER, by City Owl Author, Kathryn Troy. Turn the page for a sneak peek!

You can also sign up for the City Owl Press newsletter to receive notice of all book releases!

SNEAK PEEK OF CURSE OF THE AMBER

BY KATHRYN TROY

The sun seems to have forgotten Wales. I didn't think there was any place on Earth that could make me long to be in Egypt again, but I couldn't escape the memories that flooded me. I shivered in the absence of the Valley's merciless heat, where for summers on end its oppressive dryness sucked the life out of my lips and baked my skin into hardened, sand-beaten clay. That dryness had followed Ramesses, Amenhotep, Aken-aten, and his son beyond the world's suffering down to their resting place, and kept the divine kings ready in the dark, empty stillness.

But the day's oppression had always faded with the sun. The perfection of those nights on the Eastern Bank, at our host Hani's home—that was what I missed. Invigorated by the fresh, life-giving breeze off the Nile's surface and snuggled between my parents under thin woven blankets was a warmth I knew I would never feel again. The cold and damp of Britain, once the stronghold of the Druids, was relentless. The gnawing feeling at the pit of my stomach grew, and the thought I'd pushed away more than once made itself more insistent.

This was a mistake. I shouldn't be here.

My fingertips numbed to the statuette in my hand, a solid representation of the wet chill in the air. Its faceless form was as alien to me as the bog in which I crouched. The shape of the stone fetish was at least interesting, a long, slender column with a severe "V" etched into it. It held more promise than the dozens of thin rings fashioned out of iron, bronze, and even gold, heaped together in a tangle, the clay pottery, now in shards, and scraps of linen that appeared to be tossed desperately into the bog as a last-ditch effort to avoid Roman destruction. But I couldn't enjoy it for what it was. It was inscrutable, too disconnected from anything familiar. Its primitive, obscure expression reminded me of my own cold thoughts, and as I squeezed the chilled stone in my hand, I doubted if I would discover anything that had once been warm —made of flesh and blood. We were as deep down as the famous bog bodies had been, more so in certain places, and still we had nothing, or rather no one, to show for it.

I lifted my head, trying to shake off my melancholy and averting my eyes from the stone carving that would not reveal its secrets to me. I was too low down to inhale even a whiff of air that wasn't saturated with the grassy pungency of the bog wall. From my vantage point, huddled low in a deep, man-hewn pit, the sodden depression of the bog appeared even more overgrown on all sides. Birch trees poked out of humble clusters of willows, red-speckled buckthorn, and mountain ash. Except for these trees skirting its outermost edges, the sunken area was wide and open. The cauldron bog retained its secluded atmosphere, despite being carved into a series of waterlogged cavities.

My somber mood deepened when I saw my advisor approach. Up until then I'd been successful at avoiding him. I deliberately didn't linger, and always found a reason to visit another pit when the one we were in suddenly emptied of other researchers. I'd resisted the wrenching feeling in my gut too long, but as our excavation wound down, it was impossible to ignore, with nowhere for my thoughts to hide—there was nothing left of what used to be my life.

"How's it going?" Alex asked, and knelt beside me.

"Fine," I answered, not bothering to look up from the peat I was brushing off of a link of iron rings sunken into the over-saturated soil.

After a long, awkward silence, he said, "It's okay, you know."

"What is?"

"If you don't...if *we* don't find one."

I swallowed hard. The only place for my rising fury to go was back down.

"I just don't want you to think that this whole thing was a waste—"

"A *waste*?" I shot back. "I've got enough to keep me occupied for the next decade, thank you." It was true, but that didn't make the prospect of studying human sacrifice *sans* a human sound any better. Nothing would tell us as much about the Druids as human remains that had, willingly or otherwise, undergone their practices. It may have been more than anyone else expected, but the bar had been set impossibly high. A human discovery might have been the only way to exceed my father's own discoveries in the Valley of the Kings and earn the same level of respect in my own right.

"All right, all right," Alex said, contrite. "I didn't come over here to upset you."

"Then why are you here?" There was more bite in my voice than I meant, but he had that amused eyebrow raised again, the one that made my anger meaningless and painted me as a silly, wide-eyed novice with dreams of finding the next Tut.

"I thought you might need a refill." He offered me a cup of coffee.

A gruff "thank you" was all I could manage. My brain had reached maximum capacity for caffeine, but it went down easy. Milk and two sugars, just the way I liked it. Damn.

He reached out for me but caught himself before his fingers could find their way into my hair, frowning before he lowered his voice.

"Will you come tonight, Asenath? It'd be a shame for you not to see the room. You picked it, after all."

Memories of Alex's firm, feverish grip on my hips, his moans in my ear, passed unbidden across my mind. Some days it was so easy to look at him and just see the charming, somewhat quiet young man always at my father's side, more often than not covered in two-thousand-year-old dust.

"Will you tell *her*?" I asked.

His silence hit me like a stab in the gut. It was self-inflicted—those rosy pictures and all his stale promises were just a veil, a childhood infatuation. I saw him then as he was—his chocolate-brown hair had dulled, the sharp line of his chin softened; so, had the brilliance of his eyes, their dark fathoms fading. Small lines crept at the corners of his eyes and mouth. I bit my tongue as a distraction. The imprints of his touch on my skin would fade, if I let them.

I sipped my coffee again. It had a bitter taste the second time around. When I let the silence settle between us, he rose to his feet, stifling a groan on the way up. He disappeared again to the other side of the dig, and I went back to work.

I ended the day uploading my latest round of pictures as usual. Dr. Pryce, the head of the Aarhaus team, walked into the makeshift tent and took up the seat beside me.

"Good evening, Miss Hayes."

"Hi, Dr. Pryce. I'm almost done here."

He nodded. "Time for your daily report. Carew was preoccupied, so he asked me to come in his stead."

"Preoccupied with what?" I asked, then mentally kicked myself the moment the words escaped my mouth. It was too familiar, but my patience with Alex was thin. Dr. Pryce didn't seem to notice, and only smiled, a sly thing with a hint of amusement. "Right," I answered, shaking my head. "Well, according to today's soil readings, we're anywhere from fifteen to twenty-five hundred years down, and some of the wells were definitely dug by human hands."

"Wells," Pryce repeated, bobbing his head thoughtfully, "but no mounds."

"That's right." I felt my face flush hot under the electric lamps swinging overhead. The Druids hadn't built permanent structures, making them an elusive lot. But I'd hypothesized that impermanent markers, made of dirt and mud, had been either destroyed or overlooked completely. The clunky peat-cutting that locals relied on for fuel had raised almost every bog body ever found by sheer accident. Any significant difference to the topography would have been ripped apart before anyone had realized its importance. I had at least hoped to map out some pattern to the ritualized deaths bog bodies had endured and give more substance to Julius Caesar's accounts of human sacrifice among the Druids. But without markers in the ground as a reference, or actual victims to study, deciphering the meaning of these haphazard bits and bobs wouldn't amount to a whole lot that we hadn't known before.

I think Pryce read the disappointment on my face, and tactfully changed the subject. "It's taking us longer than we thought to hit our marks," he said. "It's unlikely that we'll be able to complete the site, this time around at least."

I blew air out of my lips in a loud puff, deflated. He'd caught me. I had tried not to be concerned by it, but we *were* behind schedule. Cerriglyn Bog couldn't support the weight of bulldozers. The ground was too unstable. We'd been left to do the grunt work with smaller machines, sometimes only by hand. It made just reaching our intended depth a daunting task. I pursed my lips and wondered if I would ever feel the African sun on my face again, or see Hani's familiar, wizened face. He was probably still there, giving respite to obnoxious tourists, those he decried for destroying his homeland with their discarded water bottles and used-up film canisters. A hollow feeling deepened in my chest at the thought, threatening to swallow me up. I did my best to shake it off.

"Let's narrow the field, then," I finally answered.

Dr. Pryce smirked and pulled a copy of our working map from his back pocket. "I thought you might say that."

"Am I that predicable?" I asked.

"Predictable? No. But *capable*? Yes, you are that, Miss Hayes. So, what do you think?"

I examined the map centered around Cerriglyn Bog. Bordering its northeastern edge was the forest, with fainter lines indicating its prehistoric boundaries intersecting the topmost sectors of the bog. Along that corner crawled a small creek. Minus the geographic features, the map was blank. Staring at it was like gaping into an abyss, and that overwhelming feeling crept back up again, settling in my armpits and down the center of my back. I hoped Pryce couldn't smell my fear.

I closed my eyes, wishing for the meticulously plotted charts of the

Valley of the Kings, its pristine, orderly rows and markers instead of this yawning nothingness. But it too, once, had been only a mass of nondescript, transient dunes. I looked at the map again, the one in my mind's eye laid over it like a transparency. The bog beneath came to life, reacting like watercolor paper dipped in ink. Invisible markers blossomed in neat, ordered lines, woven together by unseen pathways into a modest village, one as close to the wetlands as safety would allow.

"Let's pull it in here," I said, pointing to the northeastern sector where the environmental markers overlapped—where the bog met the forest and where it touched the bank of the creek. "Take half your team out of the south and move them to the center." Those in-between spaces would have been the most sought after, the ones deemed sacred. If we didn't find anything bigger than chicken bones there, I doubted we would find them anywhere.

"Will do," he said, restoring the map to his pocket. "You know, Miss Hayes, I never really thanked you for thinking of us. This is the most exciting thing that's happened to our department in decades."

"Of course," I answered quickly. "You're right here. I thought it would be wrong not to. Although I'll admit that my intentions were not entirely altruistic—your Celts might be able to tell me something that the pyramids can't." That was the main reason I'd gone along with Alex's suggestion in the first place—I was seduced by the idea of bringing Druidism out of the shadows and drawing a line straight back to the practices that made pharaohs divine kings and praised wetlands as sacred.

Pryce smiled. "You *are* your father's daughter, Miss Hayes."

I turned my face from him and bit my lip. The sting of tears that should have run dry long ago tried to push its way forward again. I tried to console myself with the thought that, had I not already been thinking about them, it wouldn't have hit me as hard. But even I wasn't convinced.

Pryce cleared his throat. "I apologize, Miss Hayes. I—"

"It's fine," I assured him, blinking to clear my eyes. "Thank you for the compliment."

"I'd ask you to stay longer, if I didn't think Alex would have a fit.

Lord knows he wouldn't get any work done without you." He rose from his chair and left me with a knowing grin.

Pryce's parting words left me wondering just how much Alex *was* supposed to be doing as my supervisor. I shifted restlessly in a moldy dorm bed, abandoned in the nadir of the academic year. Today was not the first time that Alex was seen to shirk his duty. Sneaking breaks and doing his utmost to *not* tire himself out as much as the next man was second nature to him. It stung to have my work, my conclusions, be subject to his opinion. But it was too late to switch advisors and explaining the more pressing reason for wanting the distance was out of the question.

In the starkness of the brisk night, my boots called to me. Their plush lining was irresistible at the ridiculously late hour. I'd never get any sleep if I didn't clear my head and at least try to keep warm. I pulled the barely upholstered desk chair next to the window. After pushing down on the window to confirm that, yes, in fact, the wind was coming *through* the closed frame, I set the chair in front of the window, so that the frame sat at the leftmost corner of my vision, leaving the rest of my view looking out onto the bog which lay in the distance. Thick grasses and clusters of myrtle clutched each other in the darkness, shivering violently in the wind. Moonlight bounced off their tangled, indefinable edges, and the more I peered into the Welsh countryside, the more it divested itself of its false bluntness. The bog and its surrounding brush revealed whispers of greens, blues, purples, and yellows in its multi-layered blackness. Calm crept softly over my frazzled brain as I roughed out the scene before me in charcoals, paying attention to the angles and proportions before treating its colors and textures. I willingly lost myself in the quick strikes of my hand against the paper. Thoughts of anything but how to render the window frame fell from my mind. I considered whether to keep the aged, peeling texture of the white frame intact, or to restore it to a gleaming pristineness set at odds with the watery chaos beyond. As I worked, the untarnished frame looked too unnatural, so I weathered it once more. I worked until my eyes became blissfully heavy and drifted down into sleep.

I was still working on the image of the bog in my dreams. My charcoal strokes had become bloated with water, bleeding my greens, my blues, my whites, and my blacks together until the bog was nothing but a dark mass, a bottomless chasm. Obsidian waves shifted and swayed—something was rising to the surface. I couldn't run, couldn't scream or blink the image away as the rising wave took shape and glided across the surface of the bog. A shrunken, wrinkled face emerged from the watery depths. Its twisted mouth wrenched open to reveal a blank expanse. Vacant eyes glowed an unearthly blue, staring straight into my soul.

I woke gasping for air and wiped a sheen of cold sweat from my forehead. Raindrops pattered onto the floor beneath the window, its brittle borders unable to keep either wind or water out. The edge of my picture, laid on the nightstand, was visible out of the corner of my eye. The rain glistening on the windowpane reflected on the paper in the moonlight, making the colors look blurry and wet—alive, almost. I was afraid to turn my head, afraid in the way that you can be only after waking suddenly, still too tied to your dreams to know they aren't real. Those glowing, luminescent eyes still stared at me, *through* me, at the edge of my mind. I held my breath and looked. The only things on the paper were what I had put there—high grasses peering into the window frame, that crumbling barrier against the creeping dark without. It was splintered and cracked, losing its power to keep the fen at bay.

Don't stop now. Keep reading with your copy of CURSE OF THE AMBER, by City Owl Author, Kathryn Troy.

And find more from Lizzy Gayle at
www.lizzygayle.com

Don't miss more of the The Djinn series coming soon, and find more from Lizzy Gayle at www.lizzygayle.com

Until then, discover CURSE OF THE AMBER, by City Owl Author, Kathryn Troy!

A curse, a resurrection, and a centuries old witch hell bent on revenge.

Quintus is a dutiful son and soldier, sent to Britannia to improve his marriage prospects and ensure the Druids never rise again. Roman soldiers destroyed the last Druid stronghold in a battle of blood and fire. So, he never expects to be sacrificed to their sacred bog, trapped forever by the gods below.

Two thousand years later, Asenath Hayes discovers the most well-preserved body in history. And the last thing she needs is for him to wake up.

As the young archaeologist delves into Druidic rituals to grasp why Quintus was offered to a Welsh bog and then resurrected, she is forced to complete her research with the "missing" body, dodge her ex-lover and mentor with his own agenda, and keep her gorgeous new houseguest under wraps.

But, smitten with her as he seems, Quintus says he wants to go home.

Asenath is drawn to Quintus by the secrets they share, even if it scares her. As Asenath is pulled deeper into the mysteries of the bog, she must risk everything to keep him from hell's cold grasp as she uncovers forbidden rites, awakened deities, and an attraction that transcends the ages.

Please sign up for the City Owl Press newsletter for chances to win special subscriber-only contests and giveaways as well as receiving information on upcoming releases and special excerpts.

All reviews are **welcome** and **appreciated**. Please consider leaving one on your favorite social media and book buying sites.

Escape Your World. Get Lost in Ours! City Owl Press at www.cityowlpress.com.

ACKNOWLEDGMENTS

There will be a prize at the end of this.

So much goes into the making of a book, and THE BINDING STONE is no exception. I'd like to thank the entire team at City Owl Press, including the authors who've made me feel like family. I'd especially like to thank Tee, my editor, for taking a chance on me and making my work better. Thank you, Tina and Yelena, for all of your endless support. To my assistant Tiffany, and the team at Aurora Publicity. I also need to thank the book's original editors back when it was a YA still finding its feet, Ian and Deborah. To my family for supporting me, my friends for holding me up and forgiving me when I'm lost in my own world, and my support team of readers like my forever first beta reader, Leslie.

There are many more people that helped this book along the way since it's the "little book that could", and at the risk of forgetting a name or two, you know who you are and you have my undying gratitude.

I'd like to thank all of my characters for climbing in my head and whispering their stories to me. Without you my life would likely be quite boring.

The prize? My everlasting thanks for taking the time to read my words, both fictional and not. Without the readers, it's all meaningless. I hope I've given you something that provides comfort, joy, and imagination, as well as a little escape from real life.

ABOUT THE AUTHOR

LIZZY GAYLE loves paranormal so much, she lives it. She is both an author and a psychic. Between mothering her three kids, attempting to understand her rocket scientist husband, and consistently attempting to declutter her home (that she is convinced is a secret portal to a clutter-creating dimension), she does her  best to use her creative gifts and share them with you. Lizzy is a people person so if you contact her, it will make her very happy and she will likely answer while possibly including pictures of her bunnies and/or bird. She has also been known to write Young Adult under the name Lisa Gail Green.

www.lizzygayle.com

facebook.com/authorlizzygayle

instagram.com/authorlizzygayle

ABOUT THE PUBLISHER

City Owl Press is a cutting edge indie publishing company, bringing the world of romance and speculative fiction to discerning readers.

Escape Your World. Get Lost in Ours!

www.cityowlpress.com

facebook.com/YourCityOwlPress
twitter.com/cityowlpress
instagram.com/cityowlbooks
pinterest.com/cityowlpress

Made in the USA
Las Vegas, NV
04 October 2021